'Ian Lennox's passion for de
added to his superb story te
riddled world of cricket in

It is a story of struggle, triumph, and endeavour as the main character, Ben Linden, finds his worth as a fast bowler, and then fights his corner for respect and recognition from the upper classes.

The stark descriptive powers of the author take us into a fascinating period of history to reveal a classic love story.

The characters jump off the page with such energy, creating a terrific page-turner for anyone interested in cricket, life, or love.'

Arthur McKenzie

Arthur McKenzie was among the highest paid writers working in British Television drama. His credits include about thirty episodes of *The Bill*. His latest work includes a dramatic film, *Harrigan*, starring Stephen Tompkinson.

'Ian Lennox is a delightful writer and a true storyteller who weaves his love of sport into the tapestry of his books. Another highly commendable tale, well researched. The man keeps his standards'.

John Gibson

Executive sports Editor, *Evening Chronicle*

First published 2013
by Gordon Liberty Publishing

ISBN: 978-0-9546359-3-0

Printed and bound in the UK by Martins the Printers Ltd, Spittal, Berwick upon Tweed.

GENTLEMEN AND PLAYERS

Ian Lennox

Cover painting by Jason Zampol
www.zampolart.com

For Mum, Dad, Louisa, and Nana
My sisters, Pat, Sally, and Julie
My children, Louise, Heather, Gavin, and Emma

Chapter One

The King's beard was as stiff as a spade and he spoke with an accent that sounded strange to the boy. It was not of the valley or anywhere beyond on the vast Boutilier estate. Ben Linden stared at the great man while his mother, Beth, stood behind him bobbing curtseys like a cork in water.

George V reached down with his hand held out. Ben stayed still for a full second. Lord Boutilier stiffened in alarm. The boy seemed about to snub the King and turn the Royal visit into a social disaster that would be remembered for decades. At last the boy took the Royal hand. Lord Boutilier's face escaped from its frozen grin. He became aware that his hands were clapping softly and that the rest of the assembly had picked up the applause.

The King and the boy stood alone in the moment, and then the King drawled, 'I've been told that your father died a hero. It's because of men like him that you and I can sleep in our beds.' The boy's fixed expression unsettled Boutilier again. He recalled the stories about some ancestor who had been banished from court after a bout of involuntary flatulence in front of Queen Beth.

Mercifully, however, the King did not seem to see the boy's silence as hostility. He turned and walked down the gravelled avenue that was lined with families waving flags and handkerchiefs all the way to the great house.

Ben watched the retreating figure in silence. He wanted to tell the King that, in fact, he didn't sleep well in his bed. At least twice a week, he was chased awake by a nightmare in which he was trapped in a web and stalked by a huge black spider.

His father had died caught on the huge rolls of razor wire that guarded the trenches at the edge of no man's land; the wire which they'd said would be blown to pieces by the shells, but which had, in fact, been blown into the air only to land tangled and more impenetrable than ever.

His father's friend, the Sniper, had told him. He trusted the Sniper because he and his father had been comrades. He wasn't sure about the King and his beard. He thought it must feel like being embraced by a scrubbing brush when he kissed his children goodnight.

Ben and his mother had been summoned from their cottage seven miles up the valley in a pony and trap to meet the great man, because his father had won a medal.

They had been given a room for the night in the servants' quarters at the great house. Ben woke early to the sound of hard-soled shoes on the hardwood floors as the servants got about their work. He dressed quietly, pinned the medal to his shirt, and left his mother snoring gently on her bed. He walked down and down the stairs until he found dark carpets stretching along corridors that led him to a great hall. Two maids were tending logs under a huge, marble fireplace. Above them, for twenty feet on either side of the fire, hung a vellum parchment enclosed in a glass case. He stared at the document, which was coloured with family shields and names and dates going back to the Conquest. The maids recognised him as the boy who had met the King and gave him a curtsy as they left the great hall taking a brush and shovel with them. The boy seemed not to notice them as he stared fascinated at the crests inlaid with gold and silver. He heard footsteps behind him but did not turn. He fingered his medal, which he'd been told was made from bronze, melted down from one of the guns at a great battle. It seemed puny when set against this great display.

The boy wrenched himself from the thought. This medal

had been won by his father who had given his life leading an attack.

In the breakfast room, which was connected to the great hall by a short passageway, Lord Boutilier helped himself to a buffet of scrambled eggs, pork sausages, bacon, and kidneys. He turned to his butler who lifted the lids of the silver salvers. 'Simpkins,' he said. 'There's a small boy in the hall.'

'A boy sir?'

'Yes. He's about four feet tall and has a Victoria Cross pinned to his shirt.'

'A Victoria Cross, sir?'

Boutilier recalled the boy's fierce stare when faced by his betters. He imagined his heroic father had possessed the same look when advancing on German machine guns. 'Perhaps you could return him and it to his mother before he does any damage.'

'Certainly sir.' Simpkins left the room, his feet peculiarly soundless on the hardwood floor.

Ben and his mother were given a good breakfast of leftovers at the cook's table. Then, at the kitchen door, the cook thrust some sandwiches wrapped in greaseproof paper into Beth's hands.

'For the journey, pet.' The cook smiled. 'Your lad looks a hungry one,' She leant down and pinched his cheek gently. 'He's a grower.' She glanced at the medal and the wine-red ribbon and for a second her eyes softened as she vicariously shared their tragedy. She too had lost her husband. She wondered whether the boy slept with the medal. Probably. He seemed a strange, quiet one.

The pony and trap had been called away on more important duties, so Simpkins gave Beth six pence for the bus that ran along the river road to Wolviston. They were not allowed to walk the broad, gravelled avenue that ran grandly to the huge iron gates at the entrance to the vast estate. Instead they were directed to a lane that curled around the grounds in the shadow of the stone, boundary wall. It was narrow, rutted in places, and shrubs and bushes clung to the edge on either side.

There was an hour to fill before the next bus and Beth walked slowly, holding her son's arm in one hand and a thin canvas suitcase, held closed by parcel string, in the other. She glanced down to check that the medal was still pinned to her son's grey shirt.

'I don't like it here. That woman seems to think I'm a vegetable.'

'Which woman?'

'A grower.' He tried to imitate the cook's accent of rolling vowels.

Beth smiled to herself. 'She meant you were going to be a big man. She was being nice,'

They walked on.

The boy looked up. 'I've stepped in a puddle,' he said.

'More fool you.'

'There's a hole in my shoe.'

Beth sighed. She'd saved a little for a pair of stockings and a black, pleated skirt, but now that would have to go. Behind her she could hear a gardener mowing one of the long lawns. She breathed in the warm scent of new-cut grass. 'Come on,' she smiled at her son and pulled him to her side.

The boy rarely mentioned his father; indeed he spoke little about anything now. But he wore the medal and, at least, he had stopped wetting the bed.

It was the first warm day of spring and the wall and the

bushes sheltered them from the gentle breeze. Beth felt like sitting in the grass for a little nap, but she feared missing the bus. She walked along in a gentle daydream for what must have been five minutes when she was summoned back to the world by a sharp toot of a horn. She turned to see a shining black limousine crawling silently along the track. She stared standing in the middle of the narrow road. It did not seem real that such a magnificent gleaming beast of a vehicle should be using this tatty lane, and not the gravelled driveway that swept straight through the avenue of oaks and elms to the great house. That was where this shining thing belonged. The horn tooted again, slightly longer and more insistent, this time. Through the windscreen she could see the red face of the chauffeur, his eyes hidden in the shade of a peaked cap. She gave a start and pulled her son to the side of the road, hiding her string-bound case behind her hips. God knows who was in the back seat. It could be the King, though what would he be doing on this little leafy lane rutted by wheelbarrows? The car drew level and as it passed she saw the little girl sitting in the back seat, her blonde hair hanging in long wavy tresses and on her head a tiara of diamonds, resting like a crown. The car moved on gently and she heard Ben whisper. 'It's the posh girl from the great house. She thinks she's the queen.'

Ten yards on, the little girl ordered Purvis, the chauffeur, to halt. It was a bit much for a man who only three years ago had been ordered to advance on machine guns armed with a Lee Enfield, a bayonet, and a blood-curdling scream. However two pounds a week was good money, even if part of his duties was to take an arrogant child on a drive round the grounds so that she could wave at the workers as though they were her subjects.

He glanced into his mirror and watched as the woman

and her son drew level. He gave a start as he noticed the medal on the boy's chest. Blimey! He was driving a little girl who was wearing a diamond tiara, and now there was a boy wearing a Victoria Cross. He was glad he didn't drink.

The girl had wound down her window. She had a sharp voice for one so small. 'You there!' She was addressing the boy. 'You are meant to touch your forehead in respect when your monarch goes past.' She'd said the same thing to two serving maids half a mile back as they laid the sheets on the long washing lines, but they'd had the sense to play the game and had given elaborate curtsies that had satisfied the little horror. The boy, however, did not have a curtsey in him, nor did he seem keen on knuckling his forehead.

'Did you hear me?' The little girl's voice rose with what she supposed was dignity.

'Yes.' The boy continued to stare.

'Well get on with it then, or I'll have you in the Tower.'

Beth was on her second curtsey when her son pointed to his medal. 'This is a Victoria Cross. That means YOU are meant to salute ME.' His mother gave a little gasp and sought sanctuary in a glance to the chauffeur. Purvis merely shrugged, and his face seemed to say, 'What's to do?'

The girl was out of the limousine now, facing Ben. 'I'm Helen,' she announced. 'I'm not a queen really, it's a game.'

'Aah,' said Ben and the two children stared at each other.

At last she pointed at the medal. 'I've heard of those,' she said. 'You must be very brave,'

'I am.' He stood facing her with a solemn expression, wondering whether he was required to tell her that his father had something to do with the medal.

There was another silence between them. They could hear the engine purring and the breeze ruffling the leaves of the bushes and trees. 'You're the boy who stared at the king, aren't you?'

'I didn't like him much.' Ben heard his mother give another gasp.

Helen smiled. 'He's a bit stiff. Still, Daddy said at least he didn't chase the maids. He said it was dreadful when Lord Palmerstone came to stay. But that was years and years ago in granddad's day.'

'Why did he chase the maids?'

'I don't know. It's some sort of game for grown-ups, I think.'

'Why was it dreadful if it was a game?'

'Hmmm. I suppose the maids wouldn't have got their jobs done.'

'Aah.' There was a silence between them. Beth and Purvis found themselves grinning.

The girl pointed to her tiara. 'Would you like to swap?'

Ben shook his head. 'I can't. My father won it. He's dead.'

'This was my mother's. She's dead too.'

Ben felt his mother's hand grip his arm, but he held his ground.

'Would you like a lift?' The girl gestured to the Rolls.

Beth spoke before Ben could say yes. 'Very kind of you, Lady Helen, but we've been provided for to get the bus.' She began to edge away but the girl pulled open the door of the Rolls to its full extent in an overwhelming invitation.

'We'll take you to the gate.'

They all climbed in and the Rolls moved off smoothly.

When she got home Beth made herself a cup of tea. She found that she could not remember a single word spoken during the trip to the gate or, even more alarming, whether any word had been spoken. When she climbed on to the spluttering red bus all she could recall was the smell of leather from soft seats, and the feeling that she had chanced upon a world of absolute, bewildering luxury.

Her cottage lay to the east of Wolviston by a dried-out riverbed. She grew vegetables on a small plot and took in washing from select families to supplement her fifty pounds annual pension as the widow of a Victoria Cross holder.

That week the Wolviston Clarion carried a picture of Beth and Ben being presented to the King. Word got out that she worked by Royal Appointment and she began to take in more washing than she could handle. They bought an extra poss tub and Ben helped her when he came home from school. One day he stood for a while watching her work and said that they'd played cricket, but they'd had to stop him from bowling because he was too fast.

Beth nodded towards the spare poss tub. 'Aye, well, I won't be stopping you for being too quick. If you ever start that is.'

The boy grinned and rolled up his sleeves. 'Wouldn't last long as a fish, Mam.'

Beth herself was a fine straight-backed woman with dark hair that fell off her shoulder. There were a few men who made an excuse to call at her door, but they were never invited across the threshold. Beth herself found no need for men. She hadn't since Ben was born. Indeed she had got no pleasure from the attentions of Frank when he had come home on leave.

Frank had said nothing at first, and then, the night before he was due to return to the front, they were lying back to back in bed and his soft voice reached her in the dark. 'You know that half the girls in the valley would pay to buck me.'

She was awake in a second and wanted to shout, 'Well why don't you then?' But she held her tongue because she did not want to lose him. Years ago, she'd seen off all the girls in the factory to win him and now it had come to this. Tears ran hot down the sides of her face. He felt her sobbing and gently pushed his arm under her. She rolled herself to face him and clung long and hard, and as he made love, her nails scoured his back in a despair that passed for passion.

On his next leave he brought the Sniper with him. The man stood down the garden path like a stray dog, waiting to be allowed in.

To the casual eye they seemed unlikely friends. Frank was large and loud and he strutted about like a man who owned the space he was in. The Sniper was pale and sallow, and he moved with quiet economy. He had washed-out eyes that rarely blinked. Ben sat in silent awe of both of them. Beth sensed that the Sniper was a troubled man. Her husband was his only friend. They'd met one evening in a bar when Frank had come to his aid during an argument with some Welsh Guards.

Frank told her that his friend was an orphan and had been brought up in the poor house where he had to fight for every scrap.

The War had saved him, for the army discovered he had a talent; he was an amazing marksman.

He worked with an observer, often from behind some disguised spot, such as a false tree. The observer identified the target, the Sniper fired the shot and then they both dived into a slit trench where they remained, often for hours. On one occasion the Germans had spotted the flash from his rifle and called in artillery. When they emerged the tree had been blasted away. They'd waited until dark before retreating to their lines. They knew that if taken they'd be shot where they stood.

It was only on the third day of his visit that Beth discovered that the Sniper was called John Bart. Frank referred to him as Sam the Sniper.

As the days went by he took to Frank's son and carved him crude soldiers from Beth's wooden pegs. They stuck them on the washing line where they stood like guardsmen. Ben clapped his hands as they hovered out of reach.

Frank refused to talk about his time in the trenches. Beth had no idea about life at the front. When she asked he just said that most of most days were filled with chores. The most dangerous enemy was boredom, because you became careless.

He smiled, 'That's when people like Sam here get you.'

At the mention of his name, the Sniper looked up from his chair by the fire where he'd been puffing on his pipe. Beth could see that, for a second, he thought they were accusing him of something. He spoke softly, 'Sometimes Frank sees me as a sort of assassin. But to me there's more honour in it than sitting behind some great gun lobbing shells from two miles away.' He stopped, aware that no one had accused him of anything. 'The real reason,' he said, 'There's no one to order me about.' He caught the eyes of the boy staring at him and forced himself to smile. Then he noticed the soldier pegs. There was a group of them leaning against the fireguard and, under the table, a lone peg lay behind a chair leg, like a sniper.

Chapter Two

The cricket festival was the great occasion in the valley, surpassing the hunt, the coursing events, and even the annual agricultural show

Each year a team of professional players from the counties met amateurs from the shires and universities in a match that attracted thousands of spectators from along the valley and beyond. They filled the hotels and the pubs, and spent money in the shops, before travelling along the river road to the match. Indeed the festival attracted all sorts of business, including a team of loose ladies paid for by Lord Boutilier, for the attentions of the professional players. Only ten of these women were hired each year because Boutilier refused to provide pleasure 'for the bugger who gets me out.'

Then, two years after the General Strike, disaster struck. The rains poured throughout June and July. The river burst its banks, flooding the cricket ground. The stars could not play, the spectators stayed away, and the whole valley suffered.

Lord Boutilier had lost his festival, which gave him much prestige at the MCC, and the people who lived in the valley had lost their business.

Something had to be done. Experts were called in and, after much stomping about with maps and surveying sticks, they told Lord Boutilier that they must divert the river, in a loop away from the walled estate. Everyone agreed that this was the best solution with the exception of Beth Linden whose cottage and land would be flooded, but, as Boutilier owned her plot, and all the other land throughout the valley, her objections would normally have mattered little.

Boutilier had long since forgotten the woman and her strange son but he did remember the Victoria Cross. When he learned that she was the widow of the man who had led the charge on the German trenches he sent his agent, Captain Carter, to her cottage to offer a compromise.

Carter's big, thick boots stamped off the mud on the stone step and then he entered, his bowler held defensively in front of his thick tweed jacket. He gave a 'harrumph' and shook his fleshy, red face before telling her about Lord Boutilier's plans.

Beth started to protest. 'Where will I go? What will become of me?' Carter hastened to assure her that she would be moved to a smallholding within the estate walls. Carter pointed out the cricket pitch was important to the economy of the whole valley.

Beth could not argue with these facts. She was in awe of the great Boutilier. She had been in his presence only once since her invitation to the great house.

She'd seen him from afar riding to hounds and, occasionally, bowling down towards the town in a gleaming black Rolls. However, on this day, he'd passed her in the lane on a huge hunter and had acknowledged her curtsey with a nod before resuming his gaze on the horizon. Had any of her equals dismissed her in such a fashion she would have seen it as a snub, and something not to be forgotten. But the nod from Lord Boutilier made her feel privileged to have been acknowledged.

She knew that Lord Boutilier came from a great line. He was a man who had the powers of the realm at his table, a man who had a knowledge, understanding, and experience of the world that was beyond her comprehension.

Her new cottage was larger than her previous home and situated on a clump of land that backed on to the high stone wall that enclosed the immediate estate. It was as far as possible from the great house while still within the protective walls. Some said this was no accident, for the previous inhabitant had been Lord Boutilier's nanny, an ancient woman, who had become progressively prouder of her virginity as she advanced in years. She had died in her nineties and rumour had it that her last words were a threat to box the lord's ears.

Beth had no dealings with the Lord Boutilier, though his agent, Captain Carter, took an interest in her affairs that, some said, went beyond Christian charity.

He was as stiff as the round-topped bowlers he took to wearing, but he was an observant man and he saw pleasing qualities in Beth's quiet, straightforward manner. He favoured her above the other tenants and always left his horse in her bottom field so that she would get the benefit of the manure. Carter liked the look of Beth's long, lean figure and the way she clipped wild flowers into her hair. However he suppressed any desire for intimacy because he knew that, despite the improprieties common at the great house, affairs among staff and tenants were frowned upon, and adultery would be met with instant dismissal.

Beth's new cottage was equipped with an impressive iron range to heat the home and the oven, but she was not allowed to graze cattle within the estate's walls and she feared she and her son, Ben, would struggle. The great house would provide a regular market for any vegetables they grew, but she had lost her income from washing clothes and she knew she needed something else to survive. The answer came one autumn day when Captain Carter came up the slope on his steaming horse laden with a large basket.

'Here you are ma'am,' he grinned showing his white teeth that looked strong enough to snap a bone. He leaned from his saddle to place the basket gently on the ground.

She opened the wicker lid and two large hens flopped out and scuttled noisily round the back of the cottage. She looked up at Carter in askance. She'd become uneasy in his presence. She felt his stares whenever the wind pulled her loose dress around her body. She had no desire for him and found his interest intrusive.

Carter thrust at his reins as his hunter shook his head and gave a loud whinny.

'Two hens?'

'Brooding hens, Mrs Linden. Brooding hens.'

'Brooding hens?' She still didn't understand.

The hunter snorted and reared. Carter tapped it on the nostrils with his crop.

'The great house needs chickens and eggs. They'll take all you can supply. I've told the cook.'

Beth blinked. She was being pushed faster than she could run.

'It's real kind of you, but I know nowt about chickens. And who's going to kill them? Not me'

'That lad of yours ain't so queasy. One of the handymen has his own hens. I'll get him to come over of an afternoon and build a coop. He'll help you get a start, if I tell him.'

Beth's initial apprehension was fading fast. Carter was making sense; if only he wouldn't stare so hard at her.

She watched him as he trotted away. The breeze lifted her dress and she brushed it down quickly. He gave her a backward look. She pretended her attention was elsewhere.

John Jarvis, the handyman, arrived with a handcart full of wood the following afternoon. He had watery blue eyes and a grey moustache. He touched his old flat cap, lifting the peak, which was stained with sweat and dirt. He gestured to the cart. 'For the coop.' He was a man of few words but, as Beth watched him build the wooden walls on a flat space at the back of her cottage, she was impressed by his slow rhythmic movements that suggested an inner contentment. She could not help but compare him to Captain Carter. She much preferred Jarvis, because she sensed that the Captain's kindness had been born of other motives. She shuddered at the thought of his hot breath on her neck, his skin boiling with lust and his thick fingers plunging their way through her clothes. She splashed herself with cold water from the heavy stone basin in the kitchen to escape from such alarming thoughts. She had made Captain Carter the main character in the little nightmare; though in truth it could have been any man. Only her son, Ben, warmed her heart. As if driven by providence, he appeared beside Jarvis as the handy man hit the last few nails into the coop.

Ben had grown tall and had the black hair and dark eyes of his father, who had been a handsome man. Beth had seen the eyes of the maids and working girls on the estate follow her son.

He was a quiet youth but she knew he had depths of passion.

That summer he'd come across a crow pecking at the body of his pet cat and hit it with a stone thrown so hard that it had crushed the bird's skull. Then, the following day he'd gone to a rookery and thrown more stones at the nests high up on a clutch of beech trees. He'd thrown with amazing power and balance for one so young but still couldn't reach the clutch of twigs and dirt that made up the nests. One last shot had clattered the branches with such force that they'd risen cawing in alarm. He turned away muttering and saw Captain Carter staring at him from a hillock across the field. Their eyes met and the agent wheeled his horse back towards the great estate.

Captain Carter never spoke to him of the incident, but a week later his mother sat him down at the kitchen table and warned him against hunting the rooks within the walls. 'It's on the lord's land and the trees and the rooks are his.' She sensed his rebellion at her rebuke. 'Any road the rooks have nowt to do with eating dead cats. They don't touch carrion.'

She knew her son would ignore her argument. She remembered the boy's father confronting some youths who had barred her path in a lane. He had said little and the youths had strength in numbers, but something in his look told them that the matter wouldn't end on that day and they'd retreated muttering their excuses.

Ben took to running up the valley and into the lower hills until he came to a great forest and there he found the rooks. For a week he collected stones in the dry riverbed and placed them in a pile at the edge of the rookery. Then, for one whole afternoon he threw the rocks at the birds, but they were too clever for him. The nests were out of range and they circled overhead mocking him with their calls.

He turned to run for home, lost in his thoughts. It no longer mattered that they had not been the defiler of his dead cat. The challenge was now to throw hard and high enough to hit their nests, and was he still twenty feet short. His steps shortened on the steepening slope to the bank of the dried-out river. He burst through the alder trees and swung right towards the estate when a great horse reared whinnying in alarm at his sudden appearance. The girl rider bent into the horse's neck in a bid to retain her seat. The horse whinnied again as its rear legs slipped in the soft turf by the riverside. The girl swung her reins hard so the horse turned prancing up the slope. She was caught in the moment of fear and frenzy and lashed out with her riding crop. The blow came from nowhere but Ben was quick enough to raise his left arm to save his face. The horse continued prancing but the eyes of the two of them were locked in the moment that neither of them would forget. At last she shouted. 'You clumsy fool!'

He looked at her as she hovered over him on her high horse. Her face was pale enough to model for a Chinese vase. He knew her in an instant as the girl in the tiara and that now, as then, she belonged to another world. For a moment he was arrested by the vision of her. Then he felt the pain in his arm. He pulled up his shirtsleeve to reveal a pink weal below his elbow. He looked up at her and saw she was staring at his arm.

When he spoke he had taken time to contain his anger, so his voice was low and even. 'Thoroughbreds are high strung, Lady Helen. I'll make sure I don't disturb you again.' Then, he turned and started to run along the riverbank. She felt a rising fury, as much at her own arrogant behaviour as at his impertinence. She shouted at his retreating figure, 'It's highly. Highly, not high.' But her call only gave him the chance to ignore her. She watched him go, noting the easy balance, the still head, and the effortless rhythm of his strides. She was aware that there was something else which she could not identify. It was only later that it came to her. There was no sound as his feet touched the ground.

Chapter Three

For more than two hundred years, the drovers had passed through the county on their way to the London markets. Lumbering cattle from the highlands and bleating sheep from Wales, they all trod the drovers' road, fattening on the lush pasture land of England before moving on their last journey to the capital. Geese and turkeys from East Anglia joined them and all the herds and flocks had rough strangers to guard and drive them.

Usually the drovers' road would keep to high land and then curl its way between towns to avoid the tolls. In places the trodden way was more than forty feet wide to accommodate herds of up to four hundred cattle. In the shire, the road pointed south so straight that it might have been formed by the marching feet of Roman armies, but when it reached the lands of the great Lord Boutilier, it curled this way and that, before heading into the hills. The story that came down through generations was of a group of crafty drovers who had wagered one of the Lord's agents that their geese could travel faster than his quickest turkey. However, when he discovered that, unlike turkeys, the geese could feed on the run, a fight had broken out and the agent had been sorely hurt. From that day on, their route was barred. And so the drovers used a higher trail until the advent of the stock trains ended their way of life forever. No cattle, nor sheep, nor geese, nor turkeys had trodden the drovers' road for more than forty years but, strangely, the track itself stayed pristine and smooth, and the land, that had been manured by generations of stock, was the envy of many a farmer in the valley below.

The bracken and ferns, that grew in abundance in the hills, did not encroach on to the rich green grass.

Ben's father had taken him to the road only once, remarking how it stretched like a racetrack. His father was not a countryman. Nor was John Bart, the Sniper, though he seemed to find a home at the sight of it. He walked with Ben along the great stretches every time he came to stay. Then one year, after the War was over, he brought a rifle with him. As the man and boy walked towards Wolviston he told Ben that the gun was a German Mauser and that it had belonged to an enemy sniper. The man had shot at least twenty British soldiers before John Bart was brought in. They'd sent a German prisoner back over no man's land with a challenge. They were to hide at night in the woods near Fricourt and fight to the death after first light. The Sniper had studied the maps and knew there was only one way in from the German lines. He lay hidden for three days and nights before he picked out the German crawling back to his lines. He'd got careless and had not waited until after dusk fearing he might lose his way in the dark. The Sniper hit him with one shot from 600 yards, waited an hour, and then crawled to the scene of his triumph. The German lay dead and the Sniper took the gun as his trophy.

He carried it in a thin case and Ben watched him wrap it in oilskin and bury it on the drovers' road near a small fir tree.

'Why?' Ben asked him. But the Sniper only smiled and said, 'One day I might need it.'

On the way back to Beth's cottage he told Ben how important it had been to him to discover he had a rare talent. There were some who said he was the finest shot in the British army.

The boy looked up at him and said. 'I've got a talent too.'

'Oh what?' The Sniper smiled indulgently.

'Cricket,' he said. 'I'm a bowler.'

'Oh,' said the Sniper. 'Yes,' said Ben. 'Except they won't let me play anymore. They say I'm too fast for the rough pitches.'

The Sniper smiled. 'The big babies! Tell them there were some rough pitches in No Man's Land and to come to me if they doubt it.'

He laughed and the boy laughed with him, though he didn't know why.

Ben took to running the drovers' road to stay away from Lady Helen, her horse, and her haughty ways. It was common land and so he had as much right to be there as anyone. Each time he passed the fir tree he thought of the Sniper.

He found a rare sense of solitude as he ran. He had hardly seen John Bart since the burial of the rifle, then one evening, half a dozen miles from his mother's cottage, he appeared driving a score of cattle. He explained that this was now his new life; he'd revived the trail, driving the cattle down to a London market and using the proceeds to buy perfume and trinkets, which he could sell on the way back north.

Ben grew three inches that summer, enough to tower over Jarvis, a man three times his age. He listened respectfully as Jarvis started his lessons on how to keep hens. He had a strange burr to his accent that told Ben he came from far up the valley.

Jarvis lit a stained clay pipe before giving Ben the benefit of his wisdom on his favourite subject.

'I prefer the Sussex hens myself,' He punctuated his words with a puff on his pipe.

Beth advanced on them with two mugs of cool milk taken from the larder.

Jarvis nodded his thanks as he took his cup. 'Carter says

you know nowt about hens.' Ben and his mother shook their heads. Jarvis grinned. 'Well, I'll visit each week to keep an eye on yer.' He nodded to himself. 'A subject worthy of study is hens. Two types of eggs. Right. Those where the hen has been . . . been roostered and those that haven't. Those that haven't are eggs and only eggs. Those that have will hatch. If a chick starts to crow it's a rooster. If it doesn't it's a hen.'

Jarvis continued his tutorial over the following weeks. They started with one rooster and a dozen hens. He showed Ben the rooster's duties: sitting on a fence post to watch for danger; the different calls if a threat came from the air or the ground; how the rooster searched for food and called to the flock when successful.

Then, after a couple of weeks, Jarvis showed Ben how to kill a chicken by grasping the bird to the body and giving a sharp tug to the head. Death was instantaneous but the bird's wings still flapped for a good thirty seconds. He grinned at Ben's white face. 'Don't worry son, the hen was dead.' He handed out the dead bird to Ben. 'Give it to your mum. Tell her to put it in a bucket of hot water to ease the feathers and then pluck it.' Ben held the bird neck up conscious of the blood trickling on to his hand.

Jarvis shook his head. 'Best the other way up. Let the blood run to the neck.' He smiled again and reached for his pipe. 'It's a bit different from hitting them with stones.' Evidently he had heard about Ben's own campaign against the rooks. 'I hear you have a tidy arm on you.'

Jarvis had worked on the great estate all his life, as had his father and grandfather before him. Occasionally, on market days he caught a bus into Wolviston, but that was as far as he had been. Indeed, generations of his family had lived their lives in the valley and had never followed the river to the sea. He was a strong, simple man and Ben admired his quiet qualities.

Jarvis took Ben on regular visits to see his brother along the curling lane that ran by the inner wall, past the immaculate cricket pitch, which itself was protected from the lane by a five-foot hedge.

One afternoon, in midsummer, they were walking past the ground. Jarvis was sucking on his pipe as Ben chewed on a long blade of grass he'd pulled from the lane. They heard the crack of bat on ball and the cries of the cricketers and spectators. Ben nudged his way through a gap in the hedge and sat to watch the match. Jarvis followed him nervously. 'I don't think we're welcome here,' he whispered, though there was no one within forty yards of them.

Ben didn't answer; he just stared in awe at the huge expanse of immaculate turf, the players in their pristine white shirts and flannels, rows and rows of spectators wrapped around the ground, and across the wicket, in front of a small wooden pavilion, the good and the great lounging in deck chairs.

'Ain't it grand,' he said.

Jarvis grinned. 'Is this your first sight of our betters at play, then?'

Ben looked out across the huge expanse of grass and to the rolling lands behind. 'To have so much,' he whispered. 'What is there left to do?' As he spoke a tall fair-haired batsmen swivelled on his heel and hooked a short ball to the boundary in front of the pavilion. A man in a red and orange blazer jumped from his seat. 'Good shot sir!'

'Lord Boutilier seems to be enjoying himself.'

The ball had come to rest among a group of women who were lounging in their deck chairs. One of them rose and sent the ball in a gentle loop to a fielder, who'd approached from square leg. The fielder caught the ball and doffed his cap.

Ben heard Jarvis chuckle again. 'That should be worth a guinea on his fee. She's Lady Helen, Lord Boutilier's daughter.'

Ben stared across the pitch. He was one hundred and fifty yards away and the hair that was loose had once been hidden but he recognised her in a moment.

The ball was sent looping back to the bowler who rubbed it vigorously against his flannels as he started running in.

'That's Warren.'

'Who?'

'Warren. They reckon he's England's fastest bowler.' As Jarvis spoke Warren slapped down his left leg in his delivery stride and sent to ball spitting off the wicket, short of a length. Jarvis chuckled. 'Another who knows what's good for him, Two yards off his pace in the nets last night.'

Ben wasn't listening. He found himself staring across the pitch at the girl. He could see her ash blond hair lifting in the wind. 'How old is Lady Helen?' he asked.

'About your age. Much good it'll do you. Now if she was a scullery maid or a footman's daughter . . . ' He laughed and gave Ben a gentle punch on the shoulder. 'Bloody hell, lad. You're smitten with a lass who lives in another world.'

'I've met her twice,' he said.

'Of course you have.' Jarvis gave another laugh. 'Was it when she invited you to dinner?'

'The last time I startled her horse and she hit me with a whip.'

Jarvis stared at him. 'You frighten me sometimes, Ben. It's like everyone knows their place, but you.'

'If you're saying it's my place to be whipped, you can go to hell. And so can yon stuck-up bitch.'

Jarvis glanced around, fearful that Ben's words had been overheard. He got to his feet and brushed some grass cuttings from his trousers.

'Careful, lad. Hedges have ears. Come on, I've got a fence to repair.' Ben was so transfixed by the grandeur of the scene that he appeared not to have heard him. Eventually, he rose to his feet.

Seventy yards away, Warren bent his wrist and let the ball slide across his fingers. The batsman went to drive him and by the time he realised he was facing a slower ball it was too late to adjust his stroke. His intention had been to hit the ball over midwicket. Instead he caught it with a thick outside edge and sent it soaring on the off. The ball flew high over cover point straight at Ben who had stooped to straighten his rough trousers. Jarvis called out a warning and Ben saw the ball and instinctively leapt to his right to take a catch high above his head. There was a stunned silence throughout the ground. There was no fielder within twenty yards of the ball, though Ben could still be seen to have interfered with play. Then a voice rang out over the square. 'Well caught, young man!' Ben looked across the ground and saw Lord Boutilier applauding his catch. Encouraged the spectators broke out in a smattering of applause.

Ben grinned and took a step forward before sending the ball back to the wicketkeeper. The throw was even more spectacular than the catch. It never rose above twelve feet before hitting the wicket keeper's gloves with a smack that was heard over the square.

The fielders and batsman froze in combined astonishment, the intrusion forgotten for a moment.

Ben heard Jarvis mutter. 'Don't push your luck. Let's away.'

He lifted his peak cap in what he hoped would be seen as a gesture of respect and then the two of them pushed their way through the gap in the hedge.

Lord Boutilier watched the two figures disappear in silence. He heard his daughter whisper. 'That's the young man who frightened my horse, Daddy.'

'The fellow you struck with your whip?'

Helen did not answer.

'Have you apologised?'

'I haven't seen him since,' she lied quickly.

The two of them were aware that talk had ceased around them. Her father said quite deliberately for their benefit, 'You know Helen, if this is the way we treat our servants, some would say we don't deserve to have any.'

Helen flushed at this rebuke in front of her friends, but she said nothing. Thankfully, the bowler, Warren, sent down a loose ball, which the large, fair-haired man dispatched to the boundary amid a new burst of applause. Helen stared out at the pitch, furious at her humiliation. The batsman seemed to be smiling directly at her. She noticed a cravat stuck into the top of his shirt and thought it absurd. He was called Peregrin Bowden and was a friend of her brother, Charles. They'd arrived fresh from Oxford the previous evening in a vulgar, little red sports car. She had no doubt that Charles's had brought him down for his own designs, but Peregrin seemed encouragingly heterosexual. She'd noticed his glances at her. She thought she might flirt with him. Unfortunately she discovered that he was not very bright. Charles had said that Peregrin was 'wizard at games'. The family owned extensive estates in Lancashire and Peregrin was being set up for a career in the city. Charles seemed to think this was the role of the modern man, but Helen was not impressed.

To be set up in the city meant that Peregrin had an elder brother who would inherit the family estate, as was the custom that had prevented English estates from becoming fragmented over the centuries. It had also unleashed a reservoir of talent from the great families into the professions. The trouble was, she suspected that Peregrin was not talented, and the sports hero of his public school and university would have to rely on friends in high places when he met the gritty gremlins in the world of business. She was alarmed how much Charles was in awe of him, seemingly because he'd hit five sixes to win a match against Cambridge. He was tall, pleasant to look at in a smooth-skinned sort of way, and had good strong legs, but when he started to talk he said nothing that engaged her.

Her thoughts were broken by drama on the pitch. Peregrin's lusty blows had angered the bowler, Warren. She could see it in the man's body as he started his run-up for the last ball of the over. His chest thrust into the wind and his legs pumped hard on the turf before he leapt into the air at the wicket. His bowling arm seemed to brush the ground after releasing the ball, such was his effort. From her position square to the wicket she never saw the ball against the background of hedges and trees, but she knew it was short because Peregrin pivoted on his back foot and attempted to hook it. But the ball was two yards faster than anything he'd faced that afternoon and it reared hitting him above the heart. Peregrin collapsed to his knees, and while there, fighting to rise, she saw him clothed in courage. If only he could stay in that moment of magnificent defiance, but moments were just that, moments. She looked across to the hedge and saw the young man had gone. Someone had said he was called Ben and that he threw stones at rooks. Perhaps he was an imbecile. Then she remembered his words about thoroughbreds being highly strung. She knew that he was not a fool, and that he had been referring to her and not the horse.

'Magnificent, isn't he?' One of her friends whispered in her ear in a voice low with sex and secrets as Peregrin got back to his feet.

'Careful Felicity. I doubt he's experienced more than a smooth-bottomed fag.'

Felicity giggled. 'Helen! You're awful.'

But Helen was lost in her thoughts again. She wondered whether Peregrin would be invited to her father's post-match party. The handsome virgin, with women anyway, wandering along a corridor of bedrooms, each one stocked with a woman destined to be buried in a y-shaped coffin. She laughed to herself. The idea was no more ridiculous than the image of her father creeping down the same corridor in spindly-legged lust.

She looked again across the pitch. The fielders were moving in and out following the ritual of the game. She could hear their calls and the sound of the bat striking the ball. She felt the absence of the strange, young man. She felt the emptiness of the moment. That night she slept in a spare room in the west wing of the great house, out of sight and sound of the party. The night owl called and the heavy curtains moved in the breeze from the open window, billowing like a gown gliding out onto the dance floor.

She woke hungry and was first down to the long breakfast room, which overlooked the parkland at the southern end of the house.

One of the under footmen, was on duty and he preceded her down the long buffet table, lifting the heavy lids of the silver dishes as she selected her food. He smelled of cheap soap and there was a line of light dandruff at the fringe of his grease-backed hair. She found him an unpleasant fellow, but too lowly for her to articulate her displeasure. She was halfway through her scrambled eggs and thin bacon when Charles came in, white-faced from the night's carousing. He gave her a sickly grin and sat opposite with a cup of dark coffee. He was followed by Peregrin who yawned loudly and looked very pleased with himself. Suddenly it was all too much. Her father hiding in his bedroom, as he did after all his 'parties'; the girls no doubt driven away at dawn along some back road counting their money; this idiot smirking with self-satisfaction, and some villager sneaking away with a fiver in his back pocket and his bum pierced by her brother.

She rose from the table. 'I presume from that absurd smug look that you managed to park yourself between some prostitute's legs last night.' She had time to see the astonishment come over Peregrin's face before marching out of the room. As she closed the door she heard Charles's laughter lift into the air, as clear as a bell.

Chapter Four

Helen left the house by a small door on the west wing. She could hear a vacuum cleaner droning its way down the long corridor that ran parallel to the front facade. She walked out into a paddock that dipped before sloping into a hillock on which a giant oak tree stood. Two hundred years ago her great, great grandfather had lain as a child in a blue silk suit at the bottom of the slope to have his portrait painted. She knew because the giant oil canvas stood in the great hall. The boy had long since gone, but the tree remained, and beyond it, then as now, stood the stone wall that marked the immediate boundary of the great house.

She knew the young man would be running from his cottage to the drovers' road that evening. She had wanted to apologise but couldn't find the words that would express her contrition without her losing too much face. She was after all bred from a line of lords and he bred chickens and threw stones at rooks. She looked out across the paddock.

Wolfie, her father's huge Irish wolfhound, came bounding down the hillock barking a great resounding woof as the cook enticed him home with a ham shank. There were a few who noted the dog's thick legs and suspected that Wolfie had a touch of bull mastiff in him. Thoroughbred or not, the dog lived the life of a lord. Each morning the cook let him out for his 'business' as she delicately put it. His next ritual was to sleep in his great basket by the ovens, or sometimes before the fire in the great hall. That afternoon Lord Boutilier would walk him along the lane to the cricket pitch where he would bound about while his master talked to Arnold, the groundsman, who had once bowled to the great WG Grace. Arnold was stooped with age, had a walrus moustache and fine blue watery eyes, but most attractive of all, a slow burr he'd brought from the West Country where he had been raised.

Helen felt the pleasant warmth of the early sun as she stood looking across the long lawns out to the hills that rose in a great sweep across the skyline.

On a whim she turned back indoors, and ran up the great circular staircase. She trotted along the main corridor and hammered on her father's sturdy bedroom door. She was rewarded with sounds of life. 'Daddy,' she shouted. 'I'm off to London to find a man.'

This elicited a loud, but indeterminate, response from within the room, which she chose to interpret as a question.

'To have sex.' This time her voice was loud enough to be heard by the ground floor maids, one of whom dropped a duster and started to giggle.

By the time her father had plunged into his trousers and reached the door she was gone. To add injury to insult she had summoned the chauffeur and disappeared in the Rolls.

Ben had been up for two hours. His mother had not been told of his exploits on the cricket pitch, but he knew the story would be spreading by mouth right now, like the flu, and would inevitably result in another rebuke from his mother about his behaviour in front of the 'Lord and his like'.

He recalled Lord Boutilier applauding his feats. He would make that the case for the defence, should it be necessary. He began to whistle as he busied himself with his work in the coop, stealing the eggs from the laying hens to encourage them to lay some more. He placed them all in a large basket and then visited the new coop, which housed his brooders. He pushed a dozen eggs under their warm bellies. In three weeks the fertilised eggs would hatch. The chicks would grow into chickens and then he would tweak their heads and pluck them for delivery to the great house. The unfertilised eggs would lie abandoned in the nest waiting for collection.

The chores bored him and unbeknown to his mother he had tried a little experiment. A few months back he'd bought a dozen eggs from the travelling shop and placed them under the brooding hens. Some of the eggs had not been fertilised but one in particular had yielded a spectacular result, a male duck. Unfortunately the resplendent green and grey feathers had attracted the attention of the rooster, which had insisted giving the duck the benefit of its favours.

Ben had learned two things in the following weeks. First, that the words fuck and duck might rhyme amusingly, but there were not poetry to his mother's ears. Second, each time the duck was assaulted the bird sought sanctuary in the drainage pond in the field next to the cricket pitch. Usually the rooster followed him, strutting the waterline, keen to continue his unnatural liaison.

The pond had been created shortly after the flooding of the cricket ground. A bush drainage trench had been dug across the pitch during the winter, allowing the water to flow into a dip in the land in the neighbouring field. It had been planned to provide drinking water for the Friesian cattle. However, the cows had created a deep morass of mud, that had become so dangerous that the water hole had been fenced off.

As Ben strolled down the hill, Lord Boutilier's Rolls passed silently along the lane that wriggled round the estate. He saw Lady Helen sitting straight-backed in the rear seat. He remembered the tiara and the medal from all those years ago. But when she glanced out at him he pretended he had not seen her. Once she had passed him, he followed the path of the gleaming limousine and watched it turn on to the main driveway and head for the huge ancestral gates.

He moved in easy strides feeling the pleasing warmth of the sun. He could hear the rooster crowing away, but, as he reached the lane and began to walk past the cricket pitch, there was a new sound, the deep bark and loud whining of a dog in distress. He ran up to the pond. The rooster was standing on a tree stump and the duck was paddling in the deep dirty waters. But between them, ten feet out in the quagmire created by the stomping feet of thirsty cattle, the great wolfhound stood sinking in the mud with a strand of barbed wire around its neck. For a second Ben stood staring in panic. The one bar fence was too sturdy to be dismantled for use in a rescue. There was no other wood, no rope, nothing that he could use to pull the great dog to safety. Then he remembered that over the hedge, at the edge of the cricket field, stood a rambling old shack used to store grass cuttings and old tools. He ran to the gap in the hedge and along the whitewashed boundary lines to the shed. Across the field he could see old Arnold watering the square. He shouted and waved but Arnold, glancing up, saw some wild man and chose to ignore him. Seconds later, Arnold heard a loud crashing noise and saw the same lowly fellow dismantling the shed door with kicks from his heel. By the time Arnold had crossed the ground Ben was emerging from the shed carrying a length of hosepipe and the unhinged door.

Before he could speak Ben gestured over the hedge. 'It's Wolfie. He's in the swamp.' With that he burst past Arnold shouting, 'Bring some cutters, he's got wire round his neck.' Ben pointed back to the shed where three pairs of sheers were stored. Then he disappeared through the hedge.

Arnold muttered something about a 'bloody rude, young bastard who didn't know his place' before the reality of the situation took over. By the time he reached the pond Ben had thrown the door out into the swamp and was lying on the makeshift raft by the dog.

'Here you are son,' Arnold lobbed the shears to Ben who caught them and cut the wire. The barbs had raked through the dog's skin and he whimpered as Ben pulled the wire away. Ben turned to Arnold, 'Steady the door. Stand on the end.' Arnold stepped out into the swamp. His left leg sank in shin-deep but then held firm. Encouraged, he placed his right boot heavily on the edge of the door.

At the other end, Ben leaned out holding the hose and plunged his fist under the chest of the dog. 'Steady now, for God's sake!' Ben pushed his left hand down into the mire on the far side of the dog's chest, caught the hose, and pulled it to the surface. For a second his own face had been forced under the surface of the foul swamp and he came up retching and spitting. He repeated the process again creating a loop round the dog. He turned to Arnold. 'Stay your ground mister or I'm a dead man!'

Arnold stared in shock, not contemplating what was to come next. He heard himself shout 'I will! I will!'

Ben had fed the hose round the dog so that he had about three feet spare at Wolfie's near side. This he wrapped around his left elbow and then his hand. He stood up and stooped over the dog, which by now was whimpering pitifully. Ben grasped the dog's thick leather collar in his right hand and hauled with both arms at the dog. The dog stayed stuck. Arnold felt the upward pressure on his end of the door and stepped out onto it with both feet. He could see the stress beginning to bend the wood and looked anxiously out at the young man and the giant dog. The young man had seen something, for suddenly he altered his stance, plunged his fist into the swamp and pulled fiercely. He came up with Wolfie's left foreleg, which he pulled towards him so that it gained purchase on the door. The dog barked and began to push on the plank with its free leg just as Ben began to pull on the hose and the collar for a second time. Arnold saw the door bend like a bow and then, just as he thought the wood must snap, there was a loud sucking noise as the dog rose dirty and stinking from the swamp. Wolfie gave a great bark, bounded over Ben, cleared the fence, and disappeared through the hedge.

The old grounds man stayed at his end of the door. 'Come on son. Can't stand here all day.' He grinned. Ben became aware of the nauseous taste in his mouth and began to vomit. He wiped his mouth with a filthy sleeve and looked at Arnold. 'You couldn't put a hose on me could you?'

Arnold grinned. 'Better than that. There's some warm water in the pavilion.'

As they strode across the cricket pitch they heard a distant bark. Arnold shrugged. 'He'll be halfway home by now.'

Indeed, by the time the two men had opened the pavilion door Wolfie was back outside the kitchen shaking the wet out of himself and sending great globs of mud and slime showering into the air. A bespattered footman ran into the kitchen to tell cook who sent one of the downstairs maids to tell the butler who, in turn, informed Lord Boutilier that his dog was back.

The great hound was hosed down while they waited for the vet to come rattling ten miles from Wolviston, in a little Morris, on his day off.

Chapter Five

Bunty Williams leaned back from the table so that her tight sequined dress glinted against her lean body. She flourished her long cigarette holder vaguely towards the band. 'Darling, you really must let someone transform your hair into something fashionable.'

Helen grinned. 'Never been one to pay much attention to fashion.' She gestured to her friend's short-cropped hair. 'What do you call that?'

'It's the Eton crop. Just in.'

'Looks as though someone poured a bucket of water over your head.'

'Any gossip, Bunty?' Giles Smallwood gave a little giggle as he twitched his moustache. Over his shoulder Helen watched a portly couple dance with robotic movements to the anonymous music of the string quartet. The singer sang 'I've only eyes for you' with a studied lack of emotion that passed for style.

Bunty laughed. 'Giles, you know your role is to tell me gossip so that I can put it in my paper.' Giles's question had raised a question of her own. 'Which reminds me. Any secrets, poppet?'

'I hate poppet,' Helen protested. Bunty had called her poppet or something as ridiculous since they'd met at an Eastbourne finishing school. Bunty had been three years ahead of Helen and, more importantly, her family were 'new money', so a friendship had seemed unlikely. Indeed, Helen had initially been reluctant to have dealings with Bunty but had soon succumbed to her infectious, cheerful outlook. Helen was troubled by the fact that she could see her own life mapped out for her and so was particularly impressed when Bunty had taken up a job in London as a journalist for the Daily Globe's gossip column, and 'broken away from Daddy.'

Helen stayed at her friend's flat when she visited the capital, though her father thought she used the family apartment near Lords.

'Daddy held a cricket match at the weekend. Provided prostitutes for the opposing team - except for the chap who got him out.' Giles and Bunty began to splutter with laughter. Bunty took a deep pull at her cigarette holder and blew smoke rings towards the high ceiling. 'What an imagination you have, Helen!'

Helen smiled happily at her private joke. 'There was a chap called Warren. He bowled quite spitefully at Perry Bowden. Hit him in the chest. He was really quite nasty.'

'Tom Warren, the Lancashire bowler?'

'Yes, tall, red-haired man. Do you know him?'

'Dreadful chap. Drinks beer by the barrel and curses at every batsman.' Giles was becoming animated. 'Thank God, we don't have to share a dressing room with his sort.'

Bunty smiled. 'Giles plays county cricket.'

'Only in the hols.' During the last hour he had hardly spoken as the conversation had progressed through the latest film, the rise of socialism, the increasing influence of women following the war, but now his moment had come. 'I was at school with Perry. Decent chap. So Warren peppered him, eh?'

'Only after Perry had slogged him a bit.'

'Good for Perry.' But Giles was not appeased. 'Cricket's going to the dogs. Following football. Went to a soccer match recently. Aren't the working classes appalling.'

Helen who had been well schooled in cricket by her father intervened. 'But surely cricket can't survive without professionals. They bring in the crowds, and they are just working at something for which they have a skill.'

'They should go to the leagues.'

'It's a three-day game. How many amateurs can take that sort of time off regularly? It's just not practical.'

Giles gave her his 'mere woman' look and Helen flushed with irritation but managed to keep her voice calm. 'I think it's important to know when to step back.'

A waitress leaned over the table to collect their empty plates. Giles, gripped by a passion, ignored Helen's observation. 'The trouble is they might tip their caps and call me Mister, but the reality is very different.' He handed the waitress his plate and waved her away. 'Last summer, Ambrose, the England spinner, got me with a flighted ball. "Good ball, Ambrose!' I said and the bloody wicketkeeper grins at me and says, "You're right there, sir. And it were wasted on you!" '

Bunty looked out of the long window. They were one storey up and she could see the tops of the trams as they trundled along the Strand. It had been raining and the lights from the theatres gleamed on the wet pavements. She loved London, there was always something to do, someone to meet, something to engage her mind. She lived in a frothy world of gossip; she knew it was also a sad world full of desperate laughter, but even so it was a good time and place to be young. The wild merry go round of life in the city had gained pace recently and some of the riders were being flung aside. The Talkies were taking over from the Silent Movies and many of the established stars were being found wanting. It wasn't so much a question of whether you slept with anyone to survive, but who, as many who had chosen wrongly had found to their cost. It was a long way from the life that her finishing school had envisaged for her.

One day she might stop to consider the casualties, the actress found with her head in an oven, the star now reduced to busking at a station, the silent movie siren now selling her body to get work as an extra, or worse, to get a packet of cocaine; the list was long. She smiled to herself. She was not ready to move on. She was still too young, and when she tired of the squalor and the turmoil, as she occasionally did, there was always Helen and her world in the shires.

She stretched her arms behind her head and yawned. 'Gosh, this seat is hard after a time. I think I've bruised my bottom.' It was the wrong thing to say. Giles, rumour had it, had a predilection for biting ladies' bottoms and other parts of their anatomy given the chance. There were stories of his liaisons with a succession of theatre women and in particular of a chorus girl who, presumably having been paid in advance, expelled gas in mid bite. Giles had promptly attacked her with such fury that his father had had to intervene with a bribe to prevent the lady taking the matter to court.

Bunty looked across at the little man. His heavily greased hair was showing sign of melting down his red, angry face. She thought him thoroughly unpleasant. Perhaps one day she would write a sufficiently sanitised version of Giles's biting for the story to be accepted by her newspaper.

She smiled at Helen. 'I think it's time for a club.'

'Lead on.' Giles rose from his seat and summoned the waitress for the bill.

'Where we going?'

Bunty wrapped herself in her mink stole. 'Take your pick. There are dangerous dives where I know the doorman, there are dangerous dives where I don't, there's clubs for the toffs and there's clubs where the toffs mingle with the crooks and the stars.'

She could see the excitement in Helen's face. 'Oh I think the last,'

Bunty laughed. 'The Blue Moon, then. It's near here, and very good for gossip.' As they left other customers glanced up at them. They seemed unlikely companions. The women were three inches taller than Giles whose stiff white bib bulged slightly as it stuck awkwardly in the top of his trousers.

The rain had stopped and Bunty skipped laughing between the puddles linking her arms with Helen. Giles followed puffing on a cigarette as the two girls talked of their days at school. He found himself watching the swing of their buttocks in their tight dresses and their words passed him by, not that they would have interested him anyway. Bunty directed them to a dark building in a lane off Fleet Street. The doorman's battered evening suit complemented his broken face. He smiled at the sight of Bunty and ushered them in. A small man was playing quiet jazz on a tiny stage at the end of the room. A group of young men and women sat at his feet. Others danced to the slow mood of the music. Bunty hoisted her mink over a hook by the door. 'Look after it George, darling.' George gave her a swat on her bottom as she passed and winked. He made the same gesture to Helen who pushed her arms back to protect herself. 'No, thank you!' She said sharply.

She followed Bunty down some stairs. Bunty turned and smiled. 'Keeps a girl warm on a winter's night,' she said brightly.

'It's the summer, Bunty.' Helen shook her head.

'Don't be so literal.' Bunty giggled. The two of them became aware that Giles was clumping down the stairs after them. 'He gave me a whack, as well,' he protested.

'He gives everyone a whack. It's a sort of trademark,' Bunty giggled.

'Oh. Oh, I see.' Giles appeared to be appeased.

The long room was swilling with smoke. Bunty and Helen found a small table while Giles went to the bar to order cocktails. A tall, sallow-faced man with large, sad eyes waved to Bunty from across the room. Bunty waved back before sitting at the table. 'Who was that?' Helen was staring into the room trying to identify stars, though she had little interest in films.

'That was Harry Bell.'

'Is he an actor?'

'He owns the place and a few others like it. Makes a fortune from selling cocaine.'

'Good God! You mean drugs.'

'Yes.'

Bunty nodded towards a languid, dark-haired man lounging in a chair in the far corner of the room. 'Now he's more my type.'

Helen followed her gaze.

'Recognise him?'

Helen shook her head.

'Harry Law. *The Angry Soul*. You've seen it?'

Helen shook her head.

'*Before the Dawn*?'

'I don't watch films.'

Bunty smiled. 'Perfect profile. But it's his eyes that really matter. They take to make up. So does Harry unfortunately, off the set as well as on it. He likes men.' Helen took a long look at the actor. For a second he caught her stare and gave faint smile. The cigarette at the corner of his mouth drooped. He sucked and exhaled and then reached out into the dark recesses of the corner. The hand that reached back was large and had a blue tattoo at the wrist. Helen was struck by the little drama.

'What a waste!' Bunty purred in Helen's ear. 'Ah, here's the bold Giles, seemingly unaware that there is a waitress service in these places.'

Giles' small figure cut belligerently between the dancing couples with three cocktails wrapped in his hands. As he passed under the bright lights in the centre of the room Peregrin Bowden recognised him and came to the table.

'Small world, eh?' Peregrin smiled down at Helen who looked up at him coolly.

Before she could speak Giles exclaimed, 'Heavens Perry! We were just talking about you.'

'I told them Warren gave you a bit of a going over,' Helen sipped at her drink.

In answer Perry pulled up his dress shirt showing livid bruises on his chest.

'Good God! You can see the seam.' Giles reached out and ran his fingers over the ridges.' Perry pulled down his shirt and took a seat.

For the next hour they chatted and danced. Helen had four more cocktails with some exotic sounding names and began to feel slightly drunk. She became aware that rapacious eyes were following her on the dance floor and she began to feel flustered. She had none of Bunty's easy skills in dealing with different types of people; her experience was limited mainly to those who were deferential because she was their social superior.

She found herself glancing across at Peregrin. She realised that, despite her instinctive dislike of him, he had qualities. He was a hard nut. His smiles and laughter had falseness about them, but the bruises on his chest were real. She remembered the way he had stayed in line before and during the battering from Warren. She looked out into the room. There were too many men looking at her, some glancing slyly, and some staring. She recalled the strange young man who threw stones at rooks. He had stared at her from across the cricket field. She remembered his spring to catch the ball, the throw from the boundary and, most of all, the graceful glide of his run. There was something pure and pagan about him. She looked around the room and felt the tiredness of the place.

London always came at her in a rush. She needed a fix of it, like others needed cocaine. And then the effect wore off and she was left with a vague and unsatisfactory feeling of emptiness. There must be something else. The trouble was, as far as she could see, there wasn't.

It was time to go home.

Chapter Six

Beth took one look at her son as he walked up the slope, dressed in white flannels and a cream shirt with three falcons sewn on to the breast pocket. She scurried from the cottage. 'You've got the Lord's clothes on. What's got into you?'

Ben held his own stinking shirt and trousers at arm's length. 'Arnold gave me them.'

Beth moved to him brushing her floured hands on her pinafore. 'They're not Arnold's to give. Have you any idea how beholden we are to the Lord?'

'Arnold said it would be alright.'

'And who's Arnold when he's not pushing rollers?'

The dripping dirty clothes added to her alarm. 'And what have you been doing with those?'

Ben explained how he had rescued the great dog and how Arnold had invited him to use one of the baths at the pavilion, but by now Beth could see no good coming from anything. 'I hope you cleaned the bath after you,' she said. Then a new fear consumed her. 'You could have drowned, sucked under by that bloody swamp.' She looked down at his clothes, which lay in a soiled heap on the path. 'Put them in the stream and then dump them in the poss tub. On their own mind. I don't want you mucking any more clothes.'

Ben stood there grinning as she was chased by one panic after another. 'All for a bloody dog!'

'It was Lord Boutilier's dog,' said Ben. 'I would think he'd be grateful.'

'Grateful! Grateful! The likes of him to the likes of us. Don't be daft.' She pointed to the dirty clothes once more.

Get some raggy clothes on. Get those cricket ones into the wash and get them,' she pointed to the pile on the path, 'Get them down to the stream. All this for a bloody dog!' She turned and strode into the cottage, but before Ben could stoop to pick up the dirty clothes she ran out again and hugged him. 'You could have been killed. Heavens knows where this will end!'

It seemed her worst fears were confirmed the following day when a large limousine stopped in the lane leading to her gate. A chauffeur marched round to the passenger side, opened the door and Lord Boutilier emerged, followed by a huge dog.

Beth saw them from the front window and ran out the back of the cottage into the garden to where Lord Boutilier's cricketing clothes were hanging. She felt them. 'Still damp!'

Ben saw her as he cleaned out one of the hen coops. Beth pointed through the house. 'It's him. Lord Boutilier. I told you there'd be trouble.'

Ben wiped his hands on a rag and strode round the side of the cottage. His mother's antics had amused him, but now they had him on edge. The simple fact was that he had saved the man's dog, at considerable risk to himself. He had faith in the natural justice of things as a rule, and certainly could see no reason why he should be blamed for anything. Even so, Boutilier's daughter had struck him for nothing, so his mother might be right. His stride had an aggressive air, but then Wolfie spotted him, gave a great bark, and bounded to him, rearing up.

Ben buried himself in the dog's neck. His mother caught up with him. 'Careful, son. Don't harm the dog!' Even she was aware of how ridiculous she sounded as the dog had a head as hard as a cannon ball.

She turned to Lord Boutilier. He was dressed in stained flannels and a faded, tweed jacket with leather patches at the elbows. His battered walking boots and his dishevelled hair completed the picture of a model for a lost property shop. Had her own son appeared out the door dressed in such a fashion she would have berated him, but for Lord Boutilier she had only smiles, and a little dip of a curtsey. She advanced on him with a waterfall of words. 'Good day Lord Boutilier. This is a great honour. I take it you have come about the cricket clothes. I've washed them fresh, sir. The boy only borrowed them because his own were ruined in the rescue of the great dog that had fallen into the swamp and my boy went in to pull him out, which he did at great risk to himself, and at the cost of ruining his own clothes. Mr Groundsman cleaned him down and loaned him the flannels and shirt else, he would have had to walk naked to his home.'

All this came in one breath and then she stopped aware that she had been talking for a long time and that Lord Boutilier had not spoken a word. She imagined this alone might be cause for rebuke or even dismissal, save for the fact that the great man did not employ her, though she did live in one of his cottages. The thoughts scampered through her mind like frightened mice.

Ben strode down the slope past his mother with Wolfie bounding by his side.

By now both mother and son saw that Lord Boutilier was smiling. 'The dog seems quite recovered from his ordeal, sir.' Ben patted Wolfie's head. The dog took his hand in his mouth in a friendly grip.

Lord Boutilier nodded. 'He is and that is, in no small way, thanks to you. Arnold has told me all about the rescue and I have come here to thank you. It was a brave thing that you did.' He turned to Beth. 'Madam, you had a very brave husband and you have a very brave son. I congratulate you.'

Ben could hear his mother give a little gasp behind him. She'd been about to scurry to the back of the cottage to retrieve the cricket clothes for Lord Boutilier but now thought better of it. Perhaps it would not be appropriate for the great man to carry off his flannels and shirt in his chauffeur-driven limousine.

Even so she wanted rid of them. To her they were evidence of a crossing of social boundaries.

As these thoughts were scattering through her head she heard her son say, 'Thank you, sir. I told Arnold that we can replace the door.'

Lord Boutilier chuckled, 'A door's a bit of wood, but a dog's a dog, eh.'

'And the cricket things, sir?' Beth still needed closure on the clothes.

'Those old togs! Your boy is welcome to them. Indeed I think he might have better use of them than I ever did.'

Beth's hands wiped at her flowered pinafore. There'd been so much of this conversation that did not fit into her understanding of things. She could deal with Lord Boutilier's agent Carter with ease because, in the end, they were both underlings and she could see a common purpose. But this man, with all his power and the history of his name, was an awesome mystery to her.

Lord Boutilier could see she was perplexed. He gave a gentle cough. 'As I see it, Mrs Linden, I'm in debt to your son.'

'Oh no, sir! That is not possible.'

Lord Boutilier raised a hand to silence her before there was another rush of words. 'And, as such, I want, if he is willing, to offer him a part-time job working with Arnold on the cricket pitch. I understand from Mr Carter that he has helped you to create a little business with your chickens and eggs.'

'Yes sir. He has that.'

'Well, in his spare time he can work with Arnold.'

'To be a groundsman?' Beth sounded doubtful. The chicken business seemed to have better prospects than a grown man growing grass.

'No, to be a cricketer.'

'A cricketer! But he's only played at school.'

'And had to be restrained because he was too quick, I gather.'

Ben and his mother stood silent astonished that Lord Boutilier knew so much about them. Then Ben blurted out, 'The batsmen weren't too good you see, sir. Nor the pitches.'

Lord Boutilier looked at the tall, straight figure of the young man. He remembered the leaping catch and the great throw at the match. Arnold had spoken of the youth in glowing terms as they'd smoked a couple of clay pipes sat on the pavilion steps, watching the dog bound after birds with futile enthusiasm. Lord Boutilier saw Arnold as a trusted link with common people. It had been Arnold who'd taken his father's wicket with a hat trick ball in a Gentleman versus Players match in 1895. The Doctor had been one of the other wickets and Arnold had been very graceful about his triumph. In fact there were some who pointed out that he was a great deal better at winning than old WG was at losing. Indeed there were rumours of bad blood between them for a season, after Arnold had sent a ball whistling through the Doctor's long beard.

There were many who had chortled on hearing the story because the Doctor, who had played as an amateur, earned more than any five professionals.

News of the lord's visit spread through the estate in a day and throughout the valley in a week, for Boutilier had never been known to call at a tenant's cottage since his old nanny had died just after the Great War. And, as news of the visit went from cottage to cottage, so too did the tales of Ben's rescue of the dog.

There were some, who had never met or even heard of him, who now claimed first name acquaintance.

Others told tales of the cricket match and Ben's catch and throw that had dragged gasps of admiration from the good and the great. There were a few who claimed to have seen him clattering the rooks' nests with stones. Others said they had seen him collecting round, smooth stones from the dried-up river bed which he had then bowled at prodigious speeds at the beech trees on the edge of the southern wood. Doubters were taken to the wood itself and shown a tree with the bark smashed. But the most compelling tale of all came from a young crofter who drifted all over the county searching for work. He had been sitting in the Queen Victoria enjoying a pint of best ale when the latest argument erupted over Ben's prowess as a bowler. One of the field workers claimed to have seen one of the woodsmen attacking a beech tree with a hammer and the two men were all for going out back to settle it with fists when the crofter spoke up in a quiet, but deep voice. 'It seems to me of little consequence whether the tree was damaged by hammers or stones.'

'How's that?' asked one of the protagonists with muted aggression, for the stranger had a broad chest that strained his shirt.

'Because either the young man can bowl fast or he can't and the proof will be in the pudding and no amount of dents in a tree will make a bit of difference. And, anyway, I can tell you that he can bowl as quick as lightning.'

'Oh you can, can you? And how so?'

'Because I was at school with Ben Linden, up the valley at Wolviston.'

The Landlord, Jimmy Swann, looked nervously about the room at this because he had endured nights and days of tale telling about this youth, and some of it had come near to the boil. There was a silence in the room during which some of the more argumentative customers sized up the man and noted the obvious, that he was a very big man indeed; so big it was difficult to imagine him plying his trade without going through the roofs he repaired.

'Well then,' said Jimmy Swann, anxious to move the conversation on. 'Tell us about him.'

The stranger took a sip of his dark beer. 'The truth is that I don't know how fast he is when set against others, and remember he was only thirteen when I saw him.' He paused, pleased by the silence he commanded.

'Yes, yes,' said Swann sensing that at last there was a man about to deliver facts rather than conjecture. 'Well, the truth is that I have never seen your top players bowling but what I do know is that our teacher, Mr Hurley, had to stop him from bowling after a couple of overs. We had no pads or gloves you see and the pitch wasn't the flattest.'

'Yes, yes. But was he quick?'

The stranger gave a laugh. 'He was the fast as a hawk coming for the kill.'

There was a silence in the pub. Jimmy Swann had never seen anything like it.

Later, much later, the crofter wobbled his way out of the pub and along the valley road, not having bought another drink.

Chapter Seven

Helen had been home a week before she ventured to the cricket ground. She wore cream jodhpurs and a faded, red hunting jacket, which her father had forbidden her to wear at hunts, because it was deemed inappropriate attire for women . She left her hunter at home and walked to the ground. Her father had told her about the rescue of Wolfie and she stopped at the drainage pond and studied it for minutes. The dirty water was rimmed with mud and slime at the lower end, and it was here that Wolfie had bounded over the fence after the duck. Carter had announced plans to drain the pond into a ditch that ran alongside the lane.

As she stood looking across the still water, Helen imagined the great dog leaping out towards the duck, landing ten feet from safety up to its chest in slime, and sinking slowly. Just to see it in her mind was horrible enough, but to be confronted with the reality, that was something else. For the first time she noticed the door. Its front end had sunk leaving the back jutting out like a decayed wreck, a dark, stark testimony to the heroic nature of the rescue. She shuddered again. She had been trying to bring herself to apologise to the strange youth who threw stones at rooks and ran like a ghost into the countryside. Now, as she stood at the edge of the swamp reliving his rescue, she knew she must go to him straight away and make her peace.

She walked through the hedge and across the pitch to the pavilion. Arnold was sitting on the steps, smoking his pipe and sharpening pegs for the cricket nets.

'Old Arnie!"' she greeted him.

He looked up and smiled. 'Queen Helen.' He called her that on occasion to puncture her regal airs.

It was Arnie who had taught her to bat. More than that, he'd had a special bat made for her because her brother's was too big and she was wheeling her front foot to leg to get a swing, instead of playing down the line. Arnie was one of the very few people with whom Helen felt completely at ease and when she sat beside the old man she leaned her slim body into him without a thought of impropriety. Her head rested on his shoulder. 'Thank you,' she said.

He blew on her hair and she could smell the heavy aroma of his tobacco. He gave a chuckle. He knew she had more wiles than a cage of monkeys.

'Thank you for saving my dog.'

She looked out across the pitch, avoiding his gaze lest he divined her real intent. 'Aaargh,' he said. 'As you well know all I did was stand on a door. So the young man you really want to be thanking is Ben Linden. But that'll be a problem, won't it, as you've hit him with your whip.'

She looked up startled. 'Who told you that?' she exclaimed.

Old Arnie's blue, watery eyes lit with amusement. 'I hear everything.'

'When did you start to forget that you are an employee, Arnie?'

'Probably when I caught you having a wee behind yon hedge.' He warded off her punch with his right arm. 'About fifteen years ago, it would be.'

She hugged into him and felt the warmth of his body. Her father avoided physical contact, indeed he avoided expressing emotion.

Arnie stood up and brushed at his stained, wrinkled trousers. 'Are you looking for Ben?'

'No! Whatever makes you think that.'

Arnie grinned. 'I've seen you walking about the grounds

a lot recently and I asked myself 'Why isn't her royal highness on her great horse?' But, of course, if you are trying to say sorry, twelve feet up on a hunter ain't exactly humble, is it?'

Helen rose from her seat on the steps. 'What tosh you talk, Arnie.'

Arnie sucked on his pipe. 'Maybe.'

'Father says he is going to work for you.'

'He's asked me to turn him into a bowler.' Arnie began to walk across the outfield towards the square.

Helen followed him. 'You can't just turn someone into a cricketer.'

'No.'

She caught up with him. 'So it's silly.'

'No.'

'How not?' Her voice rose in irritation.

Arnie glanced at her. 'I see the queen is coming out.'

'I'll kick your arse in a minute, old man.'

He grinned and pulled on his nicotine-stained moustache. 'You've seen him run. Not the speed. The balance, that's the important thing.'

'So, have you seen him bowl yet?'

'No. But he knows how to set up the nets. I've let him settle in. He hasn't bowled for years, so I'll wait till he feels comfortable. But I know he's practising because he goes up the old drover's trail. That's why you haven't seen him in your travels. Now you know where to find him.'

She gripped his arm. 'Arnold! That's enough. Really that's enough.'

However, that evening she ordered the head groom to saddle Jasper for eight o'clock the following morning. She drove the horse at a steady gallop uphill until she came to the long winding trail that had been hollowed out by tens of thousands of hooves. She looked along the road through the morning mist and it was as if the ghosts of men and beasts could come roaming into sight. She was overtaken by a new thought. God help her if they did! For many of these men had been wild, the sort who would have carried her off into the bushes.

Jasper gave a loud snort and whinnied, impatient to gallop on. She dug in her heels and sent him rearing down the road, his heavy hooves thudding mightily into the soft turf. The wind pulled at her hair and cut through the gaps in her jacket. Her face became numb and her eyes began to water as the great horse pounded on. Jasper raced round a bend without a change in the rhythm of his hoof beats and suddenly she was confronted by a long, straight stretch. Two hundred yards down she saw three makeshift stumps stuck in the middle of the road. Forty yards from them, at the beginning of his run-up, he'd piled a neat pyramid of smooth stones. She slowed to a trot and saw that on either side of the stumps the wicket was dug up with divots where the stones had pitched. Obviously he'd been bowling at one end, the stones had pitched through the wicket, and so he'd collected them and bowled from the other end as well. She was impressed by the thought and effort he'd put into it. Carrying the stones from the dried-up riverbed to the drovers' road must have exhausted him, and then he'd started bowling.

She nudged the reins again and Jasper blasted the air through his nostrils and set off on a gallop once more, along the straight and then into bend after bend across the undulating landscape. At last she pulled him up on his back legs and turned for home. She saw Ben as she came thundering into the straight. He was way down the track and running away from her to his marker. He hadn't heard her in the wind and she watched him glide in effortlessly, leap and send down a stone at great speed. She had time to register that he had a side-on action before the turf exploded on a length and the stone bounced over the wicket and came to rest thirty yards down the track.

She had been brought up with cricket and cricketers all her life. It was her father's obsession. As she sat on the great hunter, who had slowed to a walk, she realised she had witnessed something special. She couldn't analyse it. She just knew that this man bowling on a windswept road, without proper boots, bowling a smooth stone; that this man was special. For a second she forgot who she was and who he was, and she sat in awe at the beauty and fierceness of what she had seen. He turned from the wicket to collect another stone and saw her for the first time. Jasper walked slowly towards him, but Ben stayed still and staring. When she got within twenty yards of him he moved to the opposite side of the road. She noticed that his jacket, waistcoat and cap were piled neatly by the bracken that skirted the road. He waited for her to pass, his black eyes calm and watching; his look was neither obsequious nor arrogant; he was just waiting for her to go.

Jasper gave another snort and pawed the ground. Helen stared down at the young man. She recalled Arnie's words about her being twelve feet up and swung her right leg over the horse to dismount. He stood his ground staring at her. She noticed that he didn't blink for long periods. She became aware that she still had her riding crop in her right hand. She had thought many times about the incident and how she would bring herself to apologise. Given their different positions in society, none of it seemed natural, yet it was something she knew she must do, not least because she was intrigued by this man when so many of the other people she met seemed like riders on a roundabout.

'The last time,' she couldn't bring herself to be more specific that than that, 'you gave me a fright and I just lashed out. I'm sorry.' The words came in a rush as though she had been holding her breath for weeks.

His expression didn't change and still he didn't blink. Did he not realise how much her words had cost her? She hesitated and then spoke again. 'I've wanted to say that for a while but . . . '

'It was difficult.' He finished the sentence for her.

'Yes.'

'Because you are Lady Helen.'

She gave him a hard look. Was he mocking her?

Then he stepped forward with a smile and offered his hand. The wind ruffled the bracken. On the galloping horse it had been exhilarating, now it had a biting breath. She hesitated. She didn't shake hands with tenants, let alone those she hardly knew, yet, if she refused, the offered hand would be gone forever, and her apology merely words lost in the wind.

He spoke again. 'We're in a wild place here, don't you think? It's common land, a place that belongs to people of the past, both the huntsman and the herdsman. If we can't shake hands here, where can we?'

She was struck by his sense of poetry and reached out in an instant. His hand was cold from the wind and rough from the stones, but while she held on to him she could feel his strength and obduracy. She tried to escape from the intimacy of the moment.

'Arnie says he is going to make a cricketer out of you.'

The young man laughed. 'He hasn't seen me bowl yet.'

'Has anyone?'

'Only at school. They stopped me after a few overs. The pitch wasn't good.'

'And that was it?'

'Yes.'

'Apart from some stones.'

'Yes.'

She was being seduced by curiosity. 'Arnie is a clever man. He was a great bowler.'

'I know.'

'And he hasn't seen you bowl a ball.'

'No. He says he's seen me run, and that's all he needs to know.' As he spoke the wind wrapped his loose clothes around his body and she remembered his still head as she'd watched his gliding run. 'He says it's all about balance.'

The great horse gave a shudder and a snort, as though recalling her to her other world. She reached into her saddlebag and pulled out a couple of cricket balls. 'Here. They were lying on the pitch. I thought you might like to have them.' She heard his thanks as she mounted the horse. She didn't look back as Jasper broke into a trot and then a canter, but, as she neared the end of the straight, she realised that her smooth exit had gone wrong. He knew that she had sought him out. She looked back and he was running in from his marker. He didn't see her. He had eyes only for the makeshift stumps. She had a strange feeling of rejection, which she tried to suppress.

Chapter Eight

In the space of a few months Beth had seen her fortunes change dramatically for the better. She still could not bring herself to break the necks of chickens, but she cleaned out the coops, checked the eggs that were on their three-week hatching cycle, and made sure the chicks had enough space to survive without fighting. Captain Carter appeared less frequently and was more formal. She suspected that the change had been driven by the rise of Ben's stock, following the rescue. He was however, she had to admit, as good as his word concerning the chickens and eggs. The huge house took as many as she could supply. The price was slightly less than she could have got selling round the villages but the volume and the guarantee of sales more than compensated. The head cook, Mrs Frobisher, met Ben or Beth at the door, armed with a blunt pencil and a large ledger into which she would enter their supplies in large loopy writing. She settled with them every month.

Then, in early July, Jarvis called at Beth's cottage, touching the peak of his cap.

'Well?' she said, a little impatiently, for she was about to put a stew in the oven and had had a hard time lighting the fire.

Jarvis smiled shyly and pointed to the wheelbarrow he'd pushed up the lane.

'I seen you carrying them baskets and thought this might help.'

She looked at the stained old barrow, but noted that he had replaced the spokes in the front wheel with hard beech wood, and that he had wrapped the handles in cloth to save her from blisters. Her heart warmed to him briefly. Life had taught her that nothing came for nothing, but she judged him to be a kind man, unlike Mr Carter, who had given her the hens to seek her favours.

'Thank you, John.' It was the first time she had called him by his first time.

He blushed and tried to impress her with his knowledge of local commerce. 'I thought it a good idea for you to increase your production.' He pointed to the barrow as though it was some integral part of a factory.

She suppressed a desire to laugh, but later she realised that what he had said made sense. The barrow meant that she could indeed increase the amount of produce she sent to the great house by three or four fold, providing she could increase her output.

That week she decided to extend her vegetable patch. It stretched in a neat, brown strip about a quarter way across the back garden. She and Ben toiled for days, digging up the turf and then digging out the soil and clay to a depth of two spades. Ben laid the turf face down at the bottom of the shallow pit and then took the barrow down to their bottom field and loaded up the manure left by Mr Carter's great mare. Mother and son spread the muck before filling the pit with the soil and broken clay. After that they spent a day hoeing and laying a crop of potatoes to break up the soil even further. By the end of the week they'd trebled the size of their vegetable patch. That Saturday, Beth wheeled down a dozen chickens and two hundred eggs dressed in straw and told cook that soon she would be able to provide an additional service of root vegetables. Mrs Frobisher wiped her stained hands on her pinafore. 'Fresh grown. Not like that scallywag in Wolviston?'

'Delivered on the day they're picked,' said Beth with pride. 'Though it'll be a while before they've grown.'

'Fine.'

Beth gave Mrs Frobisher a hug when saying her goodbyes. Her hands pulled on the cook's beefy back. She smelled of cabbage leaves. As she turned to pick up the handle of the barrow, she heard two horses trotting on the gravel.

'It's the Mistress and the Hon Peregrin,' whispered cook.

Beth said nothing but stared after the straight-backed couple. Lady Helen dug her heels into her mount that plunged forward. The man charged after her and their laughter mingled strangely with the squeak of Beth's barrow.

Peregrin had become a frequent visitor to the house hanging on to Charles's coat tails. He sought Helen's company at every opportunity and, as he gained confidence, he lost his affectation of smug conceit that had so irritated her when they first met.

Her father had taken to the young man, even though he was the second son. Peregrin and Helen rode out most days, usually up the hills and along the drovers' road. The trail had some long flat stretches, without rabbit holes or any other dangers to the mounts. They could slip the reins and ride full pelt until the horses' breath came in great sobs and they slowed to a canter and then a walk. However, there were days when Helen insisted on taking less exciting rides because she feared that she might reveal her strange interest in the cricket pitch, and the bowler who used it. She'd pointed it out to Peregrin on their first ride. He had shown little interest, even when she had mentioned that the bowler was the young man who had taken the catch when Peregrin had struck the boundary.

They rode the trail four times in a week and there was still no sign of the widow's son. Helen mentioned his absence and the fact that he was training to be a bowler and was to be tutored by Arnold.

She made herself give a giggle and pointed to the cricket balls. I brought these up for him out of kindness. He'd been using stones.' She pointed to the pitch marks on the wicket and gave another little giggle.

'You say Arnold is going to train him to be a bowler!'

'That's the plan. Sounds crazy doesn't it?'

Peregrin shook his head. 'He's not even practising. The balls haven't been moved all week.'

She felt a stab of alarm at the words. It seemed he had abandoned the bowling wicket, and ignored her gift. She was filled with anger and disappointment. 'How dare he treat me in such a manner?'

Their two horses had closed and Peregrin reached out to place an arm round her shoulders. She shrugged him off angrily. 'How dare he?' she asked again.

Peregrin shrugged. 'Who cares, Helen? He's just some uneducated lad who knows no better.' He reached out again, but she urged her horse forward out of his reach. 'I told you we could just be friends,' she snapped.

Peregrin was shocked. He'd thought she had warmed to him over the past few weeks, and now this. The stupid loutish bowler seemed to have angered her for some reason. He stared at her. 'My God! It's this ridiculous bowling fellow, isn't it!' He gave a loud, hollow laugh.

'Don't be absurd! Remember to whom you are talking,' her eyes flashed in anger, 'Just accept I don't, and never will, have any feelings of love for you. Never!' She dug her heels into her horse and galloped down the straight whooping with the thrill of it. He watched her bobbing buttocks and charged after her crashing down the wickets with a vandal's glee.

That evening she walked Wolfie down to the cricket ground and found Arnie sitting on the steps of the pavilion sucking on his pipe, enjoying the remains of the day.

He moved over and gave her room next to the railings. 'Been expecting you. Haven't seen you for a week. Haven't seen him either.'

'Haven't seen who?'

'The young lad. Ben Linden. Haven't seen him either.'

'What on earth has that got to do with me?'

'He's been helping his mother build up their little business.'

Helen tried to protest again, but Arnie just spoke on until she listened, as he knew she would, because she wanted news of him. 'He's coming here tomorrow. He'll make a nets bowler this summer. Maybe more.' He winked at her. 'If you come down tomorrow evening, maybe I'll let you know how he got on.'

For the second time in hours she was being taunted with Ben Linden and her face reddened in anger. 'Stop this, Arnie. Stop it now! I was at fault with him at our first meeting and I have tried to correct it.' She wagged her forefinger at the old man.

But Arnie, unlike Peregrin, had known her and her wiles since she was a child, and he was not to be intimidated. He sucked on his pipe quietly as she tried to rebuke him. 'I'll not mention him again,' he said quietly.

'Good!' she exclaimed rising to her feet and was about to walk off when he said, 'He told me something unusual though.'

'What?' Helen realised that she had betrayed herself. 'As if I care.' She began to walk away. He could tell she was waiting for him to continue speaking so he didn't.

'What?' she asked again.

'He said the balls you gave him were useless. Every time he bowled them they went two hundred yards down the track. He had to use the stones, you see.'

Ben arrived at the cricket ground at four o'clock prompt, carrying a pair of canvas plimsolls under his arm.

Arnie gave them a glance but said nothing. He pointed to the nets that had been erected at the boundary nearest the great house.

'Ready?'

Ben smiled and nodded. Arnie picked up a canvas bag full of cricket balls.

They walked to the nets. 'Do you want to mark out your run-up.

Ben shrugged. 'I've never done that. I just walk back until it feels right.'

'Well, if it works, it works.'

He watched as Ben struggled into his plimsolls. The sun was still warm and they could smell the new-cut grass. The tall trees rustled behind the nets and the cows called to each other in an adjoining field.

'Don't be nervous.' Arnie smiled. 'I'll watch some from side on and then some more from behind the net.'

Ben nodded and took the bag to the end of his run. When he placed it on the ground he knew he was at the place. He picked out a ball and, without hesitation, flowed into his run. The ball flashed down the wicket, spat off the pitch just short of a length and reared over the stumps before hissing into the net.

Arnie knew that Ben was looking at him as he retraced his steps, but he avoided eye contact.

He watched five more balls without comment. The young man had a natural side-on action, but he was jumping too high in his delivery stride and so losing power. But he was fast, very fast.

Ben was back at the end of his run when Arnie signalled him to wait as he walked to the far end of the nets and stood directly behind the stumps.

He nodded and Ben ran in again. Arnie noted the smooth run, the straight line to the wicket, the still head and the silent feet, and he felt a surge of excitement he hadn't experienced since his own playing days. This young man was the most natural bowler he had seen. The ball pitched on middle stump and reared over the wicket.

'Try to pitch on the off stump and pitch it up a bit.' They were the first words he had spoken in five minutes. Ben nodded and turned at the end of his run. The ball pitched six inches outside off stump, but he had managed to get a fuller length.

'Again.'

Ben bowled four more balls and the last of these hit the top of the off stump and sent it spinning back into the net. Arnie grinned, 'Well bowled, son.'

Arnie walked from behind the nets and followed Ben to the end of his run-up. As Ben turned he rubbed his heel in a line two yards in front of the young man. 'Start here.'

Ben moved forward to the marker.

'This time lean your upper body forward before you start your run. Your feet will follow.'

Ben did as he was bid and sent another ball just wide of the off stump.' He looked disappointed. 'What was the difference?'

'You got into your stride quicker and so saved yourself a couple of yards. That'll add up during a day, I can tell you.'

Arnie had already seen enough but he asked Ben to bowl another six overs to test his stamina. The young man's shirt was stained with sweat by the end of his stint, but was he still bowling with rhythm and accuracy.

Arnie found it hard to disguise his excitement as the young man pulled on his jacket and approached him.

'That was a good first session. Very promising.'

'Was I quick?'

Arnie laughed. 'That's a question you all ask.' He began to collect the cricket balls and Ben followed him. 'Well?'

'You're quick enough.'

'For county?' His voice was innocent and eager.

Arnie laughed again. 'My God, son. You're a long way off that.'

Ben didn't try to hide his disappointment. 'You said I was quick.'

'You are, but so are the county batsmen. You bowl two loose balls an over so they'll wait for those and block or leave the rest.' He watched as Ben's body sagged in disappointment. Arnie was reluctant to praise the boy too extravagantly because he could see no good coming from it, but it was time to give him a carrot. 'If you are willing to work hard, I can make you a good bowler.'

'How good?'

'You can be two yards faster, more accurate, and you will be able to move the ball both ways. It'll take time, but you have my promise.'

He watched as Ben seemed to grow a size and wondered whether he had said too much.

They began to walk back to the pavilion. Arnie felt for the keys in his pocket. 'Do you want a bath? You're sweating.'

'No point. I've got to tend to the chickens when I get home.'

They arranged to meet the following evening and Arnie watched him stroll back across the field. Cricket had given him about twenty days that he would remember for the rest of his life, and this had been one of them.

The following morning Boutilier took Wolfie on his walk to the cricket field. Boutilier knew that something was up because Arnie rose to his feet and approached him across the pitch.

'Fair goings on yesterday, sir.'

His lordship didn't appear to hear as he looked across at the small wood which stood to the west of the pitch. The keepers had told him that the trees were stacked with game but there was no obvious place for the beaters to drive them.

Arnie persevered. 'It's about the boy, sir. The young man who rescued Wolfie.'

'Ah yes.' Lord Boutilier continued to stare at the wood. 'He was last heard of bowling stones on the drovers' road, I believe.'

A lesser man might have been discouraged by the great man's diffident manner, but Arnie knew from many conversations with Boutilier that this was an affectation.

'The fact is sir, I watched him bowl eight overs last evening, and he's fast.'

Boutilier whistled for Wolfie who ignored the great man, preferring to follow the scent of a rabbit. 'How fast?'

'I think he may become as fast as there's ever been.'

Lord Boutilier stared at the groundsman. 'You're serious?'

'Yes.'

Lord Boutilier turned his back to Arnie and stared at the nets where the great drama had taken place. He had known his groundsman since childhood. His father had brought the man from London at the end of his county career, and it was he who had taught Boutilier the rudiments of the game. Boutilier had never shown any skill as a bowler but, like many of his class, was a keen batsman. Arnie had been honest enough to admit his deficiencies in that respect, but had brought in a batsman who'd recently retired from the county game. During the years that followed Lord Boutilier had heard Arnie give a thousand opinions on cricket and its complexities and he knew him to be a shrewd and honest judge.

For him to praise the young man so highly on such scant evidence was extraordinary. His thoughts were interrupted by the sight of his daughter bursting through a gap in the hedge. She was wearing a long grey cardigan over a fair isles sweater, and pleated grey skirt. Her legs gave off a ruby sheen from her lisle stockings and her fair hair fluttered as the breeze caught it.

She was carrying a shallow wicker basket. 'Can't find any plovers' eggs.' She showed her father the empty basket.

Lord Boutilier smiled. 'You're a townie, Helen. They've been out of season for two months.'

'Oh! We've only just run out.' She smiled at Arnie and turned again to her father. 'Has he been telling you about our stone bowler?'

Lord Boutilier nodded. 'Yes, he has.'

'And?'

'He's very impressed. I intend to watch him myself this evening with a view to hiring him as a nets bowler.'

Helen looked at her father. She was irritated by his habit of talking to her in the language of a solicitor's letter.

Arnie was waiting for Ben at the nets that evening.

The young man was wearing his plimsolls and, though it was warm, had a pullover tied around his neck. He heard a giggle from the pavilion and looked across to see Helen seated between her father and Captain Carter.

'Ignore them,' Arnie whispered.

Ben stared at him. 'Ignore them!'

'They're just spectators. You're the player. For all their rank, they're sitting on their perfumed arses watching, and you are doing the doing. This is about you.' He gave Ben a wink. 'Just warm up for the first over. I don't want you going flat out yet.'

'When?'

'I'll tell you.'

His approach was as smooth and straight as ever for the first three balls, but his arm whirled over without effort. Helen turned to her father remembering the stones. 'I thought he'd be faster than that.'

'Wait, Helen.' Lord Boutilier stared intently towards the nets. Carter gave a herrump and wriggled his neck in his collar.

Three more balls went by without any appreciable increase in pace. At the end of the over Arnie walked back with Ben to the end of his run-up. 'Ok. Let's see what you've got.'

Ben felt warm and free and his gliding run gathered pace until he leapt into his delivery stride. Arnie had told him to keep his upper body forward as he jumped and to keep the leap low and long. He was far from perfecting the technique, but this time he got it just right.

Neither Lord Boutilier nor his daughter saw the ball, but they heard it crash into the wicket and saw two stumps spear into the net. Lord Boutilier stared at the scene. One of the stumps was stuck in the netting, broken halfway up. 'Good God!' he said.

Ben did not bowl as fast again that morning, but even so

Boutilier knew that he had seen something remarkable. With Helen in his wake, he walked up to the young man who was towelling himself after his exertions and congratulated him.

Arnie waited until Ben had said his goodbyes before approaching Boutilier in his blunt fashion.

'He'll need some boots before he turns his ankles.'

Boutilier frowned. 'Well, he can buy them out of his wages, surely.'

Arnie shook his head. 'The family have an uncle in Wolviston who's lost work at the mills. Ben's money goes to help him out.'

'Well, give him some extra work here. Mow the grass. Cut the wicket or something.'

Arnie was the one man who worked on the great estate who could stand face to face with the great man. 'He runs and walks twice a week to Wolviston to give his uncle produce. He does most of the work in his mother's poultry business. If he does any more he'll be too tired to bowl.'

Helen pulled at her father's elbow. 'Daddy! It's only a couple of guineas.'

Boutilier turned to her. 'Once I grant such a favour, others may ask for the same, and what can I say to them?'

'You can say that they didn't risk their lives to save your dog.'

Lord Boutilier stared at his daughter and Arnie thought that he was going to rebuke her, but eventually he nodded his head. 'Very well. I shall employ him as a net bowler this summer and his wages shall be deducted until he pays for the boots. I shall instruct Carter to see that he is fitted.' And with that he walked off.

Chapter Nine

Ben had never taken to his Uncle Joshua and nor had his mother, though she never admitted as much. She was a practical woman who rarely dwelt on what might have been, but when she looked at Joshua with his fat, pale face, his pink, wet lips, and his bulbous stomach, she could not but help wonder why he had survived the War while his brother, her husband, a fine strong man, had not.

The answer was obvious: her husband had done six months training in home-made trenches, had been armed with a Lee Enfield, and been sent to France, while Joshua, a great bag of wheezing bad breath, had been armed with a ladle and sent to the kitchens.

There had never been much love lost between the two brothers. Joshua, two years older, had always looked in envy at the ladies Frank had brought to their home. He was however more taken with Beth than all of Frank's previous girl friends and they had struck up an uneasy friendship, helped by the fact that Joshua had started courting a girl of his own, Edith, 'the plump lass from the fish and chip shop' as Frank had described her.

More importantly, both she and Beth read the gossip papers and were addicted to the personal letters in the Daily Mail. Later they became devout readers of all the film magazines that flourished with the advent of the Talkies. Each day Joshua scoured the bins at the mill and retrieved a variety of magazines and papers, which he gave to Edith, by now his wife, who duly posted them on to Beth, usually with a chatty letter. When he was laid off at the mill the little parcels stopped. In their place Joshua sent a pleading letter on which Beth felt obliged to act because he was 'family'.

Ben, who felt no such obligation to his uncle, who smelt of sweat, grease and beer, argued that they should send the man a little money each week to help Edith and their two children. But Beth knew better. 'It'll go down his gullet or disappear even faster into the pockets of the street bookie,' she said.

So each Saturday Ben was given the task of walking and running ten miles to Wolviston carrying a couple of chickens and a dozen eggs packed in straw in a rucksack. Ben could have followed the Valley Road but the track was rough on his feet, so, after a couple of trips, he decided to favour the lush turf of the drovers' road.

The trail swept away from Wolviston to avoid the old toll road and for the last mile of his journey he was forced to crash his way through bracken to cut to the town.

Before he set out, he helped his mother clean out the coops and steal the eggs from the laying hens to encourage them to lay some more. His mother cooked him a breakfast of egg and bread, fried in dripping, and then packed his rucksack with the produce. Last of all she placed a thick sandwich at the top of the rucksack, together with a billy-can of sweet tea.

On the first trip, Ben discovered that three of the eggs had cracked during his journey across the countryside. Joshua had frowned at the sight of them.

'Perhaps if we boiled them first?' Ben suggested.

'Perhaps if you wrapped them properly,' said his uncle.

Ben was about to give an angry retort when Edith came out of the kitchen in a rush. 'What sort of talk is that to a boy who has walked twenty miles to help us, Joshua Linden?'

'It's not twenty or anywhere near it,' was all Joshua could think to say.

'Oh yes.' Edith's voice rose with scorn. 'And how's he getting home? You'll be carrying him on your back, I suppose.'

Ben looked up in gratitude at Edith for she had saved him from betraying his true feelings for his uncle, which were that he was a lazy man, who lacked enthusiasm and ambition and who, consequently, was always going to be the victim of circumstances, for which he was going to blame anyone but himself.

Ben had become increasingly conscious of the need to take control of his own life during Arnie's coaching sessions.

Arnie in his clever, quiet way had set about giving Ben a master class in the art of bowling.

He was to be paid seventeen shillings a week and for that his duties included attending the pitch under Arnie's supervision and bowling at the nets for three hours each day during the Boutilier festivals.

For the first two weeks the old pro did nothing but work on Ben's basic action. Then he taught him how to use his non-bowling arm. This, he assured Ben, was more important than the arm that bowled the ball because if you brought it down quickly brushing the hip, the rest of the body came round quicker and made for a fast delivery.

He taught Ben to bowl nearer the wicket. Ben, who liked to spear the ball in from a wider angle, asked why.

Arnie took Ben to the bowler's end at the nets and stood him near to the stumps. 'Now look you, if you bowl from here you pitch in line for lbw when you aim for the wickets. There's another thing too. Put one in short and it's coming straight at them, not across them. There's nowhere for them to go.'

They practised day after day. Occasionally Ben was

weary after his trek to his uncle's home but he was always willing, a fact noted by Arnie who knew that the difference between a good bowler and a great one can sometimes be the determination to battle fatigue.

Three weeks before the cricket festival, Arnie stood at the nets watching Ben come down the hill from his mother's cottage. As the young man approached he held out a parcel. 'For you.'

'The boots.' Ben grinned, the tiredness gone from him. He opened the parcel. 'They're beautiful.' He held up the buckskin boots and rubbed his hand across the studded leather soles. 'They're beautiful,' he said once more with a kind of reverence. That evening, Arnie did not give Ben any instructions, but let him bowl for the pleasure of it until his feet started to blister.

The following day, Ben rose early and had cleaned the coop before his mother had prepared his breakfast. She loaded up his rucksack with chickens and hard-boiled eggs. She noticed he was wearing his boots. He grinned. 'I'm breaking them in.'

Bess shook her head in exasperation. Her son had no sense at times. 'They'll break you in, you stupid lad.'

But he was not to be dissuaded and set off up the hill towards the drover's road. He made the ten miles to his uncle's home with some discomfort but it was on the return journey that he began to realise his folly. His heels and toes felt as though they'd been scalded. He writhed in pain as he pulled off the boots. His socks were stained with sweat and blood. Both were holed at the heel and he savagely tore them away from his feet revealing a mess of burst blisters and burning flesh.

He sat against the slope by the side of the track. For the first time since the death of his father, he felt empty and helpless. So much for being in control of his own life. He couldn't even walk home. He buried his head in his hands and fell into an exhausted sleep sitting hunched by the side of the trail. He woke to find Wolfie sniffing his feet with his huge, wet nose. For a second, he thought he was dreaming and then he heard the thump of the horse's hooves and Helen's voice. 'Are you hurt?' Her tone seemed to contain more curiosity than concern, though she smiled when he looked up at her as she held the stamping hunter in check.

He explained what had happened.

'What a stupid thing to do!'

'My mother said the same.'

Helen flung her leg over the back of her horse and knelt at his feet. Straggles of her long hair escaped from under her riding cap. He guessed she pinned it when out on the horse. She smelled of scented soap. She'd laid her crop down by her feet and pulled off her leather gloves, no doubt to protect them from his blood.

She gave a little whistle. 'You need to get these cleaned when you get home.' She looked up at him and he was taken by her clear blue eyes. 'Can you walk?'

He shook his head. 'I can hobble, but it's at least three miles.' His voice sounded empty and deflated. Wolfie started to lick his feet. He winced at the scrape of the sandpaper tongue.

'Can you ride?'

He shook his head.

'Well, you can at least sit on Jasper while he walks.'

She helped him to mount. His hand pushed hard on her shoulder as he struggled to lift his leg over the far side of the horse. The pressure stretched her jacket, revealing her long, white neck.

She held the reins and nudged the horse forward with her shoulder.

Wolfie began to bound about barking. She shushed him in case he alarmed Jasper. Ben felt her body against him, and then, most shocking of all, her hand curled round the inside of his leg to get better purchase.

For a while his pain was forgotten as his fevered mind asked one question. Could it be possible that this proud, wilful lady was attracted to him? Surely not. Yet, she had sought him out previously on the drovers' trail. No! That had been to apologise for striking him with her whip. Then, as though sent by a devil's messenger, he felt her hand squeeze gently on his leg. In his half conscious state he was never sure that she was aware of what she had done. He fancied she gave a start and the squeezing stopped. Perhaps he had imagined it all; it so seemed the stuff of fancy. Despite his excitement he dozed in and out of an exhausted sleep. She looked up at him and saw that his head had dropped and his body was swaying to the rhythm of the horse. Even at rest he had a natural strength and power. She felt the bare flesh at the back of his leg and shivered. She was honest enough to admit to herself that she had been caught out by circumstances, and now the desire she felt for this man had escaped like a bag of snakes. She knew that her father tolerated, or ignored, her casual affairs because that's what they were, casual, and therefore of no great consequence. But with this man casual was the exact thing she could not be. She sensed his spirit and determination. She valued him. He was set for a long journey and the truth was that she didn't dare to become a fellow traveller.

She was suddenly angry at everything and most of all at herself.

They came to the top of the rise and way before them

stood the great estate with its stone walls. The two of them would be clearly visible to any casual eye. She stopped the horse and the change in motion woke Ben. He stared at her in sleepy innocence and she almost relented. Then she forced herself to speak. 'You'll have to wait here while I summon help.'

He said nothing, but she knew what he was thinking.

'Look,' she said.' This place is full of gossips. If we're seen like this tongues will wag.' Still he said nothing. 'I can't . . . I can't risk it,' she said lamely.

He gave a short laugh and she saw the anger in his face. He swung his leg across the horse and gave a cry of pain as he dismounted. She caught him as he fell and for a moment their faces pressed side by side, then he slipped from her grasp and sat on the ground.

'I'll get help for you,' she said.

'No!' The word came out like a gunshot. 'I'll see my own way from here.'

She knew he was not referring merely to that evening. Her eyes filled with tears as she mounted the hunter and she kept her face away from him as she said, 'You don't know how lucky you are.'

'That you rescued me.'

His sarcasm hurt her but she kept her voice steady. 'You know what I mean.' She pressed her knees into the hunter urging him forward, alarmed lest he should see she was in tears. She wanted to reassure him that she would still send for help but didn't dare lest her voice betrayed her emotion.

When she reached the stables she ordered one of the grooms to seek out a young man she'd passed on the drover's road, as he seemed to be in distress. An hour passed before one of the maids knocked on her bedroom door to report that the groom had found no one.

It was Ben's mother who helped him into the house after hearing him crash through the wicker gate at the front of the cottage. She was so alarmed she started to shout at him as he lay groaning on the path clasping his bloody boots to his chest. Then she saw his feet and even in the gloom she knew he was in great pain. She could not lift him so she draped an arm round her shoulder and helped him to limp, groaning, to the cottage. Once inside, she bathed his feet in warm water, which stung him so deeply that he called out. His face was covered in sweat and she feared he might go down with a fever. She covered him in her husband's old greatcoat, which she had kept for ten years and more. Then she wrapped his feet in rags she tore from an old sheet.

Mercifully, he fell asleep. He slept through the night and through the next day. She woke him only to feed him with a thin chicken soup.

Arnie called on the second day. He could see Ben lying in his bed from the front door and was startled by his pallor. Beth told him that he had been trying to break in his cricket boots by walking twenty miles across the moors, which gave her some focal point for her anger. 'Stupid bloody lad. Stupid bloody game. What's it good for, eh?'

Arnie said nothing because he wasn't sure how to answer. Indeed, he was not sure whether there was any answer that would satisfy this irascible woman.

Beth ushered him into the cottage and he stood over Ben's bed shaking his head.

'Daft young bugger!'

Ben gave a weak smile.

Arnie leaned closer to him so that Beth couldn't hear him speak. 'I know all about her ladyship. She's been fretting, if it's any consolation.'

He thought that Ben had drifted into sleep again, but after a while the young man opened his eyes. 'She fretted more about people gossiping.' The young man's face had become as hard as a sculpture, and like Ben's mother, a few minutes before him, Arnie knew Ben was not for turning.

It was a week before he could leave his bed and when he did rise he was a stronger, colder man, forged by his bitter experience. His mother had placed a chair in the front garden and as he looked out at the great roll of the land across the paddocks and fields and woods, he knew he must leave this place. As it had grown through the ages it had become a place of boundaries, the drovers' road, the river, the wall, the cricket pitch, the pebbled roads over which only the grand limousines were allowed to travel; they all were there keeping people in their place. If he had any doubts he had only to recall the way Lady Helen had left him lying in pain.

As the days went by his body became stronger as did his confidence and resolve. God had given him a weapon. It was called cricket.

Chapter Ten

Arnie took time to call on Ben each day. They sat in the garden and Beth brought them cool glasses of milk. Gradually the colour returned to Ben's face and he began to take an interest in the nets that were being erected in preparation of the festival. Lord Boutilier, no less, had asked whether Ben would be fit enough to bowl. Arnie looked closely at Ben. 'I told him you would be ready.'

Ben nodded. 'If you think so.' He was already heavily reliant on Arnie's knowledge. He'd assume that net bowling was like any other bowling, an observation that had brought a heavy shake of the head from the old man.

'In a match you are the opponent. In the nets you are the servant.'

He glanced across at the allotment. 'Carrots are doing nicely.'

Ben ignored the hint. 'How's it different then?'

'It's simple. Your job is to bowl to their instructions. Say there's a shot they want to practise. Say a cover drive. No good you bowling at their legs then, eh. Your job is to allow them to practise what they want to practise. You understand?'

Ben nodded.

Arnie gave him a keen look. 'And, in your case, that means bowling at three-quarter speed. No good scaring the gizzards out of them. Anyway it's best not to show them what you can do at the moment. It won't help you when you come to play against them.'

The following weekend Ben walked down to the cricket pitch. The nets were lined up side by side. A group of a dozen batsmen and bowlers were practising as he brushed his way through the hedge. He stood in the distance watching them keenly. Arnie waved to him and as he strolled across the square one of the batsmen played an off drive that hit the end post of the net and ricocheted out to him. He stooped and lobbed it back to the bowler.

'Are these the professionals?' he sounded surprised.

Arnie gave a short laugh. 'God no! These are lads from the local clubs along the valleys. They're going to bowl to the pros. Most of them. Some of the best are going to join you bowling to the toffs.'

As he spoke a tall man, resplendent in a multi-coloured cap, emerged from the pavilion carrying a bat in one hand and a cigarette in the other. His walk was straight-backed but he managed to emanate a casual air like a guardsman on holiday. Lord Boutilier's son, Charles, joined him half way to the wicket. The pair took over the two nets nearest to them, shouted some instructions to the bowlers and took their stances. Charles, who had asked for balls on his off stump, became irritated by the inaccuracy of the bowling. He glared at Arnie. 'I thought father had hired a full-time net bowler.'

Arnie took this with easy aplomb. 'He has that. He will be bowling on Thursday.'

'That's the fellow there ain't it?' He pointed his bat at Ben.

Ben, who could see a nasty situation developing, volunteered. 'I think I could send a few down for you, sir.'

He heard Arnie mutter, 'Careful. He's got a childish temper at times.'

Ben picked up one of the balls that lay in a cluster at the bowler's end. Like all the others it was bruised and the seam was flattened with use. He knew he could not swing it through the air or move it off the pitch unless it found an uneven bounce. Basically, he was cannon fodder for the young toff.

He called out, 'Good length on the off stump,' and ran in soundlessly. The smooth balance of his run caught the eye of the other cricketers including the tall batsman in the adjacent net, who imperiously signalled for his bowler to halt his run in.

Ben found it difficult to hold himself back. He imagined Helen watching with a contrived indifference, whereas on the drovers' road she would have whooped like a child. The thought that came from nowhere knocked his concentration and the ball slipped from his grasp and landed yorker length outside the off stump. Charles Boutilier who was on his front foot to play the expected good-length ball turned it into a full toss and knocked it into the net in the cover area.

Ben raised his hand in apology and returned to his mark.

'First ball since his injury,' Arnie offered Charles an explanation.

Ben ran in again, this time slightly quicker. His leap and his follow through were as smooth as liquid and the ball hit a length. Charles, on his front foot again, had to adjust his stroke as the bowler got more bounce than expected. He looked back at the bowler and nodded.

Ben bowled two overs at him which he played comfortably. He looked down the pitch feeling pleased with himself, and then he noticed that the young bowler was sauntering back to his run and hadn't raised a sweat.

Charles raised his bat two handed above his head stretching his back. As he made to take guard again he saw that Helen and his father had taken a seat in the pavilion.

'Just a moment.' Charles waved his bat at the bowler.

Ben turned, at ease with himself, now that he had managed to detach himself from the situation. 'Yes, sir,' he could imagine Arnie murmuring his appreciation.

'I'm told you can bowl faster.'

The bowler nodded. 'I have been told not to. The nets are just for your practice, sir.'

'I know what the nets are for,' Charles's smooth young face flushed. 'The point is I'm facing Warren on Saturday, so I'd like to practise by facing some bowling that's reasonably quick.'

All play had stopped around them as the others sensed a conflict. Arnie intervened, 'I don't think that's wise sir. He's just back from injury.'

Charles looked down the wicket. 'He looks perfectly fit to me.'

Ben stopped at the end of his run-up as Charles hooked him with a question. 'Can you bowl as quickly as Warren? Have you heard of Warren?'

'Yes, sir,'

'That's yes to both, I take it.'

'Yes, sir.'

'Really? We're talking about the England opening bowler.' Charles smiled across to his friend who stared stony-faced from the adjoining net.

Arnie had joined Ben at the end of his run-up. 'OK faster, but not too fast. The little twerp's just name dropping.'

'Am I faster than Warren?'

'Yes, but Lord Charles doesn't know that, so don't go flat out. Not on this wicket.'

As the two men spoke they could hear Charles whacking his bat impatiently into the crease.

Even the club cricketers could see that, though Ben's run in was as smooth as ever, there was more purpose to it. The ball sped down and spat off a length a foot wide of the off stump. The width of the ball made it difficult to assess whether Charles had left the ball at the last moment, or whether the speed of it had simply been too much. As it was, the ball reared off the pitch and hit the net shoulder high.

'For God's sake bowl him something the little brat can hit,' Arnie whispered. But Ben was already in a comfortable world of his own. He'd seen the batsman's best and knew he could take him at any time, and that knowledge freed him of the necessity to do it.

He remembered the Sniper telling the family how he had drawn a sight on one of the German support trenches and a fat German cook had waddled into view. 'I could have shot him, but it didn't seem right,' said his father's friend. 'So I shot the ladle from his hand. Who'd want to shoot a cook, eh? Chances are he was doing more damage to the enemy with his cooking anyway, if he was like our own.

The whole family had laughed long at that, though they'd never told the Sniper they'd all had Uncle Josh in mind. Uncle Josh and his half-cooked dumplings.

Ben stopped a couple of strides into his run in and retraced his steps smiling. What a strange thought at such a time. Still, he knew now exactly how the Sniper had felt. He had this little bastard in his sights and he'd decided not to pin him.

From sixty yards away Helen watched entranced by the beautiful shape of the young man as he ran to the wicket, it was as though he was making a ballet of the game. The ball seemed very fast, though she knew it was by no means his fastest and it pitched on a half volley length which allowed her brother to hit it hard into the net. He stood up and walked the wicket, patting the ground. He'd given himself some personal test and he'd passed. In fact, he looked as though he was awarding himself a medal.

Helen began to giggle. Her father glanced at her. 'What's that matter?'

She shook her head. 'Oh nothing.'

Back at the wicket, Arnie approached Charles. 'Beautiful shot, sir.' The young toff beamed in pleasure. 'But I think this is all too risky on this wicket sir. It's not flat enough and it hasn't had a dose of marl.'

The words seemed to do the trick, for Charles had convinced himself he had scored a victory.

Helen took the opposite view, she knew that Ben had bowled well within himself and that if he hadn't Charles would have been humiliated.

Arnie knew better than anyone that his protégé was in a different class to the batsman who had faced him, but he sensed there was also a new, calculating air to the young man since the incident with the boots. Ben's natural friendly spirit had been replaced by a cold resolve. He'd watched him bowl before for the joy of self expression. But in the few overs he'd witness that evening he knew the young man was coldly playing a role while calculating the destruction of his batsman. The young, arrogant toff was no longer an opponent, but an enemy.

He took Ben to the centre of the square and pointed out its shiny flatness compared to the net wicket. 'So how would you have bowled against him on this wicket?

'He has many weaknesses. The first is that he moves his right foot in line with his off stump as you are coming up to bowl. So I run in close to the wicket and pitch really quick on middle and off so there's nowhere for him to go and I've got him squared up.'

Arnie grinned. 'What else?'

'He doesn't like fast bowling. And he's frightened of

being afraid of it. That's why he asked for me. He can tell me what to bowl in the nets.'

Ben had one day before the start of his official net duties, the only time he could deliver the foodstuff to his uncle. He'd missed two Saturdays, and so carried a fuller load of chickens and eggs.

The gesture did not appease Uncle Joshua who by now viewed his visits as a right, not a favour.

'About time,' he sniffed as Ben placed the rucksack on the battered kitchen table. 'Where the hell have you been?'

Ben took a deep breath to stop himself from shouting, and explained that he had been ill. As he looked at his uncle's plump body bulging in his grease-stained vest, he was consumed by a cold anger. 'I'm working every day, so if you need the stuff that badly you can walk over to mum's. The exercise will do you good by the look of it.'

'You cheeky young bugger!' Uncle Joshua struggled to his feet but Ben pushed him back into the chair. He heard his aunt give a gasp of alarm.

'When you arrive, I'll be there to thank you for coming, which is more than you ever did.'

And with that he turned for the door. He could hear his aunt crying quietly and he turned to give her a hug. 'I'm sorry but it's for the best,' he whispered and pushed a ten shilling note into the tiny pocket of her pinafore.'

Ben told his mother about his confrontation as soon as he returned home. She had known of his resentment about his uncle from the beginning and recognised that Joshua had behaved selfishly. She saw echoes of his father in Ben. She remembered Frank at home on his last leave having to listen to Joshua lecture him on the value of the support staff during combat. 'I kept on cooking when the whizz bangs came over,' he'd said while describing one particularly difficult day. Frank had said nothing, but on the way home he'd given Beth a cuddle and whispered. 'I wonder how many notches he's got on his ladle, eh!' They'd made love that night laughing about the ladle and the next day he was gone. She never saw him again.

Her son stood before her now waiting for her rebuke. She knew his action had been premeditated, but she confined her comments to, 'I'm only worried at what might become of his wife.'

Ben nodded. 'Well, let's see whether he has the guts to make the trip here. If he doesn't I can arrange for us to send her a little cash each month to Wolviston post office.' That seemed to appease her. He too was relieved to be rid of the tedious trip, and of the risk of meeting Helen on the drovers' road.

He did his chores at the coops with a light heart that night, killed half a dozen chickens for his mother, and walked down to the cricket pitch to have a chat with Arnie. As he approached the lane, Helen and Peregrin trotted past on two hunters. Helen reined her horse at the sight of him. 'I'm pleased to see that you have recovered,' she said.

'I have that, and I am very grateful for your concern, Madam,' he replied in flat voice. Helen's face flushed and Peregrin gave him a hard look.

Helen tried to recover, 'Linden here is employed as a nets bowler. He got into difficulties breaking in a pair of cricket shoes on the drover's road.'

'Ah, the stone age bowler!' Peregrin smiled.

Ben stiffened at the insult, but before he could speak Peregrin nudged his horse forward and Helen's hunter followed. She was unable to speak for seconds and then it was too late. She had used the same phrase to Peregrin, hoping to disguise her true feelings.

Ben stared at them until they reached a bend, and then he walked across the lane and through the cut in the hedge.

Arnie was sitting on the pavilion steps smoking his pipe talking to the tall man who'd batted with Boutilier's son in the nets the previous day. Ben hesitated, but Arnie waved him across. 'Ben, this is Mr Jepson, who's playing in the match on Saturday.' Mr Jepson appeared not have heard a word as he stood staring at Ben who became conscious that he was wearing rough working clothes and that blood from the chickens stained his shirt, while the other man had dressed for dinner in a silk-lapelled evening suit.

Jepson had a long, straight, still face that seemed a model for a statue entitled 'Resolution', but he surprised Ben with a sudden smile. 'Linden. John Jepson.' It was obvious from Ben's expression that he had never heard of him and this seemed to amuse Jepson.

'I was interested to see you bowl yesterday.'

Ben could see Arnie winking over the big man's shoulder.

Ben said nothing, not sure of what was required of him.

'I thought it was quite impressive. And the old soldier here tells me you can bowl even quicker.'

'Yes, sir.'

'Show me.' Jepson walked out to the nets and Ben felt obliged to follow him.

Jepson produced a shiny new ball from the pocket of his evening suit and tossed it to Ben.

'I haven't my boots sir.'

'I know.' Jepson produced a slim silver case and lit a cigarette. 'Your plimsolls are good enough for a couple of balls.' He walked down the wicket and stood nonchalantly by the stumps, a batsman without a bat. Ben stared at him in astonishment. 'Sir, I can't bowl at you like that. What if I hit you?'

Jepson stepped wide of the wicket.

Ben walked out his run. Arnie called to him, 'In your own time, son.'

Ben ran in at three-quarters speed and sent the ball spitting outside the off stump and rearing into the net. Jepson gave him a long look but said nothing as he tossed the ball back.

Arnie grinned. 'Think of something that annoys you.' Ben stood with his eyes closed at the end of his run. He could see Peregrin's red, jeering face. He turned and sprinted to the wicket. His bowling arm whipped over like a fishing rod and his fingers scraped the ground on the follow-through. Jepson wasn't quite sure which stump the ball hit first, possibly the off and then the middle, certainly both spun out of the ground and danced in the net. Jepson inhaled on his cigarette and blew a thin blue flute of smoke into the air. The ball was at his feet. He picked it up and lobbed it to Ben. 'This is yours, I believe.' He smiled and turned to Arnie. 'How long, do you think?'

'Aah, Mr Jepson. There's a question now. Two months and he could hold his own with all but the best batsmen. At the moment he's got two balls, from wide of the crease, and near the wicket. But he's got two speeds. Bloody fast and bloody hell.'

Jepson gave a laugh at this and Arnie encouraged, continued. 'Also I need to work on his slower ball and his action is a little too high for an out swinger.'

Jepson nodded. 'I will speak to you in a month and see where we are. Meanwhile don't let him bowl any bloody hells out there,' he gestured to the nets. 'No point in killing anybody. Unless they're Australian, eh.'

'Well done!' Jepson acknowledged Ben for the first time since the demonstration. He turned to Arnie. 'Keep him at it every day. Sundays too if necessary. I'll see it straight with Boutilier.' Then he strolled off towards the great house, his patent leather shoes slipping slightly on the flattened grass and a curl of smoke rising from his cigarette up the arm of his gleaming dress jacket.

Ben bowled well within himself during his days at the net. Jepson faced him for a number of overs each day. Ben noted how quickly he got in line and how comfortable he was directing the ball on the leg side. He called out 'Well bowled!' at least once an over and Ben knew that his encouragement was for the ears of Charles, Peregrin, and the other young wolves.

Under Arnie's tuition he began to practise rolling his fingers across the ball to create a slower delivery. He spoke when spoken to and kept a civil tongue, even when Peregrin tried to goad him at the nets.

'He doesn't like you,' whispered Arnie.

'It's mutual.'

Arnie gave a little chuckle. 'Watch him bat tomorrow. One day he'll face you for real and then we'll see.'

The festivals were the greatest events in the whole valley, and this festival was, by common consent, the greatest festival in its history.

Never had such an array of great names been assembled, both on and off the pitch. The players were summoned predominantly from the three great northern counties, Yorkshire, Lancashire and Nottinghamshire while Boutilier's team had access to the cream of the two great universities, Oxford and Cambridge as well as the best players, both amateur and professional from the Home Counties. In addition it was accepted that Boutilier could play as an additional member of the team, though only eleven would be allowed to field at any one time, an arrangement which suited Boutilier, who had always thought fielding was the sort of thing servants should do. Finally, and most sensational of all, the home side was to be led by JWR Jepson, captain of England, and , in the opinion of many notable critics of the day, the shrewdest skipper ever to have led out a side.

The assembly had created a few minor problems. Boutilier's team, for the first time consisted of both amateur and professional players. The increased number of professionals necessitated the creation of an additional dressing room for 'the men'. There was nothing remotely suitable in the small pavilion so a marquee was erected by its side. Jarvis, the handyman, was instructed to build some benches, and a long hanger for the clothes. In addition, two large cast-iron baths were placed in the tent and two manservants were instructed to furnish them with warm water, gathered from the pavilion tap via two large milk churns. Boutilier, pleased that all the proprieties were now addressed, let it be known that the players would be given an extra ten shillings a day for their inconvenience.

Ben's duty consisted of helping Arnie brush and roll the wicket before, and between, innings. Guests included three members of the Cabinet and, more important, three high ranking officials of the MCC. Both Arnie and Ben had been provided with neat dark slacks and white shirts. The locals were allowed in through the great gate free of charge and ushered along the rutted lane that swung towards the cricket ground. They were assembled on the opposite side of the ground to the pavilion where sat the great and the good. There were a few benches provided, but most of the common people lounged, as Ben had done, on the grassy slopes by the hedges. Across the field, there was a twinkle of silver trays and other finery. Lady Helen and her friends slumped in long deck chairs. Servants stood deferentially in the rear waiting to attend them.

Ben glanced in her direction as he and Arnie pushed the heavy roller out on to the wicket. At one point Arnie stopped to tie a shoe lace and Ben strained to push the roller on his own. Arnie caught up with him. 'Sorry,' he grinned, 'Though the ladies seemed to notice your performance.'

Ben smiled grimly. He knew he had grown into a remarkably attractive man. Black hair, dark eyes, and a gliding walk that was full of danger.

One hundred and fifty yards away Helen stared at him through a pair of opera glasses mounted on a lunette. She was still angry with the ridiculous Peregrin and angrier with herself for not having the courage to help Ben when he'd been in pain. In wilder moments she imagined them meeting like pagans on the drovers' road, and running barefooted on the soft turf. There they could be themselves, or at least a primitive version of themselves, before returning to the great estate and their separate lives. It was not, she persuaded herself, as ridiculous as it sounded. Some of her married acquaintances had conducted affairs in which the most attractive aspect was that they were secret and illicit.

She felt a gentle hand on her arm. 'The strong young man hasn't noticed that you are staring at him, but others might.'

Helen lowered her glasses. 'Oh Bunty.' Her friend saw that there were tears in her eyes.

Normally, the rollers were housed in a large shed near the pavilion, but as it would be distracting for the special guests to have the squeaking cranking things trundle past, a special hut had been erected at the opposite end of the ground. It was here that Arnie and Ben sat, having completed their chores. They had a clear view of the proceedings and Arnie insisted that Ben concentrate closely on each of the batsmen. At the end of the day he made him reel off a list of their faults. At the mention of Peregrin's name he said, 'Back lift too high.' Arnie nodded his approval. But when Jepson's name was mentioned he shook his head. 'I haven't noticed anything, yet.'

Arnie smiled. 'An honest answer. His weakness is that he has too much courage. If fear is involved he won't play the odds. He's a strange man that one, as hopefully you'll find out.'

Ben walked home happier that night. He had avoided even glancing at Helen and had persuaded himself that soon cricket and his career would be the main concern of his life, not the hopeless love of a beautiful girl who had cruel, haughty friends.

Chapter Eleven

When Ben arrived at the cottage he found his Uncle Joshua, leg cocked over a rusty bicycle, about to leave.

'You look like a dog wetting a tree,' he said. His uncle smarted before this mockery but, before he could make a rejoinder, Beth intervened to tell Ben that his uncle had been at the cricket all day, before calling to collect his produce. Beth had packed him a bundle of chickens and eggs. One of Josh's friends had loaned him the heavy, rattling bike. Mention of the cricket spurred the riposte he had been seeking. 'I saw you working.' He smiled maliciously. 'Fine job that mind, sitting on your arse all day.'

'Well, it's nice to get an expert opinion.'

Ben's mother gasped at Ben's cutting tongue. She had seen changes in him over the past few months. He'd become confident enough to release his demons like dogs of war.

Uncle Joshua stared at Ben whose silent manner he had always taken for weakness. This new adversary had him on the retreat. 'I can't help my health.'

'Everyone can help their health. You've made a career out of yours.'

'How dare you! Squirt of a kid talking to your uncle like that. I was like a father to you.'

'You were never like a father to me. You were like the uncle who wriggled out of work, and who gambled and drank, and who's been selling the chickens and eggs round the doors, so you can go on the beer. People talk.'

'That's a lie.' Uncle Joshua set the bag of produce against the handlebars and turned for one last glare as he wobbled down the path. 'A fine upbringing you've given him!' he shouted at Beth.

The mother and son watched him go. 'Well,' she sighed. 'That's the last we'll see of him.'

'He'll be back. Unless he finds out about the money we're sending his wife. It's true about him selling the chickens by the way.'

Beth gave him a weak smile. 'That was quite an outburst, son. How long has that been brewing?'

'All my life, I think. But it's just lately I've realised it.' He turned from looking down the path to face his mother. 'You know I'm set on leaving.'

She nodded her head, but said nothing.

'I've been speaking to Mr Jarvis. I've helped him to buy a little pony and trap. It's big enough to carry both your produce, and he says he'll kill the chickens for you.'

She gave a little gasp of panic. 'You've got it all planned. So soon. So sudden.'

They watched Joshua give one last comical manoeuvre on the bumpy track. Ben gave a harsh laugh and turned to the door. His mother followed. 'Be careful. There's too much anger in you, son.'

He smiled, 'Not to you, Ma.'

She pulled him into her and he saw there were no little flowers in her hair. He realised they'd been missing for a while.

Suddenly he found himself telling her the whole story: how Helen had ridden up to seek him out on the drovers' road and of the evening she had found him in pain, given him her horse, then left him at the top of the hill because she feared being seen with him. His mother listened in silence, realising there was much more behind the tale. When he'd finished she still said nothing for a while, and then she began to speak in a calm, low voice. She told him that one day when delivering eggs to the cook she'd had to use the great door because the carpenters were working on the kitchen entrance. There she had seen, right across the great fireplace, a long scroll of the Boutilier family history, dating back to the Norman Conquest.

'I've seen them,' he shrugged.

'You might have seen them, but you don't understand their meaning.'

She took her son to the door of the cottage. They looked out over the wheat and hay fields, the ploughed land weighty with planted crops, the open pasture where Helen had sought the plover eggs, the rolling paddocks and the trimmed lawns, the hedges and trees that lined them, and the woods and forest that stretched a glazed, dark shape in the distance.

'What you see there is nature,' she said quietly. 'But it's not natural, it's all man-made, and as far as you can see this has all been made by the Boutiliers. That's how powerful they are.' She smiled at her son. 'So you must know that neither she or her father could ever allow you to go on that scroll.'

His eyes softened. 'Yes,' he said, 'So I must get away, Ma. It's strangling me. It's unnatural.'

His decision was out in the open and he felt a great release. He had a month in which to prove himself to Arnie and Jepson. He did not doubt he could do it, but if he didn't he would find something else, find somewhere else. He could join John Bart, the Sniper, and drive the cattle up the drovers' road.

He worked with Arnie every afternoon and evening now. His buckskin boots, once the cause of so much trouble, were now a major attribute. They fitted him like a second skin and the long studs enabled him to get better purchase, especially on his leading foot. Arnie allowed him to bowl full speed in the nets for bursts of five or six overs making him target patches of sand placed at different lengths and lines. 'Never more than seven overs,' Arnie said. There's some who can bowl all day and hold down and end, but you're a different league to them. You're an attack bowler. You're the one to come in with two or three wickets in a burst. And if you don't you'll get wickets for other bowlers because batsmen will take risks to score before you come back on again. You are the one.'

Ben felt a harmony with the old man. In their different ways, Jarvis, with his quiet certainty about his role in life, and Arnie, with his ambitions for him, became surrogate fathers. But the real driving force, the thing that gave him a point of focus, was the way he had been treated by his so-called betters. He drank in the bitterness and thrived on it.

He stayed well clear of the drovers' road in case Helen still rode it, but on the night before Jepson came he walked up the hill in the dusk and stood by his improvised pitch. The stones were still there, as were the cricket balls that Helen had left. He picked them up and threw them all into the bracken. When he left he wanted no record of his having been there. He wanted no record of the stone-age bowler left for her or her friends.

Jepson came strolling down the slope from the great house with Boutilier. Both were in evening dress. Boutilier with a clanking row of medals strapped in a bar across his thin chest and Jepson, even more ludicrously, wore white pads and cricket shoes.

'Dashing off for dinner,' Boutilier explained. 'Got the butler to put on John's pads. Keep the crease, you know. Good at that, Simpkins.'

'A very promising umpire too, Milord, if I may say so.'

Arnie grinned, referring to the many benefits of doubt Simpkins had given to his employer.

Boutilier turned to Jepson. 'Always know Arnie's smoking me when he calls me Milord.' He gave a chuckle which was a signal for everyone to laugh with him. He was in good humour, and that pleased Arnie and Ben.

Jepson's long, large face returned to its solemn norm. Arnie handed him a bat and gloves which he'd brought from the pavilion.

Jepson took his stance at the stumps. Arnie had refused to tamper with the wicket for the past month because there wasn't time for marl to take effect. However he had watered the batsman's end and rolled it each day so that was as soft and flat as it would ever be.

Jepson took a guard of middle. Arnie whispered to Ben, 'It's so he knows where his off stump is.'

Ben stood at the bowler's end. 'Sir. Do you want me to call out what I intend to bowl?'

Jepson shook his head and patted his bat on the wicket. 'Just a minute.' He stood up and took off his jacket. His shirt had a large plasticised front that bent to accommodate him. Gold cuff links gleamed at his wrists.

Ben stared in astonishment. The whole thing didn't feel real, yet he was about to bowl the most crucial overs of his life to the greatest batsman in England. They'd given him a shiny new ball. He felt nervous until he broke into his run and then the smooth rhythm took over. His first ball swung in at three quarters speed. Jepson didn't seem to move until the last second and then with virtually no back lift he pushed forward and prodded the ball gently into the covers. Ben tried four more balls at his slower pace trying to get the ball to move in the air, but the clear, hot weather was against him. He had however kept his length and line and

Arnie whispered, 'You're doing fine.' Ben looked anxiously down the pitch at Jepson who seemed to be playing with a depressing serenity. 'Don't worry about him,' Arnie whispered. 'He never shows what's what.'

Ben pitched the sixth ball shorter and Jepson stepped back, raised his bat in front of his face and released his right hand as he played the shot making the ball drop at his feet.

'You've just bowled a maiden to the captain of England,' Arnie whispered.

Ben wasn't listening. He was beginning to see a way through Jepson's defence.

His next four balls were slightly quicker and he brought Jepson forward each time. But the fifth came down a yard faster than anything he'd previously bowled. It was just short of a length outside Jepson's off stump. He shouldn't have played at it but he did, bat high, the right hand falling away. The ball struck the bat at the neck knocking it from Jepson's one hand and the bat fell on to the wicket. The ball looped for what would have been an easy catch behind the wicket. There was a silence for a while, then Ben heard Arnie coughing gently. Jepson's expression didn't change. 'It would appear you got me out twice with one ball, young man.'

The rest was a formality. Ben bowled five more overs, very fast, but on off stump or outside. Jepson played and missed at two balls and scrambled to keep out a slower delivery. At the end of it he strode down the wicket and shook Ben's hand. 'Well bowled, Linden!' Ben noticed Jepson was sweating slightly at the arm pits and this pleased him for some reason. He imagined the butler having to make some repairs with eau de cologne. Jepson walked back down the wicket to retrieve his jacket, lit a cigarette, and then he and Boutilier strolled off to the great house. As they reached the corner of the field Helen joined them. She had been watching unnoticed. She was dressed in a long, tight, lime-green cocktail dress that blended with the beech hedge at her back. Ben was taken by surprise. He stared at her and she smiled, knowing she had won a little victory. Then she turned to catch up with her father and Jepson, linking arms with the two of them. Ben's stare followed them until they were out of sight beyond the hedge.

'Forget that proud bit of aristocratic arse,' Arnie's voice was soft behind him.

He turned alarmed, as though someone had discovered him naked. 'I'm trying to,' he said.

'She's a kingdom away, lad.'

'I know.' His voice was low with misery.

His stare had given Helen real pleasure. It was better than any caress she had ever felt. A warm glow filled her body. He might pretend, but she knew he still dwelt on her.

'How did it go?' she asked her father, though she knew the answer.

Boutilier looked at Jepson. 'Well?'

Jepson drew on his cigarette. 'How old is he?'

'Twenty, I think.' Helen wondered whether she had answered a little too quickly.

'He's the fastest I've ever faced.'

'Faster than Warren?'

'By at least a yard. Possibly two.' Jepson bent to unbuckle his pads. Helen and Boutilier paused with him.

Back in the pavilion Ben towelled himself down. As he stretched the sun warmed his muscles until he felt he was clothed by the air. Arnie looked at him from the doorway of the dressing room and wondered whether there had ever been an athlete like him. Never a bowler, he was sure of that.

Ben heard nothing directly from Boutilier or Jepson, but a week later Arnie called excitedly at the cottage. 'They want you to play for Midshire next season.'

Ben's face clouded. 'Mr Jepson plays for Surrey.'

'Midshire is nearer to here. It means I can keep in touch.'

'And Midshire have agreed to all this? They know nowt about me.'

'You have powerful backers, lad. Boutilier sits on the MCC. Jepson has been chosen as the man who might beat the Australians.'

'I'm here until next season?'

Arnie could see that Ben was still unhappy. 'You thought you'd be away,' he said.

Ben nodded. 'It's her. There's no end to it.' He told Arnie of Peregrin's insult. 'I'll pin him if I get the chance,' he scowled.

Arnie waited for the worst of Ben's anger to subside. 'She'll be away for most of the time,' he said quietly. 'The Boutiliers winter in France.'

Ben smiled. 'So how long have I got here?'

'Until April.'

Chapter Twelve

'Good news about Perry,' Boutilier glided up to Helen's side as she stood on the balcony of her apartment watching the wealthy and the wicked basking in the sun along the Promenade des Anglais. Across the road, beyond the line of palm trees, a couple emerged from a small bell tent and ran across the hot white pebbles towards the sea.

'Really?' Helen tuned to face her father.

'Yeers,' Boutilier dragged out the vowel sound to give the word an enthusiastic inflection. 'His brother's got God. He's going into the church.'

'And that is good news because?'

'Because it means that Perry will inherit the estate.'

'Aah.' She saw where he was going.

'He adores you, Helen.'

'No Daddy, he and his thirty thousand acres adore me. That's what you are thinking, really.'

Boutilier smiled. 'I've seen you together. You enjoy his company.'

She glared at her father. 'Has he told you he proposed to me?'

Boutilier shook his head, but she knew he was lying. She continued as though she believed him. 'I said no.'

Boutilier started to protest, but she waved at him angrily. 'I have been thinking. So far I have half a dozen days that I will remember for the rest of my life. The trouble is Perry isn't in any of them.'

She was wrong. Perry was in one. The day he'd called Ben Linden a Stone Age bowler. But that was because she remembered the look of hurt on Ben's face.

She found the conversation with her father stifling and

turned abruptly to the door. Her father called after her but she ignored him.

Outside on the Promenade the prosperous classes of Nice sat in the warm winter sun. The men, plump and ponderous, found shade under their large hats, or larger newspapers. The women, fleshy and overdressed, sat under parasols with small dogs yapping at their feet. Across the walkway, over the gilded balustrade and beyond the white pebbled beach, a sea plane rose from the clear blue water, slow as a bumble bee. Perry had used similar transport to come and go. Helen had assumed he was visiting Charles, but it soon emerged that he had come to see her, armed with his thirty thousand acres.

She remembered how he had blinked in surprise when she had turned down his proposal, and then he'd tried to fondle her. She'd sliced savagely into him. 'Is your preoccupation with my buttocks something to do with your public school education?'

The truth was she found him shallow. She'd told him that they were friends to set up a base from which she could retreat. They were not even that. They were simply people on the same social stratum who met frequently. There were times when she sought refuge from his company, and always in these moments her thoughts turned to Ben, and the look of pain on his face when Perry had so casually wounded him.

Her heart had lifted as she'd watched the plane rise from the sea outside the harbour to take Perry along the coast to his parents' villa. He was gone.

She strode quickly along the Promenade towards the harbour from where she turned up the slope into the old quarter. A man peddled a large tricycle past her. The rear was loaded with copies of the Daily Telegraph.

Some women were scrubbing their clothes in a trough and above them sheets and shirts hung like flags from the windows in the high, narrow street. Further on she sat at a rickety table that teetered on the cobbles and ordered roasted onions and vegetables wrapped in the thin pasta. The food was cooked in homes nearby and transported on people's heads in what looked like large dust bin lids. The people here were dark and swarthy proclaiming their ancestry, for the city had once been an Italian dominion, famed as the birthplace of Garibaldi. She looked down the narrow road that led to the harbour. Ben could be at one with the people here with his black hair and passionate, black eyes. The sun would soon burn his white skin, and he would rise like a king among them. She began to shake. It was as if the tall, narrow streets were closing in to crush her. She felt she was trapped between two walls: what people wanted for her, and what she wanted for herself. She rose quickly and walked towards the harbour.

The streets had become crowded. People were throwing flowers at each other as huge floats carrying masked figures were drawn past them by donkeys. A large banner proclaimed 'Carnival de Nice.' All around her people were laughing and dancing. A brass band was playing somewhere. She felt none of the merriment, but consoled herself with the thought that Lent was coming and soon they would be going home. She wished she had Bunty with her, to hold her hand and to talk. The swirl of the crowd picked her up again. She imagined she was on the drovers' road throwing flowers at Ben. She shivered in alarm as wild thoughts invaded her mind like intruders that had to be driven away because they were dangerously seductive. She needed Bunty here to guide her. She guessed Bunty would tell her that the cricketer was out of bounds and therefore more attractive. She would ask what they would find to talk about and, perhaps, suggest that there was no harm in such an affair, provided she knew that it could never last. But that was what frightened Helen; he seemed to communicate to her in a way that was beyond conversation. She assumed by now that her father knew his son was homosexual, and while Charles might marry out of duty and provide the necessary son, he might also find the process too repugnant. If that was the case she was her father's only hope of maintaining a direct line, and Boutilier was a ruthless man over such matters.

The noise of the carnival pushed its way into her thoughts once more. She looked out at the crowds of whirling happy people and wished the flowers they were throwing would turn to stones.

It took Ben weeks to free himself from the disappointment at having to stay on the Boutilier's estate over the winter. He had hoped to travel to north London immediately and settle in to his new life in the capital. However the delay turned out to be a blessing in disguise for, although his bowling was curtailed by the weather, there was still much that Arnie could teach him.

They met in the pavilion each evening and sat by an old coke stove. Arnie drew into his clay pipe and watched the blue grey smoke swirl towards the paraffin lamp as though it contained his dreams. 'What do you think of Jepson? As a batsman,' he asked suddenly one night.

Ben hesitated not knowing where the conversation was heading. 'He's the best I've bowled at,' he said at last.

Arnie gave a warm chuckle. 'He IS the captain of England!'

'I don't understand your question.'

'I mean how many shots has he got?'

Again Ben hesitated. 'Well, he definitely favours to leg.'

'He's got six scoring shots.'

'Right. So?'

'There's a young Australian called Bradman who's got the lot. You can't bowl to any area and stop him from scoring.'

Ben stayed silent. Arnie pursued him. 'How many balls has Warren got?'

'I don't know. I've only watched the batsmen.'

Arnie sucked on his pipe. 'He's got four balls. He has a high action so he can't swing the ball away, so he is limited.'

Ben nodded. 'OK.'

Arnie tapped his pipe on the stove making a soft metallic clang. 'You've got seven balls. You swing the ball in and out, though only if you bowl three-quarter speed, you've learned to slip the ball across the fingers for slower ball, you've got a fast Yorker, another ball that bounces on the cross seam, an off cutter, and a bouncer delivered from close to the wicket.'

Ben smiled. 'That's good eh?'

Arnie nodded. 'Yes. I won't deny it, but you can be better. I want to show you another ball. It's a fast ball.'

'I thought I was fast already,'

'You are. But you bowl side on. That's your natural style and we mustn't change that.'

'So?'

'So we can practise another action. Three quarters on. It means that your back foot is not side on so your delivery stride is flatter and your body and bowling arm come through faster. It's a ball you will use rarely, but it might get you wickets against the really great batsmen.'

'How come? Surely they'll spot the change in action?'

'Yes. But supposing you slip in an occasional slower ball?'

As he walked home seeking the light from the cottage it came to him that Arnie had always encouraged him, but had never been extravagant in his praise. But that evening he had compared him favourably with a Test bowler and here he was walking home on a dark night in worn-out plimsolls, a man who had never even played for a county second team.

However he had become increasingly aware of his own standing throughout the estate during the late summer and early autumn. Each evening at least thirty of the staff, estate workers and small holders gathered to watch him bowl at the nets. His pattern remained the same; he bowled three quarter speed for the first three overs trying to swing the ball both ways. Then for the fourth fifth and sixth overs he bowled full speed. He remembered the first ball of the first evening that he had bowled flat out. The ball flashed past off stump and reared into the net. There was a silence for at least a second after he bowled and then a roar of approval from the spectators.

The next evening the number of people watching had trebled.

'You're their man,' Arnie told him. 'Never forget that. These people will live another life through you. When you take a wicket it will be as though they have taken it with you. You are a custodian of their dreams.' He gestured for Ben to run in again. 'You can lift their lives. Never forget your link to them. It's a gift and a burden. And it's given to few men.'

The old man looked around the crowd and noted a fair number of young women. He watched them watching Ben as he glided with effortless grace to the wicket, then the long low leap, his left foot hitting the wicket and his shoulders whirling round whipping his bowling arm through the line. They didn't have to know a thing about cricket to see the beauty of it, to see the beauty of him. It was as if someone had poured him down the wicket. Arnie felt close enough to the young man to act as the father Ben had hardly known. 'No scandal here,' he whispered to him one night. 'Wait till you get to London. The girls will be waiting for you there.' He grinned warmed by his own memories. 'And remember the convention is that you play for England before you screw for England.'

Ben looked at him. 'Arnie, I need to think about nothing but cricket, until I can get away from here. I need a clean break from this place. No scandal, not even gossip. They'll use that against me if it suits them.'

Arnie looked at him keenly. He had never spoken of Helen the whole time she had been away. 'She still hurts you, eh?'

Ben nodded. 'They all do. They all think I have a value but no worth.'

'Even Jepson?'

'Especially Jepson. To him I'm a useful weapon in the coming battle against the Australians.'

Arnie sucked on his pipe, alarmed at the lad's bitterness, but shrewd enough to realise that it might be the making of him. He had become a driven man.

As the months had passed Beth Linden had come to terms with Ben's planned departure. She too had seen the increasingly bold advances from some of the girls towards her son. She feared a scandal because she knew that he was set on leaving. She neither knew about, nor cared for, cricket but she recognised that he had a great gift; one that he was bound to use. She'd seen girls in the past declare themselves with child to some prominent man when the truth was they'd lain in the hedgerows with any tramp that had passed. But that danger was relatively slight when set against his attraction for Lady Helen. If she turned to Ben, no matter how briefly, Beth had no doubt where the pot would spill when it came to the boil.

She tutted at the thought. She heard a curse through the window and looked out to see that John Jarvis had struck another stone with his spade. She'd told him the ground was too hard to dig up after the frosty mornings but he'd insisted on extending the vegetable patch. She had to admit that plan made sound economic sense because she was selling or using all the vegetables she could grow. Even after her weekly payments to Cath, she was making such a surplus that in the week before Christmas the money box she kept under the sink was stuffed full. Jarvis had advised her to open an account and had driven her to the Wolviston Valley Bank in his pony and cart. The whole process was a mystery to Beth, who had to be persuaded to give her money to the clerk in exchange for a receipt, a process which she found extremely dubious. But, in the end, she returned to her cottage with a pristine bank book. She opened it a dozen times while she and Jarvis waited for the kettle to boil. She smiled at him, a natural, happy smile and he gave her a grin. He was by now her most frequent visitor. At first, he'd worked extending the coops and killing the chickens for her, but from there it was as though he had grown into the house. Draughty windows had been refitted, a door re-hung, a kitchen table built, and a cupboard attached to the kitchen walls; all done with the man's slow relentless rhythm and accompanied by tuneless whistling.

Mr Jarvis had become John and John had become

Johnny, and on days when he didn't appear, she was conscious of his absence. John Jarvis gave no outer sign of awareness of her increasing affection for him.

He was then a little started on the day of the cash book when she'd given him a hug as he took his leave. 'Thanks for all your help, Johnny,' she whispered, and, as she stepped back, he realised that at some point she'd dabbed her neck with perfume.

That evening she surprised herself with her thoughts. She began visualise them both as they grew older. She stopped when she got to sixty and he to seventy five. She remembered how strong his back and shoulders had felt when she had held him. He was such a reserved man that she had never looked for his qualities. He made no demands on her, never crowded her space, and yet was always there when she needed him. She realised that she might have been describing a pet dog. Not even that. Dogs demanded to be taken for walks. The fact was that he had grown on her in his quiet way. She missed him when he was not around the cottage. She'd even grown to find comfort in his tuneless whistling. She wished she had given him a kiss at Christmas.

The Boutiliers were back. Ben was given the news by Arnie, a week before he was due to leave for London. He saw fleeting glimpses of her in the next few days, but always managed to avoid direct contact. Her absence in France had given him time to arm himself with the dreams of his new horizons.

Then she came for him. It was dusk and she crept out like a shadow in a grey dress as he walked the narrow lane from the cricket field. In the gloom she appeared as a weak silhouette but he knew her walk in an instant, that and the flutter of her hair. His heart leapt in both alarm and hope. He knew she had come here with him in mind.

'Good evening, miss.' He touched his new flat cap as he made to walk past her. She grabbed his arm and swung him round with surprising strength.

'You're leaving, I'm told.' She fought to gather her scattered thoughts. 'I thought we could be friends.'

He gave a harsh laugh. 'No, Miss. People like Mr Bowden are your friends. People you can go riding with.'

The riding reference cut to the heart of it. She rode the grounds with Peregrin for whom she cared nothing and she'd dumped Ben from her horse and he haunted her.

'Why don't you use my name? Miss, miss, miss,' she mimicked him.

'Because that's my place with you. And it's best I recognise it.'

'We shook hands once. Remember? You said it was possible to be friends then.'

'I was wrong. You can't live on the drovers' road.'

'And you were going to leave without speaking to me.'

'We said our goodbyes when you left me on the moor because you were afraid of some gossip. Where's the friendship in that?' Try as he might he could not hide the bitterness that had festered in him.

He saw her face turn tight with shock and felt the futility of revenge. Behind her, from two fields away, came the pleasing sound of axe on wood.

He watched her eyes fill with tears. 'Oh, that's a wicked thing to say.' Her voice went low and trembled. He could see the wind shiver through her summer dress, and stir the wild roses in the hedge behind her. He had enjoyed saying the words in the moment, but a second after he had spoken he knew he had gone too far. His voice softened. 'Your friends ridicule me. I'm bitter, miss. I must leave here to try to find my own worth.'

She saw the misery in his frowning face. 'Goodbye then,' her voice faded to almost nothing.

He smiled and made to pass her. This time she let him go. He walked on a few yards and then turned. 'I hope,' he said. 'I hope you find someone or something to engage you.' He smiled. 'Perhaps one day I'll remember all the kind things you did, and forget everything else.'

As he turned to walk away he heard her weeping softly.

The axe rung out again. A blackbird took off, scurrying low across the lane from hedge to hedge. He and she had talked as equals for a few seconds, and much good it had done them.

He walked on and turned again, but she didn't see him. She was holding her head in her hands. For a second he wanted to go back to her for he knew that, although they had spoken of friendship, they had in reality been talking about love.

Her hands came away from her face and she stared at him; her eyes were red and sore. Some strands of her long fair hair stuck to her damp face. Behind her he could see the slope of the fields and beyond that the grey hills that formed the border of the estate. All of it was hers, and it had left her with a greater poverty than he had ever known.

His own destiny was in his own hands. That was his wealth. But his thoughts hung hollow in his mind. The truth was that he was walking away because to do anything else could only lead to disaster and doom.

He rose early the next morning and walked along the gravel path at the side of the great house. Two of the maids were pounding the dust from a large brown carpet which was hung over a thick line stretched between two apple trees. The south façade of the house presented a united front of drawn curtains. He gave it one last look before turning to the lane where Jarvis awaited in a horse and trap.

'Travelling light.' Jarvis nodded to Ben's small brown, leather suitcase which he carried under his arm.

Ben smiled. 'Just a change of clothes and my cricket stuff.'

He climbed into the trap and Jarvis swung the pony round with a flick of his long whip. 'Let's take the posh way out eh! There's no one about.'

He steered the pony along the broad gravelled drive. Ben looked back at the long avenue of oak and elm trees as they passed through the huge stone gateway.

'We're going to miss you sir. You were a breath of fresh air to this place.'

'I'm not 'Sir', John! For heaven's sake, you're my mother's best friend.'

'You are Sir to us. We've seen you in the papers. There's some as says you'll play for England.'

'Well, I haven't played for anyone yet, never mind England.'

Jarvis laughed. 'Old Arnie says it, and he knows more about the game than anyone I know. Old Arnie says you can be the best.'

'Does he?' Ben tried to keep the thrill out of his voice.

The pony trotted on, its hooves punching a rhythm on the road.

'I watched you bowl in the nets.'

'When?'

' Against the Honourable.' He gave a chuckle. 'He was scared. I could see it.' Jarvis smiled at the memory. 'He's not a well liked man is the Honourable.'

'No, he's not. Though I expect he's better than he's painted.' He retreated into his thoughts. Jarvis had reminded him of Arnie's last words to him before they'd said their goodbyes the night before.

'The one thing you've got to learn is to keep your mouth shut. They don't want to hear it from the likes of us. If you're trouble they'll say you're a Bolshie and cut you out. No matter how good you are. Remember this. The world is moving forward slowly. But they want it to move backwards.' He drew on his pipe and gave off a mischievous grin as he found the devil in himself. 'Our day is coming. The trick is to still be there when it does.'

Part Two

Chapter Thirteen

Major Carpenter's thick leather soled shoes rang heavily on the hard wooden floor of the long room. The tall, young man turned from studying the photographs that covered the far wall. He was holding a large, brown, paper parcel wrapped with thick, frayed string.

Carpenter didn't bother to hide his disdain. 'Linden, right?'

'Yes.' Ben nodded.

'You're one of a batch of three. If you succeed here, and I must warn you that will be difficult, you will be a player. I am a gentleman. At the moment you are not even a player. You will address me as Major Carpenter. You will address all other gentlemen as Mr followed by their surname. Never their Christian name. I and they will address you as Linden.'

Ben did not reply, but shifted the parcel under his arm so that he held it against his side. He gave Carpenter a level look taking in the heavy build, the red, flushed face, the angry eyes, and most of all the brown, thick-soled shoes that looked as though they could kick holes in a wall.

Carpenter gestured to the paper parcel. 'What the hell is that?'

'My kit.'

'You haven't a case?'

'I left it at my lodgings.'

Carpenter glanced out of the window. 'Well, get it on. I'll see you in the nets in five minutes.'

Ben hesitated as he looked for somewhere to change.

'Don't worry. All the maids have gone home.' Carpenter turned heel and strode heavy-footed towards the door.

Ben knew that Carpenter had lied. He could hear the clatter of crockery coming from an adjacent room. He stripped quickly and pulled on his cricket flannels hopping on the wooden floor as his right foot got caught in the leg. He could hear the sound of approaching feet and the shiver of glasses on a tray. With one desperate lunge he thrust his foot clear and jerked up his trousers.

He was buttoning his flies as the waitress entered. She stopped, gave a little giggle. 'Don't worry, sir; it's all part of the job.' She looked at his broad, dark chest, caught his flustered look, and summed him up in that one glance. 'Just arrived, eh?'

He nodded as he pulled on his shirt.

'Nets?'

'Yes.'

'Watch out for Major Carpenter, he's a swine.'

Ben nodded. 'I know.'

'He'll bowl to you.' She placed the tray on the long table by the window. Her right arm swivelled. 'Short and fast. On the body. Every time. I've seen him.' She nodded her head to emphasise the truth of what she was saying. She had black eyes and a white face that seemed to hide her small nose. He thought she looked like a pretty mouse.

'Take some advice.' She leaned towards him conspiratorially. 'Shift your right leg towards off stump as he's in his bowling stride and then hook the swine.' She grinned

'You seem to know a lot about it.'

'My dad played.'

'Ah.' He grinned. 'Well, wish me luck.'

'Do you bat?'

' I'm a bowler.'

'What sort?'

'Fast.'

'How fast?'

'Fast.'

She smiled. 'What's fast where you've been may not be fast in county cricket.' She hesitated fearing she had gone too far. 'Sorry, but it's true.'

'I've bowled to county cricketers. I was a net bowler on Lord Boutilier's staff.'

'Were you any good?'

'They sent me here didn't they?'

She turned and began to lay out the wine glasses wiping each one with a thin white towel. 'If you get a chance to bowl to him take it three-quarters speed for the first couple of balls and then go for his shoes flat out. Make him hop! Make him hop!.' She repeated the words so forcefully that he wondered whether they had a history.

She leaned back, displaying a large bust, and flung her arm in a bowling action catching the edge of the tray which she had lain overlapping the table. 'Crikey. The Calamity Kid. That's what dad calls me.'

She smiled and he noticed lipstick stains on her teeth.

He showed his own teeth and pretended to brush them.

'Ooer, I've done it again have I? I should put on my lips before I do my teeth.'

She gave him a long look. 'We should be friends. You and me. What you say?'

He smiled. 'Okay.'

'Don't want any romance, mind. It's nicer just to be friends. Gives you more space, don't you think?'

He made to answer but she overtook him with another thought. 'You'd best be off. It wouldn't do to keep Major Slapbottom waiting. I'm Lizzie, by the way.'

He held out his hand. 'Ben.' He was immediately conscious of the last time he had shaken hands with a young woman.

Major Carpenter was waiting, tapping his large-bowled pipe on a single stump at the bowler's end of the net. 'Where have you been? Never mind, get down to the far end.'

'I've got no pads.'

The Major gave an exaggerated sigh. 'Well, we'll just have to make do without them. I'll not take a run-up, eh. That's fair.'

A dark, oil-stained bat was resting against the three stumps at the batsman's end. Ben lifted it cautiously feeling the weight and balance. He noted that Major Carpenter was holding the ball with the seam across his fingers. He remembered Lizzie's words. It looked as though she was right. He was trying to get the ball to spit up off the seam.

'Ready?' It was more a warning than a question. Major Carpenter didn't wait for an answer and took two steps before leaping into his delivery stride.

The ball came down just short of a length pitching on the line of Ben's middle and leg stump. He gambled on the maid's advice and, as Major Carpenter's bowling arm swept in a forward arc, he danced his right foot to off stump and hooked at the ball as it came chest high. The ball shot off into the side netting with such power that it ricocheted across the wicket. Major Carpenter scowled down at him. 'Caught on the boundary,' he announced.

Ben suppressed an obvious retort and contented himself with, 'Out first ball, eh.' He smiled and handed Major Carpenter the bat. 'I bowl better then I bat.'

'One would hope so.' The Major took the bat and

smacked it vigorously into the popping crease.

Ben studied the stance while going through the motion of polishing the ball. It was orthodox enough with the left shoulder pointing towards the bowler but the feet were heavy and flat. Like the Major, he took no run-up and whirled his arm over in a smooth, easy motion. Just as he released the ball, the Major moved his back leg to the leg side turning his shoulder slightly out of line. Ben pitched the ball just outside off stump on a forward length, but the Major had time to push out his left leg and drive the ball fizzing along the ground into the net. 'Four I think.' He gave a little herrump and settled into his stance again. Ben fed him another ball outside the off stump and the Major dispatched this one as well. The third ball he held with a looser grip and pushed it with the palm of his hand. His arm speed was similar to the first two balls but the flight slightly slower. The Major plunged his left foot forward again but was early on the stroke sending the ball soaring into the net. He gave another 'herrump' 'Cleared cover,' he announced aggressively. 'I was told you were quite quick,' he injected a hint of sarcasm into his voice.

'You have no pads.'

'Herrump,' the Major shook his head like a blowing horse. 'Fair enough. Pitch one up and let's see.'

Ben strode back eighteen paces and marked out his run-up. He advanced in his smooth, balanced stride. The ball pitched on a full length just outside off stump. The Major met it with an angled, block- bat that sent the ball squirting away through point. Ben looked at him closely. 'Good shot.'

The Major shrugged, 'That was medium pace in county cricket, Linden.'

Ben collected the ball and turned back to his run-up.

This time he hit his marker running. He reached the crease with his body full on to the wicket; his arm whirled over and his knuckled scraped the ground on his follow-through. The major was still bringing his bat down when the ball exploded on the shoe of his front foot and from there it reared up to flatten two of the stumps. Major Carpenter heard the clatter of the wicket and looked down to see that his large brown shoe had burst open like a grinning fish. He looked back and saw that one stump had speared through the net.

'Was that fast enough, you bastard?' Ben thought the words but did not speak them.

The Major gave Ben a hard stare. 'Just wanted to see what you could do.' He contained his anger in a smile. 'Well, Linden, we appear to have run out of stumps.' He walked away to the pavilion ignoring his split shoe.

Ben's lodgings were a ten minute walk beyond the gasometer. His landlord, Mr James, worked as a clerk at the local power station, but he and his wife, a large, buxom woman who looked like she could model the before advert for a line of corsets, supplemented their income by taking in lodgers, usually from the theatre. Mr James referred to his wife as 'Mum' while she called him 'Pop' unless they had had a row in which case he became 'Reginald.' They had a daughter called Lottie, who sniffed a lot and had a lazy left eye. The James' were the first family in the street to have a radio. It sat in the front room and gave off classical music through what sounded like a storm at sea. There were two chorus girls staying on the top floor, thick-thighed young women, who giggled a lot at the supper table and flashed inviting eyes at him. Mr James had an hour in the front room listening to the radio each evening, sitting by the hearth blowing his pipe smoke up the chimney at the behest of his wife. Mrs James had a large visitors' book resting on the hall table. Only 'theatricals' were required to sign it, in the, as yet unrewarded, hope that someone at sometime would become famous. Mum and Pop discussed the likelihood of Ben becoming a worthy entrant but decided to restrict the book to the theatre. One evening, a week after he'd arrived, and the day before the dancing girls departed for Stoke, Lottie beckoned him to the hall where she opened the pages. She smiled. 'Can't understand Pop and Mum. I'd say you had more chance of becoming famous than those two clatter feet'. She gestured to the top of the house. Lottie insisted on showing Ben the book which was peppered with such comments as. 'A pleasant stay.' 'Very hospitable.' She gave him a sly grin as she turned a page.

'Here's an interesting one,' she said as her mother called them to supper and the chorus girls came charging down the stairs.

'LDDAB.' Ben looked at her. 'What does it mean?'

Lottie giggled and whispered. 'You mustn't tell Mum or Pop.'

Ben shook his head. 'No. Of course not,' he said.

She gave a little giggle. 'Landlady's daughter does a bit.' She gave him a conspiratorial wink, slapped her rump and wiggled her long pleated dress as she walked all innocent eyed into the dining room. The episode quite put Ben off his Irish stew that evening. He began to go to great lengths to ensure that he and Lottie were never alone in the house.

The following day he sought out Lizzie at the pavilion and asked her a 'great favour.' Would she call at his lodging from time to time and pretend to be his girlfriend. She gave out peals of laughter when he explained his problem, but agreed on condition he took her to the cinema once a week. The Talkies were a new experience for Ben, as was almost everything else in London. Each Saturday evening they took a tram into the West End, ate fish and chips at one of the bustling tea rooms off Leicester Square and then queued outside one of the huge cinemas that were patrolled by ushers dressed in bright uniforms with gold braid epaulettes. He sat through each film like a child at Christmas astounded by the scale and scope of it all. Sometimes Lizzie's hand would worm its way into his and squeeze him gently. He felt alarm that she might be seeking to take their relationship beyond friendship. He knew if they slept together, he would wake up eventually in a cold bed with neither a lover nor a friend. He was then, relieved to discover that her hand left his at the first note of the national anthem and, though she sometimes clung to his elbow on the way home, she never hinted at intimacy.

She watched him at the nets when her duties allowed. The trialists and the second team players came back early. They were followed by two or three toffs who were hoping to get the odd game during their summer vacation from university. A week later the established first team players sauntered in and finally Midshire's great amateur star, A. J. Sinclair, put in an appearance on his own armchair, which had been placed like a throne on the balcony outside the dressing room. There he sat in his pomp until he felt the need to have a net.

Ben was bowling at just over three-quarter pace. Major Carpenter said nothing on the matter, though occasionally Ben caught him staring. Carpenter's behaviour was noted by Myers, one of second team's fringe players. Myers had been discovered batting in one of the colliery leagues. He watched Ben closely in the nets before facing him. Like Jepson he got into line very quickly and played the fast bowlers with little back lift. On the second day he introduced himself to Ben. Then he gave a boyish grin and asked 'Why?'

'Why what?'

'Why aren't you bowling flat out?'

Ben shrugged. 'I don't trust the nets' pitch.'

'Bollocks!' Myers grinned again. 'It's as flat as your girlfriend's chest.'

Ben laughed at Myers' joke. All around them the air was punctuated by the sound of bat on ball and the cries and calls of the cricketers. He moved close to Myers so no one could hear his words. 'I'm waiting my time.'

'For what? For who?'

Ben grinned. 'For an arrogant toff who was rude to me once.'

'What's his name?'

'Bowden.'

'Perry Bowden! That's his brother in law.' He gestured to the balcony where Sinclair reclined with exaggerated grace. Myers wiped the mop of blond hair from his face. 'You're going to bounce him?'

Ben shook his head. 'No. They'd call me off. I'll just bowl fast at him.'

'You're a deep one, mind.' Myers stared at Ben as though suddenly seeing him through a new light.

Ben grinned, 'The silent assassin.'

Myers gave Ben another hard look. 'Just how fast are you?'

'It's first team day on Thursday. You'll see then.'

The following two days passed quickly. Ben began looking for new lodgings. He knew that Lottie would hunt him down eventually and, at the very least, create a scene which would get back to the club and provide ammunition for Major Carpenter to damage his career. On the second day he found cheaper rooms nearer the ground and nearer the gasometer. Lizzie disapproved because it was a longer walk from her home. However, he pointed out that his move meant that she no longer had to pretend to be his girlfriend. He looked for a sign of disappointment in her eyes, but saw none. She was at the nets on the Thursday though, standing next to Myers as he padded up. The county had invited reporters and cameramen to the ground, though only after a prolonged discussion by the general committee on the dangers of losing standards by popularising the game. The modern men, it seemed, had won the day, their arguments enforced by the need to raise money.

It had been announced in advance that Mr Sinclair would not be batting as he was resting a slight thigh strain, though a number of established players as well as Mr P. W. H. Bowden would be putting bat to ball and be available for brief interviews. Mr Bowden, the statement added, was a newcomer, fresh from Oxford University, where enthusiasts would recall, he had made a dashing hundred in the varsity match last season. No mention was made of a promising fast bowler called Ben Linden, who had been given his chance after rescuing Lord Boutilier's favourite dog.

And so, at prompt eleven o'clock, the first team men and those on the fringe, advanced on to the pitch, the players through one gate and the gentlemen through another, to meet in one group by the nets.

The second team players and the trialists were herded into another group to await instructions. Six of the batsmen were assigned nets and the bowlers divided into three per net. Bowden spotted Ben immediately and turned to one of his fellow batsmen. He said something for the other man turned to look at Ben before giving out a loud laugh.

Ben felt the heady strength of a cold rage. Evidently his fame had preceded him. He was called to a net two down from Bowden and his friend, but he knew they were watching him. He ran in, gliding to the stumps and sent down a medium paced off cutter that surprised the batsmen with its sharp turn off the seam. The ball flew through the gap between bat and body but over the stumps.

'Well bowled, son!' the batsman, a gnarled old pro with skin like leather, who'd almost played for England ten years ago, acknowledged the ball.

Ben smiled to hide his disappointment. He hadn't intended to beat the bat and hoped his success hadn't deterred Bowden from facing him.

He walked back to the end of his run. Myers was standing there padded up and hoping to get a bat when the first teamers had had their fill. He'd heard the compliment from the batsman. 'That's high praise from Jimmy.'

'Jimmy?'

'Jimmy Sawyer. He got a hundred against the Australians on their last tour.' Myers grinned. 'You didn't know?'

Ben shook his head. 'Why would I? I'm just a country lad.'

He ran in and sent another medium paced ball at full length on the off stump which Sawyer hit through the covers. The ball squirmed along the net and Ben stopped it with his foot.'

'Nice shot.' He walked back to his mark and Myers moved to his side once more. 'By the way, there are two startlingly good looking ladies sitting over there and they seem to be taking an interest in you.'

Ben glanced across and saw Helen and Bunty sitting under a parasol. His heart leapt and he almost stopped in mid stride. Fortunately he had the presence of mind to drop the ball and managed to regain his composure while he retrieved it.

'No,' he said as casually as he could manage. 'They're friends of Bowden.' As he ran in to bowl to Sawyer he knew his plans were in ashes. If he humiliated Bowden, as he knew he could, he would now look like a childish show-off.

The next ball he bowled was a yard faster but Sawyer got into line and played it back to him. Ben was half way down the wicket on his follow-through and pretended to fumble the ball so that he could get nearer to the batsman.

'I'm going to bowl flat out,' he said in a quiet voice.

Sawyer, the veteran of twelve seasons in the top class cricket, the scorer of three centuries for the Players against the Gentlemen, and another hundred against the Aussies, stared at the young man, who had never even been seen on the county circuit. 'Cheeky young bugger,' he scowled.

Ben grinned. He'd taken a liking to the old pro. He ran in with the elation of a dog off the leash and kept his body forward on his delivery stride. His leading leg crunched into the hard wicket, his left arm whirled past his hips bring his shoulders and bowling arm round and when he released the ball his arm thrashed in an arc. Sawyer had barely begun to bring his bat down from the back lift when the ball flashed past him and the stumps and reared into the net. 'Bloody hell!' He stared at the young bowler.

Ben was caught in the moment, but he became aware that some cameramen were snapping at him and that there was a murmur of astonishment from both press and public. He didn't dare look toward Helen and Bunty, but he noticed Bowden giving him a hard stare. He was no longer making jokes about him to his friend.

Ben walked down the wicket to retrieve the ball. 'I'll give

you a few more on the off stump, if that's ok?'

Sawyer nodded and took guard.

He was as good as his word and Sawyer, who adopted his back lift to almost nothing, stonewalled each ball. Ben became aware that play around him stopped each time he ran in. He bowled a second over and then a third but pitched the last ball short and wide of the off stump. Sawyer went forward as usual and the ball spat past him a foot away and shoulder high. He nodded in appreciation. He knew Ben had bowled wide deliberately and was saying, 'Supposing you don't know where I'm going to bowl next.'

It was the signal of a real battle between batsman and bowler and for four more overs Ben bowled at almost full pace. The balls used for the nets were old and worn, but twice Ben got the ball past Sawyer's bat, and on another occasion found the edge.

At the end of it all Sawyer advanced down the wicket grinning and offered Ben his hand. A smattering of applause broke out from the press and public. Ben didn't dare look to see whether Helen had joined in. He pulled a thick sweater over his head and began to walk away with Sawyer. Carpenter caught up with them. 'Linden. No one has dismissed you,'

Sawyer looked across at the Major. 'I've dismissed him, Mr Carpenter. He needs a rub down.' He gave a push to Ben's back moving him on.

'Major. My title is Major,' Carpenter growled at the retreating figures.

Chapter Fourteen

Lizzie walked with him from the ground chattering about his great day. 'The reporters applauded you,' she shook her head in wonderment. 'I've never seen that happen before. No one has.' One thought chased another. 'That's because it's never happened.' She gave a giggle and punched him on the arm. 'What did Sawyer say?'

They paused on the kerb as a bus spluttered its way up the hill along Farrier Street. They strode out across the road. 'Not a lot.'

'Oh come on. He must have said something.'

'I told him where I was going to bowl.'

He heard her laugh. 'Why do that?'

'Because I didn't want to ambush him. He thought I was medium fast after the first few.'

'But you ambushed Carpenter.'

'I did.'

She gave a loud laugh. 'I saw his shoe that night. Before he could change it. He came up muttering something about dangerous stairs. But I knew.' Lizzie's face gleamed in triumph. 'I told myself, Lizzie! The new lad's done him.'

Ben said nothing. The words were whirling round him. He needed to take stock of what had happened in the morning. He needed to think about Helen's sudden presence. He needed to forget all about her, but that was a different thing from doing it. He glanced at Lizzie crossing the road in her usual excited fashion, her arms going three ways at once. He felt a sudden affection for her. He wanted to tell her everything but knew that would be folly. And, anyway, it wasn't as though her inevitable advice would have the Wisdom of Solomon about it. He reached out and squeezed her hand affectionately.

'Eeh heck! I'm on tables.' She turned and left him calling 'Bye!' She ignored the hooting cars as she scuttled across the road. He waved at her grinning. On the way home he asked himself, 'Why can't I fall in love with Lizzie?' There was only one answer. He hadn't.

He turned off into a street of small terraced houses with front gardens small enough to cover in a stride. It was market day and Mrs Frampton, his landlady, was out.

The house was dark and smelled of cooking fat. He left tuppence on the kitchen table and went upstairs to run a bath. He lay in the cast iron casing until the water began to cool. Then he wrapped himself in a large towel and went to his room at the top of the house where he fell asleep. He woke at four thirty, dressed and went for a walk along the grimy streets whose bricks had been stained by fog, and smog, and smoke. He could smell the chimneys, even on a warm afternoon. All his life he'd taken fresh air for granted, and now this. He supposed he'd get used to it, that and the noise, and the litter whirling about in windy streets.

Mrs Frampton did not have the airs of his previous landlady. She had no ambition to provide a bed for a future star. She, like his own mother, had lost her husband in the war and had taken in lodgers to survive. She preferred long-stay tenants, or 'my regulars,' as she called them.

The most regular of her regulars was Mr Long who was always first to the breakfast table, his hair oiled, a frown on his shiny white face as he perused the pages of his Daily Mail. He worked in the accounts office of the gasworks and, when Ben looked at his body stooped over the breakfast table, it seemed merely a prelude to him stooping over his desk and ledger in a gloomy room with a window seat overlooking the glue factory. He was in his mid thirties, though he could have been aged ten years either way, and referred to Ben through Mrs Frampton as 'our young friend here.' Today, however, he chose to address Ben directly as he thrust his paper across the table. 'I see you had a successful day,' he smiled.

Ben glanced down and was startled to see a picture of himself under a headline, 'Youngster makes his mark at the nets.'

The article went on to describe how Ben had bowled eight very brisk overs at the experienced batsman Sawyer J.G. who had later described the young man as 'quite the fastest bowler I have ever faced.' The writer went on to describe Ben's gliding run in and smooth side on action, and added that though it was early days it was, surely, just a matter of time before the Linden was gracing the great grounds of the country and startling the very best batsmen with his pace. It went on to quote the second team captain, Major Carpenter, whose role it was to polish the obvious talent of this young cricketer, as he had done with so many youngsters in the past. The article continued, that wisely Major Carpenter had introduced a note of caution to the general euphoria. Linden, he had said, had the gift of great pace, but was still very young and very raw and needed to be brought on slowly.'

An hour later, as Ben walked down the pavilion steps, Major Carpenter was less temperate in his opinions.

'This is not the way we do things here, Linden.' He waved copies of the day's newspapers in the general direction of the nets where a crowd of about three hundred people had assembled.

Ben stood before him, confused. 'I'm not responsible for the articles.'

'Really. I watched you. You played to the gallery.'

'I didn't. I bowled fast because that's what I do. I'm a

fast bowler.' He didn't try to keep the sarcasm from his voice.

'Only when the press are here it seems. You were medium pace for two days before.'

'I was warming up, saving myself to bowl against Mr Bowden. Then, when I found myself bowling to Sawyer I thought he'd do.'

'You were saving yourself to bowl against Mr Bowden.' Major Carpenter made the words sound as ridiculous as he could.

'Yes,' Ben found the lie he was looking for. 'I saw him bat well against Warren, and wanted to see if I could do better.'

'Warren?'

'Yes.'

'The England opening bowler.'

'Yes.'

'And who do you play for again?'

'I want to play for England one day.'

'You'll not play for our seconds unless you change your attitude.' He gestured to the crowd. 'This is disruptive. We're going to tell them that you have a muscle strain.'

Ben blurted out the words before he thought of the consequences. 'I'm not feigning injury. I'm paid to bowl and I'm going to bowl.'

'I beg your pardon!' the major's voice made it clear he was doing anything but.

Ben stared at him and his voice was resolute. 'I'm going to bowl unless you tell them the truth as you see it. That they are just a bunch of awful spectators who shouldn't be there and I'm being withdrawn because I bowled fast and gave the correspondents a story to write.'

As the two men stared at each other, Major Carpenter knew he had gone too far. The decision to withdraw Linden had been his own, as had his criticism of the young man. It was obvious from Sawyer's comments that Linden had the support of senior players and who knew where it would all end if there was a serious confrontation. He contented himself with a steely look, 'Be very careful, Linden. Be very careful.' And with that he turned away.

Ben looked after his retreating figure knowing he had won the battle, but not the war.

Whether by accident or design, Ben suspected the latter, he found himself facing Perry Bowden in the nets at the end farthest from the bank of spectators seated in the east stand.

Bowden made an entrance like the golden boy he had been at university, his pads freshly whitewashed and a sharp crease in the flannels above them. His cream shirt was tapered at the wrists and a white cravat covered his neck. His long blond locks fluttered in the breeze, and he approached Ben as though he owned the ground. When he got close he smiled for the gallery and said in a low voice. ' I'd like to practise full length on my off stump.'

He was treating Ben as a net bowler which wasn't the correct protocol, as both they knew. Ben was bowling for a place with the county and he could have refused, or simply ignored the request. Instead he said in a loud voice that he knew carried to the spectators. 'Would you like me to bowl medium pace as well as on your off stump?'

If Bowden recognised the sarcasm he didn't show it. Instead he gave a laugh and twirled his bat. 'No! No! As fast as you like.'

As he walked back to his mark, Ben considered his options. He knew that Bowden had instructed him to bowl in the area for his favourite shot, the cover drive. Furthermore, as he already knew the line and length of the ball, he could push forward early so giving himself a crucial advantage against Ben's pace.

There were five other nets but the eyes of all the spectators were on Ben as he glided in to the wicket. There was a murmur of appreciation at the smoothness of his run. His leap to the wicket was low, his upper body was forward of his hips, his left arm thrashed down past his thighs bringing his shoulders round and his right arm came over like a whip. There was no attempt to swing the ball or pitch it off the seam. This was pure pace, a ball that threatened injury to a bowler who had not had time to warm up. Those side-on to the nets never saw the flight of the ball, some noted that Ben's bowling arm scraped the turf on it follow through, others saw Bowden's high back lift as he lunged forward; but they all saw the off stump rear out of the ground and hang half and half through the nets, and all this as the bat barely started its downward path to block the ball that had already gone before.

There was a seminal moment of silence before the spectators, who had now swelled to about eight hundred, bellowed their appreciation.

Ben walked down the wicket and retrieved the stump. Bowden called out. 'Well bowled, Linden!' and then in a lower voice growled, 'I asked for a length ball.'

'I know, I got carried away in the moment.' He smiled. 'Mind you, I think your high back lift had something to do with it.'

Ben bowled eight overs at Bowden on the requested line and length. Bowden, who was essentially playing the same shot to every ball got into a rhythm and played some impressive strokes into the cover area, though he did have trouble when Ben pushed in a faster one or got the ball to spit up off the seam. At the end of it Bowden advanced down the wicket smiling and called out 'Well done, Linden!' though there was none of the genuine admiration in his voice as in Sawyer's the day before.

As they shook hands, he added in a patronising fashion, 'You're quite quick.'

Ben gave him a stare. 'Oh, believe me, I can bowl faster than that, Mr Bowden. Bowling all those stones seems to have worked. Well, I'm off to my cave.' The two then walked away to their separate gates. As Ben neared the pavilion steps the spectators began to applaud. Ben smiled shyly. He didn't know how to deal with admiration.

Once in the dressing room he gave himself a brisk rub down with a rough towel, drank two glasses of water, and left by the deserted back entrance.

He had not gone fifty yards before Sawyer came alongside him and patted him on the back. 'Thanks for that.'

'For what?'

'Bowling that twat Bowden first ball.'

'I didn't do it for you.'

'I know. He told you to bowl line and length, didn't he?' Sawyer didn't wait for an answer. 'It's the oldest trick.'

'You don't like him, I gather.'

'He took my place once,' Sawyer bristled at the memory. 'Came home from university and said he'd rather like a game. So they dropped me.'

The two of them were out of the ground by now and passing The Last Wicket. Sawyer seemed appeased by the sight of one of his favourite places. He gripped Ben by the crook of his elbow. 'Let's have a drink.'

They were in the lounge before Ben could make an excuse. Sawyer strode to the bar, leaving Ben in the middle of the high ceilinged room that was swilling with smoke. A couple of the barmaids flashed him friendly smiles and he smiled back, but quickly lost eye contact. This was his first visit to a pub, though he would not have admitted that to Sawyer, and he felt slightly ill at ease, not least because he, a trialist, had been befriended by a senior pro.

Sawyer returned with the drinks and gave him a wink. 'Dotty fancies you, I see.' He grinned, and cracks appeared in his leathery face.

He handed Ben a glass of heavy ale. 'I don't like his airs and graces. Golden Boy. Golden Bollocks! He's no bloody good.'

Ben said nothing, which Sawyer took as a sign of disagreement.

'Do you think he's any good?' He stuck his chin out like pugilist inviting a punch. Ben laughed; he was beginning to like the crusty old pro. 'His back lift's too high.'

'Aye and there's something else. He likes his cover drive, but if you block him with fielders he opens the face and tries to run through gully. A good bowler will find his edge eventually.'

Ben knew that Sawyer was right but the veteran was just warming to his theme. 'There's some of them are alright, but him, he's too hoitey toitey for me.' He glanced around the room like a conspirator and tugged on Ben's jacket cuff. 'They may be cleverer than us, but it's on the pitch, that's where it matters. And on the pitch we're their betters.' That said, he wandered off to the bar and reappeared with two more pints. He bought two more rounds and Ben bought one, before Sawyer declared that his whistle was whetted and he was off to town. Ben weaved his way home. Thankfully the house was empty and he collapsed on his bed and fell asleep.

Chapter Fifteen

Carpenter was angry with himself after his row with Linden. The young man had shown more spirit than he'd expected; that was bad enough, but the fact that his little rebellion had been heard by some of the senior pros was infinitely worse.

The attitude of some of the top professionals was becoming an increasing problem. Some were crudely scathing about the abilities of the amateurs. Carpenter was a man of private means, who'd 'had a good war', which made him the ideal choice for captain of the seconds. However he was under no illusions that he had been awarded the post following a crucial meeting with Lord Boutilier four years previously. Boutilier had no formal connections with the county, but everyone knew he was the power behind a number of thrones.

Boutilier had said in that whispering voice of his, 'I wonder, Major, how you saw the position of Lord Hawke?'

Carpenter had looked at the small, slim figure leaning gently in a sloping chair, and had wondered what he was talking about. 'With reference to what?' he'd asked at last, convinced that he had failed some test.

Boutilier had smiled, his slow, cold smile. 'Why, with reference to his statement of "Pray heaven a professional never captains England." '

Carpenter had sipped at his whisky to give himself time to think. Hawke's utterance had caused a terrible storm. The repercussions were still swilling about two years on. Carpenter had glanced around the room, aware he was being tested. He had also felt a sense of relief. Boutilier knew his general views about amateurs and professionals.

He had leaned forward and spoken in a low voice. 'I agree with him one hundred per cent.' He'd glanced at Boutilier's face which had remained unhelpfully impassive and then had added. 'Though of course he was bloody fool to say so. Brought the whole thing into a public debate. That's not what we want. Why start a fight over territory you already have?'

Boutilier had smiled and said, 'Indeed, Major, indeed.'

Two months later he was confirmed as captain of the seconds and given a place on the county selection committee.

The two men formed a natural alliance for they both despised the rise of the professionals in the game with their crude conversation, their rude wit, and their desire to win above everything else.

However, the crux of the matter was that there were too few amateurs with too little time to play the three day game, and so the influx of the professionals was inevitable. The question was: How to control them? Carpenter was more useful than most in that respect. His tall, beefy body towered over the young professionals in the second team; his thick shoes rasped on the gravel paths and scraped the wood of the dressing room with ill-concealed menace. He was used to ordering men about, and for those men not to question him. His methods were effective with the fledgling players in the second team, though he did have difficulty when the senior pros were brought into his side to bolster form and fitness.

Boutilier saw Carpenter and others like him as defenders of the faith.

He'd watched the rise of young Linden with some reservations. On the one hand there was no doubting his potential, and he might help them in their ultimate goal, winning the ashes, but on the other, he recalled the day the boy had met the King and had seemed reluctant to shake hands.

Boutilier had met and played with many a fast bowler. They were not men to whom you'd introduce your mother. But Linden was different. He was not outwardly fiery, Boutilier suspected he possessed a cold rage that was twice as deadly.

And so it was on the eve of Linden's move from the estate that the Major was summoned to Boutilier's apartment overlooking Lords.

Boutilier had sat the Major down with large malt and told him that he would be getting a young fast bowler in his charge, a special talent.

'Really?' Carpenter had looked up and wondered, not for the first time, where Boutilier was taking him.

'Jepson thinks he might win back the ashes.'

Carpenter flinched at the mention of the England captain's name. It had been Jepson, as captain of Surrey, who had banned the University amateurs from getting an automatic game for the county, so preventing Carpenter's son from playing during his vacation. The Carpenters had played cricket for five generations and all of them had, at some point, got a game for Surrey. Then Jepson and his 'modern' ideas had come along and scuppered all that. Carpenter found it difficult not to curse at the mention of his name.

Boutilier continued in his smooth tones. 'If he is to become our next national hero, it would help our cause if he learned some respect for his betters.'

Those words haunted Carpenter now. He had tried to bully the youth into shape, but had mistaken his quiet demeanour for lack of confidence, and that had been a serious error. His talents were obvious, but Carpenter had completely underestimated the rate at which Linden's reputation would rise. The top players sought him out at the nets, his name and pictures were appearing in the quality papers, and all this before he had even played game.

A week after their confrontation at the nets, Carpenter called Ben into his private office, a small room at the top of some rickety stairs. There was no carpet and the floor boards were raked with studs. A tiny window looked out over the ground and through it Ben could hear the sounds of players practising in the nets. Carpenter looked up from behind his small desk and surprised Ben with a smile as he rose from his seat and extended his hand. There was nothing Ben could do but take it.

'We got off to a bad start, Linden.' Ben met his stare but said nothing. Carpenter didn't appear to notice his lack of reaction. 'Everyone has been impressed by your performances. Time to take it on a step. There's a club representative match against Lancashire next week and we want to take you with us as the twelfth man. Basically it means you'll be looking after the kit, but will have the experience of travelling with the players. It's a rare opportunity to gain some experience.'

Ben knew enough about Carpenter now to pick his own time and place for his battles. The words kit man ran through his head like an angry horse, but he kept his cool for he knew that any protest would be reported back and used against him.

'Thank you Major,' he said in a flat voice.

Carpenter warmed to his theme. 'This is a big step in your career,' he affirmed. 'Both sides will have first team players who feel they are in need of practice.' He paused. 'I'm told Lancashire is fielding three Test players and we will also have a very strong team. You'll be mixing with the great and the good,' Carpenter gave a smirk of satisfaction as he waited for Ben to thank him.

'I'll do my best, Major.'

Ben was more frank in his opinions when a grinning Sawyer came up to congratulate him.

'What for? For carrying the kit!' He slammed his locker door shut.

'All will be revealed, my son,' Sawyer said in a pious voice.

All was revealed a day before the match when Lomax, one of the first team bowlers, called off with a thigh strain.

'Groin strain more like it,' said Sawyer with a grin. 'He's got the hots for a barmaid. He's on a promise.' Sawyer gave an extravagant wink. 'Actually the lads raised ten bob in a whip round, and that persuaded her. That and a story that got about that Lomax had a ten inch todger.' He gave a laugh. 'She asked me whether Bobby was as big as his shoes. "Meg," I said, "You may have noticed that Lomax is not the prettiest of men. But often God gives a man strange compensations."'

Ben started to laugh, 'So I'll get a game.'

Sawyer nodded, 'Yep, though you owe the lads ten bob. Mind you, God knows what will happen when Meg gets a sight of Bobby's winkler.'

Carpenter sought out Ben on the morning they were due to travel to Manchester and told him that, even though he was now playing, he would still have to look after the kit as it was too late to summon a replacement.

Carpenter had his suspicions about the sudden withdrawal of Lomax, but knew he couldn't prove anything. The professionals were told to take a tube to Euston, but ironically Ben, like the amateurs in the team, was allowed to hail a taxi to transport the bulky kit bags.

Carpenter summoned a porter for him at the station and they supervised the loading of the large canvas bags into the luggage carriage. Ben made to follow Carpenter. The engine crew were piling coal into the furnace to stoke up the boiler as Ben walked down the line of carriages. A young woman stopped him. 'Mr Linden isn't it?' She held out the lid of a cardboard cake box for him to autograph. As he reached for his pen, Carpenter intervened. 'No time for that.' He made to usher Ben away, but the young cricketer avoided his grasp and signed his name in a quick scrawl.

'No harm done,' he said brightly.

'We're late.' Carpenter's voice lowered to a growl. He stopped at one of the first class carriages and pointed down the track. 'You're three down,' he said gruffly smarting that once again Linden had defied him, even if it was on such a slight matter.

Ben started to look for his carriage and was relieved to see Sawyer stick his face out of one of the carriage windows. 'Come on young 'un. Leave the ladies alone.' Sawyer saw Carpenter stiffen as he realised his little confrontation had been witnessed. Sawyer grinned pleasantly. 'You're first class, Mr Major.'

Carpenter glared as he climbed aboard. 'Damned impertinence,' he muttered as he stormed into his carriage. 'Are we all here? Where's Mr Huntingdon?'

Abercrombie, one of the four amateurs in the side looked up from his Telegraph. 'He's in the third. He always travels third.'

'Pardon?' Such an action was incomprehensible to Carpenter. Not only was Huntingdon a mainstay of the first team and rated the best off spinner in the country, he was from a titled family.

Abercrombie nodded. 'I know. He's a strange chap. Says he only travels first class when he's abroad as the locals there expect it of an Englishman.'

Dobie, another first team regular, smiled to ease Carpenter's discomfort. 'It took a bit of time for us to get used to it. But . . . what can you do?' He shrugged and unbuttoned his dark gleaming jacket as he settled back in his seat.

Carpenter said nothing and sat down pulling his Telegraph from his leather attaché case.

Three carriages down some of the second teamers looked doubtfully at Huntingdon as he raced his way through The Times crossword.

Sawyer grinned. 'It's OK. Mr Huntingdon doesn't tell tales.'

Huntingdon did not look up from his paper but, as he filled out yet another answer, the players could see a faint smile light his face. Perhaps it was because he had just solved a particularly difficult clue. Perhaps not. They settled in an uneasy silence as the train jolted into motion.

Sawyer and Huntingdon were the only regular first teamers in the carriage. Sawyer picked up the atmosphere almost immediately and tried to play the gallery.

'Is it OK if, in the confines of the carriage, we choose to call you Basil, Mr Huntingdon?'

Huntingdon looked up from his paper. 'No, it bloody isn't.'

'Oh,' Sawyer retreated into silence.

Huntingdon looked up again, 'Would you choose to be to be called Basil?'

'Oh right.'

'It's bad enough that I have to cut my vocabulary in half to communicate with you.'

Sawyer flushed, aware that he was losing on points, 'Aye, well, our day is coming.'

'It is, and I just hope you make a better job of it than we did of ours. However, in view of what has happened to poor Gibbs it may be a longer fight than you anticipate.' He looked across at Sawyer. 'Anticipate, by the way, means to eagerly expect, Sawyer.' He grinned and the young cricketers laughed at Sawyer.

One of them asked, 'Who is Gibbs?'

Sawyer turned on him seeing an easier target. 'Who's Gibbs? Who's Gibbs? Do you know nowt? He's the Lancashire spinner who played for England and wrote in a newspaper column that he should have been given more overs. The county have got rid of him and he's lost his column. Pure spite.'

Sawyer looked across to see whether Huntingdon was going to argue. He was disappointed.

Ben found himself in awe of Huntingdon. He seemed so able, and everything he did was effortless. Apart from Helen, he was the only toff he'd taken to.

Huntingdon rose to his feet. 'Fancy a drink, Sawyer? I'll buy.'

'Not like last time. You get, 'Look at Mr Huntingdon, he's tiddly, teehee', and I get fined.

Huntingdon nodded, 'Class does have its privileges. Come on. I'll buy the beer and pay the fine.'

Sawyer rose with enthusiasm. 'Right,' he said, 'And I'll not call you Basil.'

Ben arrived at the hotel in the centre of Manchester an hour late after dropping off the kit bags at Old Trafford.

He was just in time for the cooked-out remains of an Irish stew before being shown a bed under the rafters by a rattling radiator and a small window that picked up the noise of the traffic.

He returned to the lounge in time to see Sawyer and the rest of the professionals about to embark on a night on the town.

He turned down an invitation to join them, pleading tiredness. It was only half true. He was indeed worn down with tension. The next few days might define his career, but there was more to it than that. Even though tomorrow would be his first game of any note, he had already become someone who was talked about both in the newspapers and in the game. He'd found that women were anxious to meet and to greet him. He fended them off politely and waited for Helen's power over him to fade.

He watched Sawyer and his team mates disappear through the revolving door, like children out to play, and turned into the bar where he ordered a pint of dark beer.

He became conscious that people were staring at him and realised that he was the only person in the room who was casually dressed. As he rose to leave Huntingdon appeared before him, resplendent in a silk-lapelled evening suit. He was smoking a cigarette from a holder and plumes of grey smoke spiralled into the high ceiling.

'May I join you?' Huntingdon sat down and Ben stood up reversing their positions from a moment before. Ben smiled. 'I was just about to go.'

Huntingdon gestured to Ben's full pint.

'I'm not properly dressed. People are staring. I think they're about to object.'

'Well, let them.' Huntingdon gestured for him to sit down.

'I don't want to cause a scene.'

Huntingdon grinned. 'Don't worry. We'll win any argument hands down.'

'Will we?' Ben felt very much the stranger, surrounded by people of a different class.

Most certainly.' Huntingdon settled himself back into his high backed arm chair. 'You see my family owns the hotel.'

Ben began to laugh. 'You're having me on, Mr Huntingdon.'

Huntingdon shook his head. 'No.' He raised his right arm and a waiter came at him like a moth to light. 'Whisky, Appleby. The usual.'

'Certainly sir.' The waiter disappeared and returned with the drink.

'Appleby.'

'Yes sir?'

'There are people staring at us. Perhaps we could have a strategically placed screen?'

'Certainly, sir.'

The screen was duly put in place by two waiters. Appleby danced nimbly round it.

'Anything else, sir?'

Huntingdon considered the question. 'Perhaps you could place on it one of those signs you have. Area Reserved for Special Guests.'

Certainly, sir.'

Ben looked uncomfortable. 'I don't want to be the cause of trouble. If it gets back . . . '

Huntingdon ignored him as he leaned back and looked round the screen. 'They're staring at the VIP sign now. I think Appleby has explained to them that I own the hotel.' He gave a laugh. 'Your reputation is secure. You could come down in your pyjamas and they'd fawn over you. Now if I could just persuade Carpenter to give you a brisk salute, that would round it off nicely.'

Ben found himself grinning. 'You don't seem to like them.'

'I prefer Sawyer's type. Take the word fuck out of his vocabulary and he'd make a Trappist monk. But he says what he thinks. The trouble is, as I've told him, he doesn't think very much, beyond drunkenness and debauchery.'

'And cricket.'

'Aah. There you have me. I've never met a man who knew more about cricket. Strange isn't it? The most complicated and complex of all games and Sawyer is the master of all its nuances. I sometimes wonder what would have happened if my school had got hold of him. Though Sawyer in the Cabinet doesn't bear thinking about.'

The two of them sipped at their drinks feeling pleasantly comfortable in each other's company.

'I've never seen you bowl.'

Ben smiled. 'Nor me you.'

'Sawyer says you are very quick.'

Ben wriggled to escape such praise. 'I burst Carpenter's shoe once.'

'Did you really! Oh, well done!' Huntingdon gave a deep chuckle. He rose from his seat and extended his hand. Ben took it. 'You are not anything like what I was expecting, Linden.'

'You sound relieved, Mr Huntingdon.'

Huntingdon smiled and left.

Ben gave him thirty seconds and then finished off his beer. He was aware that eyes were following his progress as he walked across the room.

Appleby called out, 'Good evening sir.'

Ben affected a nonchalant wave.

Chapter Sixteen

If Carpenter was disappointed at Ben's sudden elevation he hid it well. However the reason soon became apparent. He gave a slow smile. 'I know you'll see this as a great chance, Linden, and so you should. But Lancashire have a very strong batting line up and I think it best to break you in gently.'

Ben held his peace until he reached the professionals' dressing room. 'Break me in! Does he think I'm a bloody horse?'

Sawyer grinned and reached for a hip flask. 'What he'll do is bring you on when they're two hundred for one and the ball has less bounce than a harlot's arse.'

Melchott, one of the opening bowlers, shook his head at Sawyer's vulgarity. 'No wonder they give us different dressing rooms.'

'Well, that's another thing you've got to thank me for.'

Melchott just shook his head, but Sawyer wasn't finished with him. 'Anyway it'll never happen. Supposing we discovered that we all had bigger todgers than Carpenter. What'd that do for discipline eh?' He gave Melchott a stare. 'Though come to think of it, he'd not mind having you in the changing room, eh!'

Sawyer's forecast about the match, however, was depressingly accurate. Carpenter opened the bowling with Melchott. Both bowled at a friendly medium pace and failed to move the ball under a clear sky. Once the shine had been knocked off the ball Carpenter brought on Huntingdon, but the pitch was slow and the batsmen, who were well set by this time, simply adjusted their strokes to accommodate the spin.

By lunch Carpenter had gone through five bowlers and had become increasingly irritated by Sawyer, who continuously offered advice about field placings.

As the players strolled off the pitch Sawyer moved up alongside Huntingdon. 'You need to tell him. He'll not listen to me.'

'Tell him what?'

'Tell him to give the kid a chance.'

Huntingdon shrugged. 'He may have a point. Bowling to top players on that wicket, it might break him.'

'He might take five between lunch and tea as well.'

Huntingdon shook his head. 'Not on that wicket.'

Sawyer put his face closer to Huntingdon. 'The kid's got guts. If he does get carted he'll come back. He's faster than anyone you have ever seen. Trust me, Mr Huntingdon.' They walked on a few strides. 'At the moment he's a bit like one of your lot. It's all been too easy for him. He thinks it's a game when really it's a job to us. If he gets carted that's what he'll learn.'

They were coming to the point when they would have to part to go to their separate gates. Huntingdon smiled. 'You know what Sawyer? You have a certain cunning intelligence.'

The amateurs dined in the same long room but at separate tables from the professionals. Sawyer made a point of sitting next to Ben. Half way through the soup he said, 'You'll be bowling soon.'

Ben looked up surprised. 'How do you know that?'

'I sorted it.'

'I haven't noticed him paying much heed to you so far.'

Sawyer patted him on the shoulder. 'He don't. But Mr Huntingdon does and he's got the ear of the Major.'

Ben took a wicket in the sixth over after lunch, but it

wasn't as a bowler. His strong, low throw from the midwicket boundary caught the batsman, Maynard, a yard short of the crease. As he walked back to the pavilion Maynard gave Ben a long, hard stare. There was nothing personal. The throw had been exceptional and when he regained his composure in the dressing room after hurling his bat across the room, Maynard asked: 'Who the hell was that?'

'Linden,' came the reply from someone on the balcony. 'He's meant to be quickish.'

'Well, why the hell hasn't he had a bowl then?'

'He is now.' The spectator on the balcony gave a whistle. 'Heavens! The wicketkeeper's back thirty yards.'

Carpenter handed Ben the scuffed ball. He motioned to the batsman. 'Miller turns everything to his leg side so I've given you an extra couple of men out there.' Ben looked at the field and saw two men sweeping the boundary.' He knew the placings were wrong but knew there was no chance of persuading Carpenter to change his mind. He walked back to his run, polishing one side of the ball out of habit. Sawyer sauntered over from mid off. 'Just warm up slowly,' he whispered. Ben knew the advice was sound and bowled at three-quarter pace for the first two overs. The wicket keeper moved in ten yards and the two slips followed him.

Ben sidled up to him before he started his third over and whispered, 'Better move back.'

The wicket keeper, who had hopes of making the first team that season smiled and said, 'I think I'll be OK.'

Sawyer heard him and growled. 'Do as he fucking says.' Then to Ben, 'Bring him forward on his off stump. Fast as you like.'

The ball Ben bowled pitched six inches outside the

stumps. Miller, who had taken leg guard and had a habit of moving his front foot to off stump, lunged across the wicket and not down it, and was trying to bring his bat round his pad when the ball thudded into the keeper's gloves head high. It was a toss up as to who was the more startled, the batsman or the wicketkeeper. As Ben glared down the wicket he could hear Sawyer laughing from mid on. 'Aye Miller,' he called out. 'Wait till he warms up proper.' It took Ben another over to find his rhythm and by then word had spread round the ground, and the bars, and committee rooms stocked with members, who normally had little interest in second team matches. The two batsmen survived another four overs, edging a couple of fours through slips before Ben got them in consecutive overs. The opposing captain had scarce time to adjust his multi-coloured Harlequins cap before he edged through to the wicketkeeper. Three wickets had fallen in the space of two overs, but that was the end of it. The wicketkeeper's face was white with pain. He'd cracked two fingers taking the catch. There was no batsman left remotely competent to take Ben's bowling, but neither was there a wicketkeeper who could hope to take him if he bowled at full speed. Ben ran in for a further four overs at three-quarters pace, but even that was too quick for the emergency wicketkeeper. Sawyer watched from mid off with increasing admiration. It was true, this young man was faster than any bowler he had seen, but he noticed too Ben's frustration at being told to bowl slower. He ended his spell with a fast yorker that scattered his incompetent opponent's stumps. His bowling had changed the match and wickets were falling at the other end as the new ball was taken. Ben was brought back and his last ball moved away off the seam. Carpenter, who took the catch, called out 'Didn't carry!' The startled batsman glared at him. 'Yes, it bloody did!' And then he walked off the pitch.

Carpenter was sensible enough to realise that the time had come to accept that Ben's talent had taken him into another world, far away from second team cricket. To do anything else would be to invite ridicule. He patted Ben on the back and congratulated him before walking to the gentlemen's gate.

Back on the Boutilier estate Arnie heard of heard of Ben's 'five-for' and waited for Helen to come for him as he knew she would. She had ridden the drover's road many times since Ben had left and always looked for the wicket that was no longer there and the bowling stones that had been hurled into the bracken. It was as if Ben was trying to say they had never met. She knew she had done him a great wrong when she had left him lying near his cottage, and the tears welled in her eyes. It was not her true self who had acted in this way but she, the person, battling with powers beyond her control. If she had carried him down the hill like a wounded warrior, and if the gossip about them that was already fermenting, had reached her father, she knew he would have broken Ben ruthlessly. He would have viewed sexual contact with as much interest as a passing pigeon at a grouse shoot. But love . . . if Perry or Charles had whispered such a deadly word in his ear, her father would have torn down the world to keep the family name unsullied.

She came in the evening across the field wearing a loose white skirt that fluttered in the gloom. She sat by Old Arnie and nuzzled her head onto his shoulder. He could smell the sweet soap from her body and then he felt the warmth of the tears on his shirt. He put his arm around her and pulled her to him.

'What can I do, Arnie?' she whispered.

'Do you love him?'

He heard her sniffle. 'I've been trying not to, but it's hopeless. I don't know why or how, and I know I don't want to. But I do. It would be much better for me if I loved Perry, but I don't.'

'Easier, not better.' He felt her head move against him and remembered the little blonde girl piddling behind his pavilion, crouched over a little puddle and looking up at him defiantly. The two of them had stared and then she had said. 'I don't need you, Mr Groundsman. Carry on with your duties.'

That had been the start of the chain. She had never been able to play the lady with him after that. Over the years it had become a bond. Many times she had come to him for advice, or to talk of the thoughts that she could not share with her father, but now Arnie hesitated because he feared the wrong words might destroy her. He heard his voice as though it was another person speaking. 'You can do two things. You can stay away and hope that your love fades; you can hope that you meet someone else in time.'

'And always compare, always wonder.' She sounded bitter.

'Yes. But it's safer.'

'What else?'

'You can chase him. You may find happiness among the ruins. You may just find ruins, but at least you'll know.'

Her tears had stopped. She squeezed his arm. 'What would you do?'

'I'm not you, Helen. I'm a working man so it would be easier for me. But you know what I would do.'

He became aware that his pipe had gone out and he reached for his pouch of tobacco.

'I went to see him,' she said in a soft voice. 'I went with Bunty to watch him in the nets. I pretended that we had gone to see Perry. He knew I was there, but he didn't look till he sent someone's stumps scattering. Then he looked. It was only then I realised how much I'd hurt him. When he walked off a young girl linked his arm. The sight gave me an electric shock. There was something in their bodies, touching yet distant. I knew they were not lovers. They were friends. And I can't even be that.' She stopped, shocked as though she'd been caught naked in a window. 'I never believed I could confess that to anybody,' she said. 'I've given you too much power.'

Arnie looked down at the slim figure leaning into him and brushed the hair from her face. He smiled. 'I never told anyone about you behind my pavilion, did I?'

She smiled. 'Only me. A thousand times.'

When Ben returned to London the great rumbling beast that was the press was beginning to stir. His performance had brought him mention in the Manchester Evening News and the Lancashire Evening Telegraph, as well as a few brief paragraphs in the Manchester Guardian.

The cricket correspondents did not cover second team games, so his performance had only been witnessed by juniors, men of the same status as those who had watched his performance in the nets. Their words might have been dismissed had they been commenting on the intricacies of cricket, but they concentrated on one thing only, speed. Added to that, their opinion that he was very fast was backed up by the comments of men who had to know, the batsmen. And so it was that the great scribes of the day overcame their reluctance to admit that anything could have happened without them noticing it first, and had begun to take an interest in Ben Linden.

A clutch of them attended Midshire's next match, a second team game at Essex, and watched him take ten wickets over the two innings, seven of them bowled, and noted that the slips had dropped six catches. On top of that almost all the runs scored against him were played, voluntarily or involuntarily, behind the wicket. As a group, the experts, having the usual human frailties, were reluctant to praise him without qualification, and so they pointed out that the batsmen were, in the main, second team players, and quite unable to deal with Linden's sheer pace. Test and County players would provide a sterner examination.

Similar arguments were put at the next meeting of the Midshire selection committee. Most of the members were at a disadvantage because they had never seen Linden bowl, not even in the nets. One of them, General A.J. Sackville VC, had recently returned from business in India and had not seen the county play for a whole season. His offer to suspend his attendance until he had watched the county play had been unanimously rejected. It had been pointed out, though not recorded in the minutes, that Midshire was the only first class county to have VC on their selection committee, and one who had the humour to wear a monocle over his glass eye.

General Sackville, a taciturn man at the best of times, spoke only one word of any note at the meeting, 'Carpenter', giving the other members to understand that he thought the Major's opinion should be given more weight than normal. After all he had captained the young Linden twice, had seen him bowl in the nets and, above all, was one of them.

Carpenter, much aware of his previous loud criticisms of Linden, accepted the obvious, that the young man was extremely quick. Indeed the experienced players were saying to a man now, that they had never faced anyone so fast. However, questions remained. Carpenter stared through the maze of smoke that swirled under the long low ceiling, and reached for his whisky and soda, only to find the glass empty. A waiter stepped forward hastily. Carpenter gave a 'Herrump', wriggled his neck in his stiff collar, and continued, 'I have to say that young Linden has gone up in my estimation. He seems capable of bowling a controlled line and length, however at his speed it is difficult to get the ball to move much in the air and I wonder how he will fare when faced with better batsmen.' He paused, which was a mistake, for it allowed another member of the committee to squeeze in a comment.

A.J. Lowther rose at the far end of the table. Carpenter glared through the haze.

Lowther, a wealthy businessman, had only been voted on to the committee after making copious donations to the ground improvement fund at a time when the county was nearly bankrupt. That was bad enough, but now there were persistent rumours that the man was Jewish and that his grandfather had changed his surname from Levy for business reasons.

He spoke in a low monotone that belied his quick mind. 'I saw him bowl in the nets to a very experienced batsman, Sawyer. He certainly gave him something to think about when he exerted himself. On top of that he has taken eighteen wickets in two second team games. Now we all know that it is common at this time of year for experienced first team players to get fit by turning out for the second team, so I did some checking. Of the eighteen wickets, four were current, or former, Test players, and six others are regular first class players. In addition he had eleven catches dropped, which, one would hope, would not occur with such frequency at first team level.'

Carpenter gave another 'herrump', if anything louder than the last. 'The boy undoubtedly has talent,' he said. 'I'm worried about damaging him by bringing him on too soon.'

'If he's good enough, he's old enough,' snapped Lowther.

'Remember Carrington, last season,' Carpenter glanced round the table and saw several heads nod in agreement. Lowther's was not among them. 'Carrington was a totally different case,' Lowther said testily. 'He was down from university and pencilled in for a couple of games during his vacation. He should have batted at six or seven but someone put him in at number three.' He looked coldly at two of the members who, he knew, were friends of Carrington Senior. 'In four of his innings he came in facing a new ball, as number threes are wont to do. Of course he lost confidence. Linden, on the other hand, is a bowler who hasn't even opened with the new ball.' It appeared to the committee members that Lowther had been researching the subject with a zealot's thoroughness. He continued, 'Linden is a tough member of what we are wont to call the working class. His father died charging machine guns, and, incidentally, winning the VC.' He glanced across at the General and knew this point was a clincher. 'The youth, himself, came to the attention of Lord Boutilier by risking his life to save his lordship's favourite hound. He is, in fact, one tough young man, who is blessed with an extraordinary talent.'

The General gave Lowther a keen look. 'You've been doing your homework, Lowther.'

He and the others knew that Lowther was desperate to become a member of the MCC selection committee. No one had said anything, but the General knew that the rumours about his Jewish faith, even if they were untrue, would make that impossible.

Lowther was ahead of the General. He too knew that once his family history was exposed doors would be shut. However, there were other ways to fight the war and Linden was one of them.

'As you all know, he said. 'I never played first class cricket, so some of you have the advantage of me. However anyone can spot a great talent. That's easy, and someone who can bowl at one hundred miles an hour is all of that. I know there are some who believe it is more important to take part in the county championship than to win it. But once we are taking part surely that does not preclude us trying to win it. Linden can do that for us, and more.' He stared at Carter. 'Gentlemen. I have watched cricket for forty years. I have spoken to all the great players in this land. And every great player who has seen this young man believes he is something special. We should be nurturing this great talent, not just for the county, but for the country and for the ashes.'

The silence round the table was intense. They had begun the night discussing a simple selection for the county. Now Lowther seemed to have turned the whole process into a patriotic debate.

He found two strange allies in Carpenter and the General. They shunned him as a 'despicable little Jew' and they both fought to the last to maintain the predominance of the amateur over the professional, but they were both men who by instinct fought to win. To win the county championship for the first time this century was a worthy goal, but to regain the ashes, that was the stuff of their dreams.

Carpenter gave one of his herrumps and said, 'I think

Lowther is a little premature in viewing Linden as one of the great players. He has, after all, played two second team games.' He was interrupted by some sniggering from round the table. The Major held up his hands. 'However, I have captained Linden and watched him closely in the nets, as well as faced him, and there is no doubt he is a bowler of extraordinary potential. So perhaps Lowther is right. The risk is still that we bring him on too quickly. But if the risk is high so are the stakes.' As he said the words, Carpenter glanced at the committee secretary and was pleased to see that he was taking notes. A peripheral place in history was better than none at all.

The meeting came to order and Linden was selected for the first match of the county season with only one vote against.

Chapter Seventeen

Any doubts that the higher quality batsmen would deal comfortably with Ben's raw pace were discounted after the first three championship matches. The young bowler took a total of twenty-two wickets. The *Times* correspondent described his bowling as 'fearsome', The *Manchester Guardian* highlighted his yorker delivered from close to the stumps as one of the most deadly balls in the history of cricket.

Within days of the county season opening he found it impossible to walk the streets of London without being approached by fans. His feats even attracted the attention of Bunty Williams, who led her column on the deadly bowler with the killer looks.

She wrote the article without speaking to the new young star. Distance gave one a better perspective, and, in any case, she had seen Helen looking at the young man, and she herself had felt the primitive magnetism of his movement from one hundred yards.

She wrote, 'His greased black hair gives him the look of a matinee idol. Indeed, this tall athlete could walk into Shepperton studios, or Elstree and embrace any of the beauties of the day and they would welcome his attentions. However, ladies, if his looks are not enough, I can recommend a trip to North London to watch him bowl. As he runs to the wicket with the balance of a great dancer, it is like watching the hunter descend on his prey; it is as if the batsman is tethered to his wicket armed only with his bat and the cat is racing in for the kill.'

When she read the article in print the following day she found herself giggling at her hyperbole, but as silly as the words seemed, she knew also that there was an essence of truth that would engage her readers. She had seen him bowl, and though she cared little for cricket beyond seeing it as a social vehicle, she too had felt the thrill of watching him run to the wicket.

Strangely, considering her profession, Bunty disliked telephones, seeing them as not so much a useful appliance as 'a bloody umbilical cord to the office.'

So it was, with more than usual irritation, naked under silk kimono, her usual Sunday morning attire, that she was summoned by the stentorian ring of her telephone.

'You've spoken to him.'

She relaxed as she recognised Helen's voice.

Bunty laughed. 'No, actually.'

'But . . . '

'I've written two thousand words about him and quoted him at length,' She completed her friend's sentence.

'Yes.'

'Nothing really defamatory in it though. The editor thinks I'm slipping. It's three months since we've had a writ.' Bunty laughed and bit into a slice of buttered toast. She hated breakfast. One had to cook one's own meals.

'Oh.' Helen sounded deflated. She obviously had rung for news.

Bunty was tempted to tell Helen to go and fuck the man until she tired of him and his doubtless quaint, simple beliefs, but she valued their friendship too much for that. She remembered how Helen had befriended her when she had been kept to the periphery of college society because she was from new money.

Instead she found herself talking soothingly into the phone. 'Look this story has got legs. I'll have to meet him, eventually. Is there anything you want me to say? I can dress up and fire little arrows at his heart if you wish, or even give him a good shagging and report back on the efficacy of it all.' She heard Helen give a giggle over the phone, 'Don't you dare!'

'Hmm. I seem to recall those white flannels pressing against his long, strong thighs as he ran to the wicket. Incidentally, did you like that phrase about the cat coming in for the kill.'

Helen laughed again, 'Bunty, you're incorrigible. I don't know how you haven't got pregnant.'

'I have, dear, a number of times.'

The two friends laughed again and then Helen said, 'I was thinking of coming to stay in London for a while.'

The second call came an hour later as Bunty was drying herself from a hot bath. She stood naked looking at herself in the long art deco mirror in her living room. Absurdly, she felt the need to cover herself with a towel when the caller identified himself as John Lowther. She remembered him well. He was her father's most important customer. She remembered too the strange way he had stared at her during visits to the family home. Even as a fourteen year old she had had enough sense to make sure she was never alone with him.

Lowther purred his way through the usual polite opening gambits of conversation before coming to the point of his phone call. 'I was interested to see that you have written about a young cricketer who has come to my notice. What did you think of him?'

In the last year or so Bunty had dealt with scum and scoundrels, and that was just the upper classes. She had too much sense to admit to Mr Lowther that she had never spoken to Linden. Besides she had enough information from listening to people like Helen to bluff her way through a casual interrogation with ease. 'A very unusual young man,' she said brightly. She told Lowther stories that were not in the article, information she had saved to use in the future; about how he had grown up on the Boutilier estate, how he had practised by bowling stones on the drover's road. She sensed Lowther found the truth so strange he believed it was fiction, so she added an explanation Helen had given to her. 'He tried with cricket balls but found they were travelling a hundred yards or so past the wickets, so he could only bowl a few overs by the time he retrieved them. He collected the stones from the river bed. They were smooth and elliptical and left a mark in the turf so that he could assess the length and line.'

She heard Lowther laugh. He asked for her impressions of the young man. She recalled Helen's words about him and said that he seemed quite bright and that there was something noble about him. He had the courage of a warrior, but then his father had won the VC.

When Lowther said his goodbyes with a promise to call later, she knew she had him hooked. But to what end? Why had he called? What was his interest in Ben Linden? She knew he was involved with the Midshire cricket club, and that Ben played for the team. But why her? And why the interest in the young man's character? They were hardly on the same social level. She assumed it was something to do with cricket. But what?

The answer came two days later shortly, after she returned from work to her flat. Again the phone rang and this time Lowther did not bother with polite formalities. He was, she guessed, an impatient man who dealt with people merely as they applied to projects. She was a cog in the wheel of some new plan. He wanted, he said, to make a contribution to English cricket, and the young man, Linden, seemed an obvious choice.

'A choice for what, specifically?'

'A donation.' He gave a short laugh. 'I want him to be able to concentrate solely on his cricket.'

'A donation? Why do you need me?'

'Unfortunately my connections with the cricket club put me in rather a delicate position. I had intended to get the young man to pose for photographs and advertisements at some of my stores. However there are people who would use that against me, against him. They would question my motives in pushing his career.'

'I still don't understand why you would want to involve me in this.' Bunty was beginning to remember the staring eyes that hardly hid his dark thoughts and was tempted to speak frankly to this disgusting man whose perspiring skin dripped with lust.

He gave another of his harsh laughs. 'Ha. I want you to open a bank account in his name into which I will deposit two thousand pounds.'

She was startled at the huge gift he was proposing, and angry that he should think to use her as a bag carrier.

'I've a better idea, Mr Lowther. Do it yourself.' She was about to replace the receiver when his voice, usually as smooth as a snake's hiss rose in tone. 'Wait! I will make sure you are well rewarded.'

She laughed at him. 'You may not have noticed during your dealings with my father, but we are quite well off.'

'I'm not talking about money,' he snapped. 'I'm talking about stories.'

He'd somehow found her one great weakness. She was addicted to gossip.

'Stories? What stories?'

'Gossip. Salacious gossip. You deal in that nowadays, I

understand.' The tone of his voice suggested that he was merely stating a fact and not making a moral judgement. 'I hear a great many things in the course of business.'

'Such as?'

He did not even hesitate to collect his thoughts. He named a seaside town and told her that it was riddled with prostitutes. They used shops as a front but in reality the girls were the items for sale.'

'Sounds more sordid than salacious.' Bunty sounded doubtful.

Lowther gave one of his harsh laughs. 'This is no ordinary brothel. It caters for the elite.' He paused. 'You won't be able to name names of course.'

'Why not?'

'Well, I do believe your proprietor is one of the clients.'

Bunty found herself laughing, 'So I can't use the story.'

'Not in the conventional way, but you could do it without naming anyone. Like in the Artemis Jones case.'

'That ended in a famous libel action!' But Bunty was sold on the idea. It appealed to her sense of humour. The repercussions once the article appeared would be highly amusing. The proprietor would object of course, but how far could he go without raising suspicions of his involvement? It was a beautiful hypocrisy, and so English.

'It's a deal,' she said cheerfully. She didn't really care whether she could print any of his stories. The gossip itself was wonderful, and knowledge was power. Also, it would give her an excuse to meet Ben.

A week later Bunty was standing outside the cricket ground when Ben emerged with a pretty, dark-haired girl who was wearing the uniform of a waitress. The girl pecked him on the cheek and headed off to the main stand. Neither of them looked back. Perhaps Helen was right. The girl was merely a friend.

'Mr Linden,' she called to him as she approached. She was dressed in a long dark coat that wrapped round her figure. She was, she knew, an arresting sight for a eunuch, never mind a red-blooded fast bowler.

He stopped and watched her approach.

She introduced herself. The sun had got to his face, giving him an Italian look. 'I know who you are,' he said in an even voice. 'You're a friend of Lady Helen. I've seen you at the cricket matches. You were asleep, I think.'

She gave a peel of laughter, 'Very likely. Though I did notice your bowling.'

'So you said in your article.'

'Ah you read it. Hoped you liked the quotes.'

'I couldn't have said it better myself.'

She laughed again. 'Perhaps I can get my next article from the horse's mouth.'

'Perhaps. If you give the horse a chance to speak.'

This was not the sort of man she had been expecting. He seemed more relaxed and confident than the one Helen had described. But of course a lot had happened in a short space of time, not least, she suspected, that he had found his worth. The appealing thing was that the process had left him with an easy-going self-confidence. He was not at all the strutting, arrogant, young man he might so easily have become. She knew immediately why Helen had found him so attractive, because she felt the same herself.

He was smiling at her. 'Have you come to find out what the horse actually says?'

'God no! That would be far too professional.'

He smiled again, which gave her time to collect her thoughts.

'I've come to you with a story actually. A strange story

about a very wealthy man who has seen you play cricket. You probably won't believe this, but then I find that a common reaction when I tell stories.' They were walking slowly along the High Street, past the shops. 'Let's go in,' she pointed to a tea shop. They took a seat at the window. She held out a little olive green book. 'This is a bank account. It's yours,' she said.

She watched him as he opened the book. It must have been five minutes later, after a scattering of thoughts and observations, that he asked, 'But why?'

Bunty smiled, 'Well, if you had been a woman it would have been because he was in lust with you. However, you are definitely not a woman,' her eyes lingered on him. 'He says it's a patriotic gesture and, that he wants to help English cricket by shielding you from the financial worries that beset too many cricketers.'

'Really.' Ben didn't sound convinced.

Bunty shrugged. 'Look at it like this. He has made no demands. He doesn't even want you to know who he is.' She was struck be a thought. 'He's a devious, dangerous man. Perhaps he's hoping that you will live on the same stratum as the amateurs. If you become one of them, or even near to it, that will open the gates for others.'

'Why should he want that?'

'He's new money you see. They don't like him, not because he's a groping, dirty, ruthless man, which he is, but because he's new money, and worse still, he's rumoured to be Jewish. Strange thing, morality, isn't it?' She gave another peel of laughter and reached out for his hand. 'I'm new money too. Or at least my father is. And so are you,' She gestured to the bank book. 'God, we should form a club.'

He grinned. 'I'm a cricketer, that's all. I'm pretty boring eh?'

She looked at his heavy shoulders and chest. 'I wouldn't say that,' she said brightly. The words, and the thought behind them, triggered a sudden feeling of guilt. Her best friend loved this man; he wasn't something for her to play with, tempting though it was.

'You do know that Helen thinks of you all the time,' she blurted out the words.

He nodded. 'She should try to forget.'

Bunty found that she had reached out and was squeezing his hand. 'Why?' she asked.

He gave a faint smile and waited as the waitress plonked their cups of tea on the table. 'You're going to have to pay,' he said. 'I've got no money on me.'

She smiled but didn't laugh. 'Why?' she asked again.

'Because if she was sitting here instead of you, she'd be looking round to see if anyone had seen us together. She made me feel that she was ashamed to be seen with me.'

Bunty sat there looking at him amid the chatter of the tea room, the clatter of the cups, and the buzz of the traffic from outside, and for once in her life she couldn't think of a thing to say.

Chapter Eighteen

Beth stared out of the kitchen window in surprise at the sight of her son striding up the garden. He was dressed in a neat grey suit and was holding a broad-brimmed hat. His hair gleamed with oil. She rushed to the door. 'You should have warned me you were coming.'

He just smiled.

'What if I'd been out?'

He smiled again. 'I'd have waited.'

'You haven't a key.'

'You never lock the door, Ma.' He hugged her.

He was just like his father, laughing at her little worries, until they seemed petty, even to her.

He looked down on her in great humour. 'Any more scolding and I'm going to hug you 'till you laugh.'

'Oh, come in, you daft lad.' She tried to admonish him and failed completely.

The cottage was lifting with the scent of baking bread. He seemed to have grown, bigger, even than his father. 'Why aren't you playing cricket?'

'We don't play every day.'

'You should have mentioned you were coming in your letters. People say you are doing well, that you frighten batsmen.' She was excited enough to scatter her thoughts. He waited for her to calm down. He could hear the sound of hammering out the back.

'Jarvis?'

'Yes.' She blushed like a girl.

'You want me as best man?'

'Ben Linden, you're not too big for me to smack your ears. He'll be in a box twenty years before me.'

'Aye, but what of the twenty before that? Enjoy them I say.'

They still fitted each other like old gloves. She lit up at the sight of him.

Jarvis appeared at the door like a cat waiting to be fed. Ben saw the two of them were closer now. He knew Jarvis to be a straight man. He gave him a wink. 'How do, old man?'

Jarvis blinked, startled at the change in him. He'd gone away a youth and returned a man.

'Fine,' he said. 'And yourself?' There was no need for an answer. He could see Ben had grown and prospered.

Jarvis, once assured that he was still welcome, made his excuses and returned to his work. Ben looked out the back window and noted the latest extension to the chicken coop. 'My God, you'll have too many eggs for Easter.'

His mother wasn't listening as she placed the ancient black kettle on the stove.

He watched her caught in a sunbeam and saw for an instant the beauty his father had seen in her. He reached in his pocket. 'I brought something for you.'

He handed her a banker's order for half his money. She stared at the draft in astonishment. 'What sort of daftness is this?'

He told her of the donation from an admirer. 'So I want you to have half. It means I know you're safe, no matter what.' She started to protest, but he knew the way her mind worked. 'Look, if my world falls apart, you can always give it back.' He grinned in case she took the words too seriously, because he knew how she worried about him in the big city. She still protested, but he held up his hand. 'I'm going over to the bank tomorrow morning,' he said. 'The kettle's steaming.'

That evening he walked down to see old Arnie at the pavilion. The word of his return had spread around the estate and kids were calling at his door for autographs. A couple of girls greeted him with inviting smiles as he walked down the lane on the way to the ground.

Old Arnie showed no surprise at his sudden appearance. He, like the others, had heard of Ben's return and had been waiting for a visit. The antics of the young girls amused him. He had had his days of similar attentions. 'Did they drag you into the bushes then?'

Ben smiled. 'I'm not used to it. It's dafter in London. I'm greeted by strangers as though I'm family. There are girls who want to sleep with me because they've seen my picture in the papers.'

Arnie glanced at the handsome young man. 'Aye, it's a cross we all have to bear,' he said drily. But within minutes it was as if Ben had never been away as the pair of them started to go through the strengths and weaknesses of batsmen. As ever Ben was amazed by Arnie's knowledge. He watched all the exhibition matches closely, he read The Times every day, albeit a day behind as he waited for Boutilier to leave him the paper, and he also wrote to old friends still connected with the county game.

By now Ben had taken fifty wickets in his first season and only a handful of the very best batsmen had looked able to handle him. There was one in particular, Brindle of Nottinghamshire, a county stalwart, who had never made the Test team, who looked most comfortable against Ben.

'I can't work him out,' he told Arnie. 'He moves his back foot to off stump before I've bowled, so I should be able to catch him in mid movement but I can't.'

'That's because he's still and perfectly balanced when you actually bowl.' Arnie sucked on his pipe.

Ben looked at him, not understanding.

Arnie spat out in an arc over the pavilion steps and on to the turf. 'He moves before you bowl and his right foot tells him where the off stump is. But when you actually release the ball he's finished his movement, and is standing balanced and as still as stone.'

Ben weighed up the words. 'How can I deal with that?' he asked.

'Practice. Try to hold on to the ball a fraction longer. The longer the arc of the ball, the faster it is, but more important he'll be used to seeing you release at a certain point. Slip in an occasional shorter or longer arc and you'll confuse him. It'll take practice.''

Across the ground in the gloom he could see a clutch of children waiting for him. Some of the bolder ones called out, but none approached across the sacred turf.

Ben turned to Arnie. 'Got a pencil. You'd never guess what they ask me to sign on in London.'

'Oh yes I can.' Arnie reached into his waistcoat pocket for the stub of an old pencil. 'I want it back, mind.'

There were children waiting at the gate in the morning. This lot were more subdued, even shy. Beth stood at the back of the garden shaking her head as he signed their pieces of paper at the rickety wicker gate. He had eventually to break away to catch the spluttering old bus that ran along the river road to Wolviston.

The bank stood just off the market square next to an old coach house. Inside, it gave off an air of staid stillness that matched the staff in their sober suits. The clerk's mouth opened in shock when he saw the size of the banker's draft. He calculated it was five years' pay and then went to summon the senior clerk, who in turn, knocked at the door of the manager. By the time Ben was summoned to see the great man, a young woman had recognised him and passed the word to the other customers.

The manager stated the obvious, that this was a large deposit. He said it was usual for the recipient to be present at such transactions. Ben realised that Mr Trumpett was, seemingly, the one man in Wolviston who had never heard of him, and that what he saw was a young stranger with a fortune in his fist, and that made him nervous.

Eventually, Ben lost patience with the cautious, pompous man and reminded him that he was attempting to put money into the bank, not take it out, which presumably was an important factor when assessing the risk. The recipient was in fact his mother, a woman well-known in the area, who was the respectable widow of a war hero. If Mr Trumpett didn't want him to deposit one thousand pounds into the Wolviston Valley Bank he should say so, and he would go elsewhere. There were, he said, plenty of banks in London who, for some strange reason, were attracted to clients approaching them with large deposits.

Mr Trumpett squirmed before this barrage of sarcasm. This youth was talking to him in the manner to which he, Mr Trumpett, talked to others, and he didn't like it, but a thousand pounds was a thousand pounds, so he forced himself to give off a glazed smile.

Outside the sun was shining and a dozen people had gathered to catch sight of the great bowler. When it all began Ben had been baffled by the attention, and then he heeded the advice from Arnie who had told him, 'Time to start worrying is when they stop pestering you. Thirty years ago, in my case.' He'd given a wry grin. Ben saw the logic in the words, and had tried to deal with the constant intrusion with as much good humour as he could manage. He signed autographs and exchanged opinions on the merits of various batsmen, before excusing himself because he had to get home. The next bus was still ninety minutes away, but the constant attention made him want to be on his way so, instead of setting out along by the river where with luck he might pick up the bus, he headed for the drovers' road.

The track was marked by the feet of beasts and he remembered that John Bart, the sniper, had taken to the trail, driving sheep or cattle from the north. Every month or so he would call at his mother's cottage, or at least stand by the apple tree at her gate until she became aware of the long dark shape of him. He was always dressed in a long greased coat that flowed to his ankles and a broad brimmed hat that sheltered his neck from the sun and the rain.

Always he asked the same questions. Was there anyone troubling her? Did she need money? And how was the boy? Usually he bought chickens and eggs. He always insisted on paying. He never stayed long before turning back to the drovers' road where he'd rested his stock. As she watched him go she noted the long thin case held by a strap along his back. She knew that that could only be his rifle.

The trail itself was heavy with memories, and among them Lady Helen, as he had become accustomed to calling her, loomed large.

There had been days when his life so bustled with new things that he scarce gave her a thought, but here, in no man's land, where they had tried to be friends, almost become lovers, here, the sense of her was overwhelming. However, whereas before he had armed himself with anger and indignation over her behaviour, those weapons had worn away in time, leaving him vulnerable. As he turned into the stretch of land where he had set up his stumps and bowled his stones he saw that the Sniper had turned his cattle off the main track leaving the wicket undisturbed. The stones that he had hurled in cold fury into the bracken had been returned and stood like a small pyramid of cannon balls. Not only that, some make-shift stumps had been stuck in the ground. He walked to the wicket and noticed that off to the right the ground had been dug up by the hooves of a tethered horse. The marks were relatively fresh, no more than two days old. He could hear his heart thumping as loud as the galloping hooves of Jasper, her horse. He found himself sitting at the edge of the bracken, his head in his hands. Even his mother hadn't known he was coming, nor Arnie, so how had she? Then he remembered Bunty calling at the small apartment he had bought, near the ground. She'd noticed the small suitcase packed in the hall. She'd wanted to write another feature about him. He'd asked her to wait until he returned. She had not asked where from. But why would she? She knew there was only one place he would be going.

It was late afternoon by the time he reached the cottage. He kissed his mother and wandered down to the pavilion. The road was free of autograph hunters. Perhaps he'd signed for them all. He looked through the hedge to check that Arnie was alone and then trotted across the field.

'I'm on the train tomorrow,' he said.

Arnie nodded.

'Can you get away to watch me play?'

Arnie shook his head. 'No need. You're coming to play here.'

'Really?' This was news to Ben.

Arnie grinned. 'They just haven't told you yet. Boutilier's arranged a match between Gentlemen and Players. Apparently they've got a good crop at the universities this year.'

'No one's told me,' Ben sounded a little put out.

'Why would they?'

Ben did not answer. As he looked out across the cricket ground, he saw a couple walking along the lane appear fleetingly through the boundary hedge. The woman was wearing a loose white dress that fluttered in the breeze.

'Has she been here recently?'

'She left for Paris yesterday. She said to tell you only if you asked. She thought it would be quite amusing, you avoiding her when she wasn't here.'

He felt like a small boy caught out in class. 'It's just she put the stones back,' he said lamely. 'I threw them away into the bracken. It was like a statement that I had gone, I guess.'

Arnie grinned. 'Yet here you are back again. No need to hide from me that you've got the hots for her, Ben. Better keep it from Boutilier though.'

Ben sighed. He was sitting by Arnie on the steps and his upper body stooped out so that his head was over his knees and he stared at the ground.

Arnie gave him a long look. The young man had put on seven pounds since he'd left and the summer sun had given his body a sheen of light gold. He was a young man who had everything, except the one thing he wanted most. He was struck by another thought. She was exactly the same.

Ben turned to him. 'When's the game?'

'A month.'

Ben rose to his feet. 'I'll see you then, eh?'

He walked slowly back to the cottage whistling, lost in his thoughts.

His mother saw him coming up the path and was struck by his resemblance to his father. He too had been a tall, handsome man and she had won him by beating off fierce competition from the factory girls. Her ace had been her terrier, Bounce, which she walked through a field that he crossed on his way home from work. He loved his dogs, did Frank. He'd whistled at the terrier, and that was that. And now, what now? There was a nice old man doing jobs around the house who had a knack of giving her space, even when he was near her in a room. She felt comfortable with him. There was none of the fierce desire she had felt for Frank, but in its place was a tender feeling for Jarvis. She was lonely, and she trusted him not to hurt her.

But when she looked at her son she recalled the love of her own youth, a love of urgent words and tumblings in lanes and in strange beds, wherever they could grasp each other. Then there was his deep laugh when she'd tried to boss him. All that lost in a second because of a German soldier who had never known him and who returned to his supper of sausages that evening and who wrote a letter home, just like the ones Frank had written to her, which even now lay curled in the dark in a rusty box.

Frank too had run like Ben, carried over the ground by soundless feet. A soldier friend had told her that her husband was first to the razor wire. They had been assured that the shells would blow it to pieces. They'd been told many things that had not been true, and then they'd died, and the people who had made the terrible errors returned to their work and their lives. She wondered bitterly whether they ever thought of the dead they left behind.

She found herself trembling at the sound of Ben's whistling. Same whistle, different tune. Same man, different life.

Cricket had been the vehicle which had taken him from her. But if it had not been that, it would have been something else. He was too big for this place. He'd grown from the boy who threw stones at rooks, who nurtured the chickens and the eggs. He was a giant who had to find something worthy of his strength, something to match the size of his ambitions and energy.

They said he had a gift for bowling as fast as anyone in history, but that was only the half of it; his real talent was his strength and courage. His father had never bowled a ball in his life, and he had had his life taken before he could live it: but the father was the son and the son the father.

She smiled to herself at her thoughts. All this as Ben strode between gate and path. His tea was on the table. She had quite forgotten about the money, indeed cared little for it. She could hear Jarvis tapping away at the new chicken coop. He too was whistling, but it was a different sound and a different tune.

Chapter Nineteen

Bunty had taken to wearing hats that reminded Ben of the German helmet his father had brought home from the front, except that it had no curled rim and the material seemed brittle, yet pliant enough to have a feather stuck in it.

She called unannounced at his apartment two days after his return. He answered the door, his grey shirt unbuttoned and drying his hair from the bath.

'Interview, please. I'm desperate.'

She was wearing a long, beige, dress that hugged her boyish figure. She refused to wear glasses, even though she was short-sighted, and had the air of someone trying to negotiate their way through fog.

He smiled. 'I seem to speak more eloquently when you don't bother to do the interview.'

She laughed and dug him lightly in the stomach. His muscles were hard and unyielding.

As they talked he discovered that she already knew a lot about him, from Helen, presumably. The interview was merely an excuse for her to call, but to what end?

He had a free day before travelling up to Nottinghamshire for a county game. She brightened at the news and suggested going for a run in her little Morris. She drove erratically to Regents Park and they sat under a large elm tree drinking coffee which she had extracted from a small wicker hamper.

Her interviewing technique was more a gift than a skill. She had such an open personality and she could talk fluently about so many topics that Ben found that he had warmed to her by the time she asked him questions about his early life.

He told her about the death of his father and his boyhood memory of his mother weeping by the door, a buff telegram crushed in her small fist. He told her of the rooks and the stones and the drovers' trail, and the strange man he called the Sniper, but he never mentioned Helen. He told her of Wolfie and the rescue and how Boutilier had rewarded him with a trial at the cricket ground. He told her of the nets and how he had bowled at the England captain. Bunty's eyes opened in delight. Within an hour she had enough material for half a dozen pieces in her column. Finally, she asked, 'And what of Helen?'

The question came so smoothly on the back of so many others that he had to catch the words at his throat to prevent himself from answering.

Bunty knew she had gone too far and so she smiled sweetly. 'I always leave the stonkers till last,' she said. 'In case you tell me to fuck off.'

He stared at her like a man betrayed. 'What is it with you rich people?'

Bunty shrugged her slim shoulders. 'I don't know the answer to that. I think we just expect to get our way, so usually we do.'

He made to rise but she pulled him down with surprising strength. 'I promise you I'll not write a word about Helen. I can't, she's my best friend.' He sat again facing her but saying nothing. 'In fact, I'll not write anything about your love life.'

He continued to stare. 'Why should I believe you?'

'I can't think of a reason that would convince you, except to say that in my job I meet hundreds of people and every so often I find someone who interests me beyond the mere writing of a story.' She smiled. 'Come on. I'll drive you home.'

The route took them past the cricket ground and as they bowled past the pavilion end Ben caught a glimpse of Lizzie arriving at the ground for the luncheon shift. He reached across and tooted the horn. They waved to each other and then the car swerved round a corner so sharply that he had to grasp the door.

Five minutes later she jerked to a halt outside his apartment block. 'That was Lizzie, right?'

He nodded and said defensively, 'We're friends.'

'I know. She's a waitress at the ground and you met when you arrived for a trial.'

'Yes.'

'And in a year's time you will probably be the star cricketer in England and you'll still be a friend with Lizzie, who will probably still be a waitress.'

'That's a lot of probables.'

'Yes, it is.'

He looked at her and then opened the door of the car. Someone tooted a horn at him as he stood up. 'I understand the point you are trying to make. I can be friends with lowly Lizzie but not with Lady Helen.'

Bunty's eyes softened. 'I'm not very good at making pleas for others.'

He reached out and squeezed her hand. 'It's not that simple, Bunty, as well you know. Lizzie and I are from the same class. Helen and I are not. I can go anywhere, meet anyone, with Lizzie and there are no social obstacles. Can you imagine Boutilier having me in for tea and showing me his bloody family tree that stretches across five rooms?'

Bunty gave an involuntary laugh.

He leaned into the car and spoke through the open window. 'There's another thing. We never were, and never will be, friends.'

He turned on his heels and walked into the entrance leaving her staring after him. She was dizzy with the passion of the man, so much so that it was only much later that she became aware that he had surprised her with his intelligence. Her mind was in a whirl all the way back to her flat. She ran herself a bath and lay in the hot water which caressed her skin like a seducer. She could not think past this extraordinary young man and her friend, Helen.

This was a new phenomenon in Bunty's life. She herself had had a number of affairs ranging from the ephemeral to the intense, but never had she encountered a tortured mutually unrequited love such as existed between Ben and Helen. This was the stuff of her actor friends, not of their own, frequently sordid, lives, but of the parts they played on screen. She found the situation intoxicating.

Ben's stock within the Midshire dressing room had risen as quickly as the number of wickets he had taken. Even the amateurs in the side sought him out for conversation and called him Ben; though he was still expected to refer to them as Mr, save in the case of the captain whom he addressed as Skipper. Indeed the social dynamic in the team environment was strange. When Carpenter had outlined the rules to him on his first day, he had assumed that the amateurs and players would operate as two distinct social classes. But the intricacies and passions of the game, and how to play it, caused conflicts and bonds that broke down the rigid wall that he had imagined would exist.

Opinions on tactics and strategies did not stay within social divides. A number of the amateurs liked to drink ,so it was natural that they should find themselves rubbing shoulders with the likes of Sawyer.

The opening session in the game at Nottinghamshire

had not gone as well as the Midshire team had hoped. Ben had taken two wickets and was quite pleased on a personal level, though irritated that three catches had been spilled off his bowling. Sinclair came into their dressing room without a knock, smoking his pipe, and started to admonish the team on their fielding. His stern reproaches were however disrupted by the sight of Huntingdon and Carstairs, another amateur, pulling faces at them through the window.

The unfortunate Myers was first to give a grin. Sinclair turned on him. 'This is not some joke, Myers. You are the professionals, so you are not meant to treat it as a merely a game.' It was at this point he glanced to the window and saw the antics of the amateurs outside. 'Bloody hell. I'm surrounded by schoolboys!' He made for the door, but turned on them before he left. 'I want a better show this afternoon.'

'He's right,' Sawyer who had only emerged from a hangover an hour ago, stooped to unlace his boots.

There was an empty silence and then Myers dug into his bag. 'Have any of you seen the Globe this morning. He spread the newspaper on the kit table displaying Bunty's latest article about Ben . He put on a coy voice and began to quote some of the more lurid prose. 'The matinee man!' Myers fluttered his eyes, 'Well boys, here's the man to get us back into Sinclair's good books!'

Ben stood smiling as the rest of the team made joking references to his looks and his success with the ladies.

'Well chaps,' he said at last. 'I need to warm up in the nets. Would anyone like to bat for me?' There were no takers. 'Can't understand it. Big hairy-arsed cricketers scared of a soft matinee idol.'

He was last out of the dressing room. He paused to look at the article once more. It was the picture, not the prose that bothered him, a sharp black and white shot of the drovers' road with the pyramid of stones in the foreground.

Bunty must have had the photograph in her possession before she had contacted him. Perhaps it was she and not Helen, who had collected the stones and Helen neither knew nor cared about the incident. Why should she brood about him, looking down from her lofty height?

Then he remembered the hoof marks by the side of the wicket, and the exact positioning of the wicket. Bunty could not have done that on her own. She did not have the information. No, Helen was the only one, other than himself, who could have replaced the stones in their exact place. Bunty, or a photographer, had followed in Helen's wake. The knowledge cheered him considerably.

He took his new-found enthusiasm on to the pitch to the consternation of the Nottinghamshire batsmen.

One of them, after surviving a torrid over during which he had failed to lay bat on ball, turned to Sawyer at silly mid on. 'What the hell's got into him?' he motioned to Ben who was retreating to the boundary.

'We got a bollocking during lunch.'

'Christ,' the batsmen stared after Ben. 'Next time could you just make it a mild rebuke?'

Twenty overs later Sinclair was congratulating Ben, and more importantly, himself on a dramatic turn around. Notts' last wicket had fallen half an hour before tea, and Ben had another five for. Sinclair put it down to his lunchtime talk to the men. They didn't seem to have taken his words on board at the time, but actions spoke louder than words.

Two days later the victorious Midshire team were back in London and Ben was soaking his tired body in a hot bath when Bunty called again.

She grinned at the sight of him draped in towels. 'I can assure you it's just coincidence.'

'Every time I have a bath,' he grumbled.

'Well get yourself a phone,' she said.

He pulled a face. 'I'm pestered enough as it is.'

She moved on. 'I've come to invite you to a party, at my place. It's on Saturday. Will you be in town?'

He nodded.

'Well that leaves only two other matters. Have you an evening suit?'

He shook his head.

'OK I'll buy you one. It's the least I can do. Your interview went down extremely well at the office. I got a raise. Not that I need the money. It's the principle of the thing.' She gave a laugh. 'Perhaps I could drag you off to a tailor tomorrow.'

'Off the peg would be quicker.'

She gave him a sharp look. 'I want you to dazzle my friends, Ben. Play the star. That's your role now.'

Ben scowled at the appalling picture Bunty was painting. 'I haven't got a part to play. I just bowl fast and everything follows from that. Leastways, that's the way my life seems to be at the moment.'

Bunty angled her head as though appraising him. 'I suppose it might work as a gimmick in polite society.'

'Otherwise known as an awful cesspool of rogues, scoundrels and scum.'

'That's on a good day.' Bunty sounded cheerful. 'You know, Ben, you really are good for my cynicism.'

'Why do you put up with the job?'

'Most of the people are bright, or at least interestingly devious, and I can't think of a more engaging way to pass my time. Also I'm good at what I do. That helps.'

They'd been playing with each other and he had got too close for her comfort. She was frightened of his ability to affect her, to make her want to do things she knew she would regret. She stepped back and said in a slow, deliberate voice. 'The party. There's something else you should know.' She paused and her anxiety must have spread to him so that by the time she spoke he was already halfway to where she was taking them. 'Helen is staying with me.'

'Helen!'

Ordinarily she would have made some witty rejoinder at his dumb response but she merely said, 'Yes,' then she waited for him to become angry.

He didn't. Instead he asked in a quiet voice, 'She knows that you have given me an invitation?'

'Yes, of course.'

He stayed silent for a while and then said, 'Well, I suppose I won't embarrass her. I'll be in a crowd.'

Her eyes never left his. Surely he wasn't playing a part. No one could be that good, and she'd seen the best. She heard herself speaking in a soft voice, 'The last time we met you talked of meeting her in another world. Perhaps London is big enough to be that place.'

He smiled a sad smile and his eyes became as wide as a woman's. 'I think she might have noticed that people like you tend to take my photograph wherever I go now. Besides London seems populated largely by her father's friends and by people like Perry Bowden.'

'Bowden! That pip squeak!' Bunty's voice started to rise. Pressing a suit for someone else really was very tiring. 'He was Charles's bum boy at school, for God's sake.'

'That doesn't seem to matter with you people.'

'Will you stop saying "you people." I'm not one of "you people". I'm first generation rich. They probably despise me more than they do you in their own behind-your-back way. Don't you see they're frightened? Their world is disappearing after hundreds of years. You and I, in our different ways, are both a threat. To them it's as though somebody had allowed cart horses to enter the Derby.' She looked at him. 'Christ, you're turning me into a bloody socialist!' She took him by the arm. 'Come on. I'm not waiting till tomorrow for that bloody suit. You'll change your mind.'

He pulled back on her arm. 'I think the least I can do is change towels.'

She saw he was grinning and she started to laugh.

Chapter Twenty

Both Ben and Bunty lived in an apartment, but there all comparisons ended. Ben's home consisted of one bedroom, one bathroom, one kitchen and one sitting room, all of a modest size. Bunty's home took in two large floors of an exclusive block near Lords cricket ground. A broad spiral staircase, art deco furniture, thick carpets, exquisite paintings and imported servants beamed its splendour from every corner. The car park was full and vehicles spilled into the street parked bumper to bumper with their brakes off, so they could be pushed out of the way to make space for drivers wishing to leave early.

Ben arrived courtesy of London transport and walked a couple of hundred yards from the tube station with the aid of a crude map drawn by Bunty. A couple of smartly-dressed children asked for his autograph outside the apartment. As he paused to oblige them, he glanced at his reflection in the window of a parked Rolls Royce. He cut a splendid figure in his penguin suit, as Bunty had called it. The bill had come to some twenty pounds, or about ten weeks' wages for a worker on the Boutilier estate. As he returned the school exercise book, which the children had given him to sign, he moved towards the driveway of the apartment, and across the path of a couple who were walking from their car.

'Good God! It's Linden.'

He smelled cigar smoke and a heavy perfume. He glanced at the couple for the first time and recognised his skipper, A.J. Sinclair. The woman, who clung to his arm, was pretty in a haughty sort of way and she had a habit of looking at people as though her sight was guided by a sense of smell.

'Mr Sinclair!'

'What are you doing here?' Sinclair was probably merely surprised to see him at the party, but Ben took it as a challenge for his right to be 'here.'

'I was invited,' he said shortly. 'But don't worry. Bunty said I'd have to have a separate cloakroom from the gentlemen.' He walked past Sinclair smiling. 'Good evening, sir.'

Sinclair watched the retreating figure in astonishment. 'Good Lord. I think he means to be offensive.'

The woman laughed a low deep gurgle of a laugh. 'He doesn't have a coat, Archie, so I think he was trying to make a point. You must learn to get on better with the working classes. There seems to be an awful lot of them, nowadays.' She laughed again and stared after the offensive young man noting that he moved like a cat.

Ben's anger dissipated as he strode to the entrance and he stamped up the stairs hoping that Sinclair would take the lift, so that they would not meet, embarrassingly, at Bunty's door.

Thankfully, a maid answered the instant he rang the bell and he walked quickly into the well of the crowded main room and from there rushed up the circular staircase. He glanced back from this vantage point and saw Sinclair and his partner handing their coats to the maid who curtsied. The woman looked up at him and appraised him coolly, as though she was valuing a mink coat in a shop window.

As he looked around the room that gleamed with jewellery and silk suits he became conscious of his own humble background. He recognised a few faces as guests at Boutilier's house parties; people whom he had observed from behind his cart as he rumbled the chickens and eggs to the great house.

His fame was stripped away in seconds as he saw himself

for what he was, a working class lad surrounded by the good and the great.

He told himself that he could talk cricket to this lot and after that he was bluffing. To compound his increasing sense of panic he saw Helen across the room.

She looked as though she'd been decanted into a white clinging dress, and an emerald gleamed darkly against the white of her throat. She hadn't seen him and he felt sick with panic at the sight of her as she sipped from a champagne glass and chatted away to Perry Bowden and some of his friends.

She looked so part of the scene, more than that, a star of it, and to see her with Bowden of all people, was just too much. Ben's rise in status since coming to London had been remarkable. He had become famous and that had given him a sense of his own importance, but here it meant nothing. He felt he had been living in an illusion. He stood there, tall, sleek, and immaculate, feeling like something that had escaped from a zoo. The more glitter in the room, the deeper his misery.

She was too far above him, and always would be. He could become the most famous cricketer in the world and, in the final analysis, he would as important to these people as a brilliant chef or a great landscape gardener. In that instant, she gave a start as she saw him and he felt the moment like an electric shock that flashed between them thirty feet across the room. Bowden too saw her reaction, and turned to glance behind him. As he did so Helen moved towards Ben as though controlled by some magnetic force. Ben panicked and turned heel, heading for the staircase and then the door. He had gone but ten feet when a small bald-headed man planted himself in his line of retreat and said in a deep voice that seemed at odds with his size. 'Ben

Linden. The one man at this party I want to meet.'

He held out his hand and Ben took it. The small man looked up at him with staring eyes. He had a self confidence that bordered on aggression, the sort of man who welcomed conflict and had had plenty of it. 'I have the honour to be with Midshire County Cricket Club. Indeed, I was present at the committee meeting that discussed your selection at the start of the season. We came to the correct decision. Absolutely.' He smiled and Ben smiled back, his mind dizzy with the rush of events, as he sought a way to negotiate his way round the little man in the press of the room. Who knows where it would have ended if someone else had not recognised him and called out his name in cheerful recognition at the same time as Bunty appeared at his elbow. 'Can I introduce you?' she gripped his arm tightly and he felt her breast against him. 'This is John Lowther, a good friend of my father's. John, you know who this is and please don't embarrass him by asking for an autograph.' They all laughed at this little joke and Ben felt like a man who broke surface after a long time under water.

He and Lowther chatted briefly about cricket. Lowther told him that he thought Ben had the best run-up he had ever seen. Ben replied that he had been lucky. He had always been blessed with a natural smooth running style. As he spoke he was conscious of one thing above all else; that he had his back to Helen and, for all he knew, she might be stalking him, or worse, smiling a superior smile surrounded by her superior friends. He stood uncomfortably numb, until Bunty gripped his elbow once more and heard her say, 'Well, John, you'll have to excuse us for a few minutes as there are people who are waiting to be introduced to Ben. We'll be back later no doubt.' With that she propelled him through a cluster of people and outside Lowther's range.

'Sorry about that,' she whispered.

'He was OK.'

'No not him; he's vile, by the way. I shouldn't have left you like a fish out of water.'

'I am a fish out of water, Bunty.'

'Don't be such a sissy,' she said gaily. 'You are not the only self-made man in the room. Lowther for instance,' she gestured to the small, staring man. ' He sacks ten workers before breakfast, yet he melts at a word or gesture from you. He'd give up his fortune to bowl out the Aussies.' She smiled. 'Well, half of it anyway.' She looked up at Ben. 'I can see that stubborn look coming on. There's no escape. It only makes you better looking.' She gushed on, fearing that once she stopped talking he would tell her he was leaving. 'Most of them look down their considerable noses at me too, you know. Upsetting at first, but once you have learned to despise them, it really becomes a delightful game.'

Ben smiled. 'I don't have your sophistication.'

'Nonsense. It's an attribute easily learned.'

'I still wish I was somewhere else, Bunty.'

'Really. And what of Helen?'

'What of her?'

'I saw the two of you catch eyes. There was enough electricity to light London.'

'She seemed to be doing very well with Bowden's bunch, before I arrived.'

'You don't know much about women, Ben. Take it from me. The little minx was putting on a performance for you.'

As they talked Bunty had been directing him towards Helen's group and she burst into them with the authority of the owner of the home.

He found himself facing Helen and staring at her. She gave him a glance and then looked away towards Bowden who was talking about his brother 'getting God.'

Bunty's grip tightened on his arm. He heard her say, 'May I introduce my friend, Ben Linden.' Bowden and his friends were forced to nod and murmur a greeting. 'Helen, of course, you know.' Helen was smiling a pale smile, like a little girl watching a large wave roll towards her and wondering what she should do. At last she spoke. 'Of course I know Linden. He's the young man who saved my dog.' She smiled again and held out a hand for him to shake, 'Nice to see you.' Her fingers were cold to the touch. 'How are you finding London?' she asked. 'A bit different from country life, isn't it?'

They chatted briefly about inconsequential matters. Ben became aware that Bowden's friends were standing in silence and that they would not meet his eye.

Bowden looked at Helen and saw she was staring at Ben. 'Linden,' he said as though grasping the name for the first time. 'You're the chap who practised by bowling stones on the drovers road. How resourceful.' One of his friends gave a soft giggle and then the company sunk into a loud silence, which was eventually broken by Ben 'Yes,' he said, 'I remember you called me the Stone Age Bowler. Very witty.'

'Come on Ben,' Bunty said brightly. 'More people anxious to meet you.'

She eased him away from Helen towards the stairs. Two maids stood as stiff as sentries by the banisters on either side.

Bunty whispered, 'The fucking jumped-up little twats!'

'They'll be jumping in a couple of weeks,' Ben muttered.

She looked at him questioningly.

'I'm playing against them,' he explained.

'All of them?'

'I surely hope so.'

Some of the guests were calling to her,

She felt him stiffen against her. 'I've got to go,' he said.

'You've only just arrived,' she protested.

'It was a mistake. We both know that.' He turned to face her. 'You saw the way they behaved.'

He looked both angry and helpless. He reached into his jacket pocket and extracted a cigarette from a silver case. She watched as he lit the cigarette. His height, his strong features, his natural grace, everything about him, gave him the look of the high born. But he wasn't. He'd bent his back pushing a cartload of chickens and then someone had found out that he could run like the wind and bowl a cricket ball with awesome speed. And so, like his father before him, he now found himself in no man's land.

Bunty sighed. She lived in a world where sympathy was in short supply, yet she knew that, given the least encouragement, she could give all of her share to this one man. She glanced over Ben's shoulder to the balcony above and saw Helen staring down at them looking like a little girl about to cry. Her friends were talking, but all she could think about was that Ben was about to leave. This was not how she had seen the night going.

Ben leaned into Bunty and kissed her on the cheek. His lips felt warm and she wanted them to linger on her mouth, but she told herself it must not to be. She smiled and gripped his arm. 'I'll call you soon. When I run out of copy.'

He squeezed her shoulder and then turned and walked away. A maid curtsied and opened the door. He smiled at her and then was out into the night air. It was colder than he remembered and he wished he had brought a coat, or rather he wished he had bought a coat. He puffed on his cigarette and moved across the silent car park into the tree-lined street. For a second he rested his forehead against the smooth grey bark of an elm tree and swallowed the bile rising in his gullet.

Sinclair, Bowden and his lackeys, even Helen and her polite conversation, could not have done a better job of putting him in his place if they had sat down and conspired. His face contorted in anger. He hoped Bowden's friends would all have a bat in their hands the next time he met them.

He ran towards the next tree and bowled an imaginary ball. His arm thrashed through the air on the downward swing and his cigarette lighter fell from his pocket on to the paving stones. He was bending to retrieve it when he heard the sound of clattering feet. He stood up and as he turned, Helen jumped into him her legs gripping his hips as though he was a wayward horse and her arms ringed tightly around his neck. Her tight dress pushed high up her thighs.'

Her breath felt warm in his ear and she said in a deep, desperate voice, 'Oh Ben, oh Ben.'

He found that he had wrapped his arms round her back and was pulling her into him, but was so shocked by her sudden display of passion that his mind went numb. He knew he must say something, but could think of nothing.

She didn't seem to notice his silence however and she licked his ear and whispered, 'Whatever you say, don't you dare call me Lady Helen.'

He laughed and then his lips founds hers and they kissed, soft and tender at first and then pressing hard and rolling their heads with passion. They came away for air and her beautiful eyes stared into his. 'What are you thinking?' she asked.

He smiled. 'I was thinking you're burning your boats with me out here. They hate me.'

She turned back fiercely towards Bunty's flat. 'They're

empty men!' She began to shiver.

'Where's your coat?' It was a stupid question. He pulled off his jacket and hung it round her shoulders.

'It was either leaving that, or missing you.'

He kissed her nose. It was cold. 'Won't they cause trouble if they miss you? If they connect you with me.'

She shook her head but wouldn't say why until they were back at his flat and warming by the gas fire.

'Bowden's the leader. They'll all follow him and he knows my father doesn't give a damn if I sleep with you, so long as I marry the right man.'

Ben shook his head. 'Extraordinary.'

'Perry will keep his powder dry until he can hit a target. Also I told him that my father doesn't know about him and my brother. He's fearful of that.' She gave a harsh laugh. 'He doesn't know father. Charles could mince after every arse in Christendom so long as he married a titled lady.' She looked at him and gave a tired smile. 'What a family, eh! Mum left Dad after four years and two kids. I don't think he noticed for a year! He didn't care. She'd done her job.'

She tried to smile, but looked suddenly tired and he began to realise what it had cost to leave her crowd to chase after him. For the first time he appreciated Boutilier's power, and his ability to apply it ruthlessly. He himself had been able to use his own increase in status to his advantage during the past few months. But set against the strength of Boutilier whose family stretched down the centuries, he could only guess how puny and limited his own influence was.

He remembered his own arrogance on the day he had left the great estate, demanding that she should flaunt him in front of that great family and their peers as a price of his friendship.

The events of the evening had shown her dilemma with cruel clarity. His hand reached out for her and found her arm just above the elbow. Her skin was soft and smooth. She smiled. Her eyes held his.

One great wave of passion had swept away all obstacles, but what would happen on the ebb tide?

'What now then?' He stroked her arm and she moved into him laying her head on his chest in an eloquent answer. He sat there stroking her hair and neck gently. He could feel the warmth of her body as she lay there so innocent. He felt as though he had tricked her with his demands, and now she was in danger of being destroyed.

She looked up at him sensing his tension. 'What's up?'

'Nothing.' His answer came so quickly as to make a lie of it. He smiled. 'I'm frightened. I've just realised that I have been asking you to give up so much. I'm putting your way of life in danger.'

She yawned into his chest. 'Don't be silly. I'm doing this because I want to.' Her hand curled around his neck and pulled his head down to hers. Their lips met in a slow kiss. Eventually she eased herself away from him. 'I need a bath,' she said. 'When I come back I want you in your bed in just your vest.'

He grinned at her. She looked so beautiful in the flickering flames of the gas fire. 'The main bathroom's six doors along and down two flights,' he said. 'However there is a basic washroom nearby.'

Chapter Twenty one

For a week they lived in his world. They held hands in the high-ceilinged tea room to which he'd taken Lizzie. They whispered to each other amid the clatter of cups and crockery. She felt his leg under the table as a white faced waitress took their order.

'Faish and Cherps twaice,' she intoned in a hopeless attempt at Standard English. Helen nipped his leg trying to make him laugh but he was made of sterner stuff than that.

Later, her hand found its way under his shirt in a dark corner of the Odeon. He flinched at her nip.

'The male nipple is extremely sensitive,' he said sternly.

'I know,' she nipped him again making him wriggle. 'It's just I'm jealous. No one ever recognises me. They don't seem to realise that I'm the important one.'

He gave a low laugh as she knew he would.

'That may be,' he whispered, 'But I didn't pay one and six to sit in the dark and get nipped by the likes of you.'

'One and six eh,' she pretended to sound impressed.

There was a 'shhh' from two rows back.

Ben turned round to apologise and a girl sitting behind him exclaimed, 'Eeeh! It's Ben Linden.'

On the way out Helen said, 'How much did you pay that girl to sit there and say that?'

'Rent a fan doesn't come cheap.'

They knew they looked like children and delighted in it. They created a world of their own for they knew that, eventually, the real world would find them.

On the Monday Ben had to travel to Lancashire for a county game and Helen left to stay with Bunty. They went out on the town together into the social whirl that Bunty knew so well; the swishy nightclubs, the haughty hotels and the fashionable tea rooms and cafes.

Bunty kept out of the way of the intellectuals and the literary figures who formed a fringe round the upper classes. Helen knew many of the people they met over the next three days. Bunty found herself looking at Helen closely, hoping to discover that her liaison with Ben was no more than a flirtation. But she knew the answer already in her heart and told herself that, however much she was attracted to the young cricketer, it must remain her secret. Confirmation of the hopelessness of her love came on the third day when Helen insisted on visiting a post office near Bunty's apartment. She sent a telegram containing three words. She blushed slightly as she showed it to her friend. Bunty smiled and kissed Helen on the cheek.

Two hundred miles away Ben had drunk himself to sleep for two nights running, ably abetted by Sawyer and some of the other pros. 'A tanner if you can knock Selby's cap off tomorrow,' Sawyer drank deeply on his eighth pint of the night.

Ben did not reply. The conversation spilled over him and he sat in a world of his own thinking of Helen.

Ben had found that Sinclair's attitude to him had changed since their altercation outside Bunty's apartment. His natural reserve had stiffened, and he spoke to Ben only when necessary, and then abruptly.

Midshire had batted through the whole of the first day and declared overnight, a decision which had Sawyer muttering because he believed that Ben should have been given half an hour at the openers before the close of play. Sinclair's decision not to allow Ben to open the bowling brought more scowls from the veteran professional. He shook his head at Ben as the two of them walked to their fielding places on the boundary and muttered, 'The stupid bastard will be giving instructions in Latin to his public school mates in the slips. They may be able to speak five languages each, but they still don't know what they're talking about.' He stalked off to long on, sent into exile from the group of toffs discussing tactics. Ben was placed at long off. Sinclair had informed him briefly of his fate. 'Going to give young Bainbridge a chance with the new ball,' he nudged his Harlequins cap. 'Just think he might swing it with the cloud cover.'

On another day Ben would have told Sinclair that he'd seen Bainbridge, who had just joined the side from university during the vac, bowling in the nets and that his arm action was too high to swing the ball away. But this day he didn't care. He knew that Sinclair was snubbing him because of their little spat, and he didn't care about that either. Normally he watched the opposing batsmen closely, noting their preferred shots, their body movements, and all the little details that gave the bowler a picture of their strengths and weaknesses. But today he didn't bother. He was dizzy with love and lost in his thoughts of Helen.

He continued in that vein for most of the morning. Bainbridge didn't move the ball and was eventually replaced, by a medium pacer and then, a few overs later, by Huntingdon who was able to turn the ball, but only slowly. Sinclair was fast running out of excuses not to bowl Ben Linden and while he might have been able to tell his county committee that he had acted to enforce discipline, that argument wouldn't wash with the cricket correspondents who were seeing the game swing back to Lancashire while the star bowler stood idle.

Ben's inactivity had been picked up by the crowd and a man bellowed in a broad Lancashire accent, 'What's up

Linden? Are you on your holidays, lad?'

Ben called back, 'I wouldn't come here on holidays, would I?'

The exchanges went on for a couple of overs, much to the exasperation of Sinclair who knew he had allowed personal matters to sway his judgement, but was reluctant to bring Ben on to bowl when it would appear that he had capitulated to the crowd.

Then, half an hour before lunch, his unwitting saviour arrived in the shape of a chubby-faced telegram boy in a tight-fitting dark uniform. The boy recognised Ben Linden who was standing on the boundary and, being a person with initiative, strode on to the pitch and handed Ben a telegram.

'For you sair.' He gave an exaggerated salute for the benefit off the crowd and then returned to his heavy red bicycle before someone could nick it from its place behind the pavilion.

Ben glanced up, waited for a break in play, and then opened the telegram. The three words were the most important delivered to him in his life. 'I love you.' He stood transfixed for seconds. Had the ball been hit straight at him he would not have seen it.

Sinclair had spotted the telegraph boy from his position at slips and deduced from Ben's body language that he had received good news. He waved an imperious arm. 'Come on Linden, I don't want to send another telegram to get you back to work.'

'It's too late, Mr Sinclair,' the wag in the crowd had a voice that carried across acres. 'He's been called up.'

Ben looked straight at the man in the crowd. 'Right Mr Lancashire man. I'm going to have you home by tea.' He seemed to swell with joy. Suddenly anything was possible.

The ball was bruised and battered and the seam flattened and soft, but it didn't matter because it still flew through the air at a blinding speed from Ben's hand. That day he bowled fast, faster than he had ever bowled before, for four overs before and six overs after lunch. The Times correspondent listed all the great fast bowlers he had seen from Spofforth to the present day and said that this was the most sustained spell of aggressive fast bowling he had witnessed. At the end of it, Ben had broken one bat, three stumps, and bruised the ribs, as well as the hearts and spirits, of the Lancashire batsmen. He took six wickets and the remaining four fell at the other end, as batsmen desperately tried to score off more benign bowling.

When Ben walked off the field at tea, it was as he said. Lancashire were all out and set to follow on. His team mates applauded him up the pavilion steps and the Lancashire crowd rose to their feet to cheer him. 'Hats were flung into the air, never to be seen again by their owners,' said the Manchester Guardian. 'Yet who cared? What's the odd homburg set against witnessing the greatest spell of fast bowling since the war, and probably before it. At last England have found a bowler to take on the Aussies. Six months ago no one had heard of him. He's the man who came from nowhere, but, by golly, he's going somewhere.'

Even Sinclair patted him on the back and, when back in London, told friends that the art of captaincy was to get the best out of his men. 'I sensed that Linden had his mind on other things. So I thought I'd get his temper up before he came on to bowl. And it worked.' He glanced around the room and saw only nods of approval, for who could doubt him when his words fitted so perfectly with the events.

Bunty had always tried to tolerate Lowther because she knew that he was an important business associate of her father. However, her sense of duty rested uneasily with her instincts which told her that her that the man, who was used to getting his way in all things, had a predatory nature. She had seen him stare at her body while a guest on her father's estate where she was used to being treated with a respect that would have satisfied the scrutiny of a Victorian aunt. In London, she soon realised, she was in a different world. She knew of three actors who had bought their way out of trouble after raping women; one of them had attacked a chorus girl backstage at a theatre, and another had left a seventeen year old bruised about the face and body when she had tried to reject his advances. In the world she had grown up in her father would have seen to summary justice on his estate, in his village. But in London, it was different. A sexual assault could disappear in a confusion of claims and a maze of motives. As often as not, the girl had slept with men to get her job in the first place. The film industry was suffering from the chaos involved in the great change from silent to talkie movies. Famous stars who could sweep an audience with a look from their beautiful eyes were betrayed by squeaky voices, or regional accents that made them unintelligible to most of their erstwhile fans. Many of them used the last weapon they had, their bodies, in the fight for survival. Meanwhile a new breed of leading lady, who could speak clearly, and thrust her pelvis with the best of them, was appearing on the scene.

And amid all the chaos, ruthless men were waiting like beasts around a waterhole, knowing that this was their time. They included the stars, the producers, the directors and, most sinister of all, the money men who helped to finance the films.

John Lowther was one of the last of these and Bunty knew from her contacts in the industry that he sought sexual favours for his backing.

On her father's estate she had seen him as a 'horrible, seedy man, who stared at the breasts of maids.' But in London, he was a different, more dangerous animal. Here, he had the power to control and manipulate.

She knew that her father's wealth and connections gave her a protection afforded to few women in the vast, lonely city. But she knew also that there were men who had a need to satisfy their lust that was so strong that they ignored any normal restraints while under its spell. Lowther was one of those. Since his donation to Ben, he had taken to phoning her, and then to calling at her flat. Bunty was so alarmed at this development that she had employed a permanent maid, a solid, middle-aged lady with a face like a potato, who could have slept unmolested in a brothel.

Lowther's excuse for contact with Bunty was always that he had gossip, usually linking some member of the aristocracy with a prominent actress. Lately however his interests had extended. The day after Ben returned to London he called at her flat without warning, his eyes and ears alert like an animal in a strange place. He heard a Hoover start in one of the upstairs rooms and his posture lost menace in an instant.

Bunty knew, though she would never be able to prove it, that he would have launched himself at her without thought or fear of the consequence, had it not been for the maid.

She was both afraid and angry. She rose regally before him and in her best haughty tone told him. 'Mr Lowther, it is a rule of this house that I never receive visitors without prior appointment.'

His eyes stared fiercely as he said, 'My apologies. My difficulty is that there appears to be two of you. The great lady of your father's estates, and the woman who writes an excellent gossip column.'

Bunty smarted at being referred to as a writer of tittle tat. Behind her the maid advanced down the spiral staircase carrying the Hoover in one hand. Lowther looked at her with undisguised disappointment. The maid didn't look at him at all, but something told him she had noticed him, and didn't like what she had seen. He sighed and the ardour wheezed out of him.

Bunty, reassured by her reinforcement, returned to the attack. 'There are no tattoos,' she said stridently.

'Pardon?'

'There are no tattoos on my breasts, which you are staring at.'

'Madame, I assure you . . . ' Lowther was lost for words, faced with the impossibility of proving a negative.

Bunty was beginning to almost enjoy herself. She had decided that she would fix a spy hole to her front door and instruct the maid that this man was never to be admitted, unless she gave instructions to the contrary. In the meantime, she would ensure that he would not seek to trouble her again without a reason beyond satisfying his venal appetites.

The maid, who had heard Bunty's observation about her breasts, said, 'I have finished upstairs Madam. If Madam needs me I shall be in the kitchen attending to the cutlery.' Her deep set eyes were as black as olives. She gave Lowther a look that would have diminished the erection on a statue, and left them with the rolling gait of a fighting man, still holding the Hoover in one hand.

Lowther watched her disappear and regained his composure. 'Madam, you do me an injustice if you consider me the sort of man who would force his attentions on a woman.'

Bunty thought the statement clearly absurd, because how else was he was he to be successful with his attentions, if not by force. However, she said nothing because she had already achieved what she had set out to do.

Lowther took her silence to mean that they had common ground. 'The reason that I called in person, rather than speak to you on the telephone, was that I have two important pieces of news which I didn't want overheard by some gossiping telephonist.'

'Really.'

Lowther disregarded her cold tone. 'First, I have been astonished and delighted at Linden's progress. That being so I intend to donate a further three thousand pounds to him if he plays a significant part in winning us the ashes.'

'Is he even in the team?'

'He will be. I have no objection to you writing a story about this donation and its terms. I'm giving you the story first.'

'And the second? The second piece of news?'

'Ah yes. It is that Linden has formed an association with a member of the aristocracy. The Boutilier girl.'

Bunty was a good card player, and she used all her skills to keep her face stone still as Lowther delivered his hammer blow. 'Ah,' she said. 'There are rumours linking him with all sorts of people. He seems to have become a new sort of sports star.'

From the kitchen they heard the sound of a knife dropping on the tiled floor. Bunty wondered whether it had caused a crack. She glanced behind her and then back at Lowther. There was a slight sheen of sweat on his bald head and, she imagined, on other parts of his body. Evidently he wasn't comfortable in the dry air of central heating, or perhaps he was merely anxious because he had arrived at the crux of his plan. She had no doubt that he knew that Helen was her best friend.

She kept her voice steady when she said, 'I'll make some inquiries.'

'I'll await the result with interest.' He turned towards the door and she allowed him to let himself out.

An hour later she was ringing the bell at Ben's apartment. She knew he was away in Hampshire, but was sure that Helen would be there waiting for him.

After Lowther had made his first donation to Ben, Bunty had made her own inquiries. She knew that Lowther would never give out such a large sum of money for the reasons he had given. She had discovered that he was detested by the establishment, but his money and influence in the business world gave him some power. One of her friends had referred to him as 'John the Jew boy' and said that he had become a bit of a joke with his obsession of being accepted by the cricket establishment. 'It's really extraordinary that a man so astute in all other matters can delude himself into thinking that we'd ever accept him into our fold.' He'd grinned in delight that the joke was on the 'dirty little Jew,' who scurried round trying to ingratiate himself with people who despised him.

Bunty had said nothing at the time, but she knew Lowther would not take his humiliation lying down and that there would come a point when he would cut his losses and take revenge.

That point, it seemed, had come a week before he made his first approach to her, when his application to become a member of the Test selection committee had been overlooked once more.

He had heard the sniggers, real or imaginary, and then with cold rage, plotted his revenge.

Helen gave Bunty a hug and then let her into Ben's tiny apartment. Bunty found the rooms claustrophobic, but Helen told her she felt at home here. There was the smell of bread baking in the oven. Bunty was astonished to discover her friend had started cooking.

She noticed that Helen was wearing a flowered pinafore and pealed into laughter. 'Is this the noble girl, who whipped the serf for startling her steed?' she laughed.

Helen smiled. 'It is.'

Bunty's eyes softened. 'Have you found happiness, Helen?'

Helen opened her arms out. 'I have. Have you ever lost control, Bunty? Really lost control.'

Bunty groaned. 'Oh God, kid, that's dangerous.'

'I know. It's wonderful. Like a little girl spinning round, making herself dizzy.'

'And then she falls down.'

'That's the risk, but I'm glad I'm one of those prepared to take it.'

Bunty sat her friend down on a hard, wooden chair by the tiny dining table. 'Have you heard of a man called John Lowther?'

Helen shook her head.

'He's a wronged, but evil man and he hates your father and his like.'

She told Helen about his gift to Ben. 'He says it is to further Ben's career and through that the quality of English cricket. But it isn't. Can I have a drink of water?'

Helen went to the kitchen and returned with a full glass.

Bunty took a sip. Her mouth was quite dry.

'What he hopes will happen is that Ben will use the

money to become a man about town and that his exploits will find their way into the papers.'

'But why?'

'To chip at the establishment. The inference will be that Ben, the working class boy, is chasing the daughters of the rich and famous and, thus, is becoming part of them. They are no longer as exclusive as they think, you see.'

'But he's not a playboy. What have you heard?' her eyes lit in alarm.

'No he's not, but Lowther's scheme has hit a jackpot, beyond his wildest dreams.'

The truth dawned on Helen. 'You mean me?'

Bunty nodded. 'He's found out and he's going to make it public.'

Helen shrugged. 'It will have to come out sometime, I suppose.'

Bunty sighed. 'What will you say?'

'That I love him and that that's a better reason to be with a man than some family alliance.'

Bunty sighed. 'All of which will go down very well with my readers. But with your lot, well, I don't think they'll take it too well.'

'They won't,' Helen said in an even voice. 'But they are not living my life, I am. It was always going to come to this.'

Bunty looked at her friend wondering whether she knew what she was taking on. 'What will you do?'

Helen shrugged her slim shoulders. 'Nothing for the moment.' She smiled at her friend. 'I'm too happy, you see. So it's best just to live in the moment, while I can.'

Bunty reached out and squeezed Helen's hand. 'It could all go horribly wrong.'

'I have always believed you should stand up and spin till you're dizzy.'

Chapter Twenty two

Ben travelled straight to the Boutilier estate after the Hampshire game. He took a train to Wolviston and then walked the river road. His only luggage was a small leather case in which he carried his boots and cricket clothes. It was a warm late afternoon in midsummer and he enjoyed the stroll along the leafy road. He was struck by how much he missed the quiet and solitude. He had never been at ease in the bustle of London, which seemed to him a city of strangers, where people struggled past each other, usually without a word, or eye contact. Of course, since his climb to fame he had been the exception and now, every day, he was approached by strangers. But it wasn't the same contact as in the country. It was either an embarrassing adoration, or a slightly aggressive attitude to him, as though they believed they owned part of him.

He stopped by a bend in the road where a lifetime ago he had burst out in front of Helen's great horse. Perhaps the blow of the riding crop had brought out the warrior in him. The irony was that he embraced her now, but for the rest of them, he felt a brooding aggression.

The thought of Peregrin and his cronies snubbing him at Bunty's party still filled him with fury. He hoped the whole bloody lot of them were playing in the match.

His mother hugged him at the door. She'd had a pot roast on for hours but he wasn't hungry. 'Where's Jarvis?' he asked.

'At home. He doesn't live here, you know.'

He raised an eyebrow and then she blushed. 'You're my son not my guardian.'

He grinned and embraced her again. Her body felt slack

and tired. He looked at her. There were lines in her face and a blankness in her eyes.

'You don't look well, ma.'

She smiled. 'Just getting old.'

They talked of his life in London, but he didn't mention Helen, or even Lizzie and Bunty. He was surprised to see that she kept a book of cuttings about his career. She didn't buy newspapers but people on the estate brought her the articles and photographs. Some of them, it seemed, bought the Times and the Manchester Guardian on match days, so as to bask in his fame with the mother.

The wobbly clock on the mantelpiece chimed six and she smiled. 'He'll be waiting for you, on his second pipe by now.

He said his goodbyes and she called, 'I'll not lock the door.'

'You never do, Ma,' and with that he was down the path.

Arnie saw him coming across the field from the swamp end as he called it, in memory of the rescue of Wolfie.

He rose from the pavilion steps and met Ben in the cricket square. The two shook hands.

'Is this the wicket?' Ben looked down at the close-mown strip.

Arnie nodded. 'As flat as the wife and twice as slow.'

Ben shook his head.

Arnie grinned. 'Boutilier's a batsman of sorts. It's his bat, it's his ball, and it's his wicket. And don't you forget it.'

'I'm not bothered about him.' He told Arnie of his treatment at the party.

Arnie listened quietly until he's finished. 'It's nothing personal, you know.'

'It was to me. And they knew it.'

Arnie spat on to the square. 'You can't fight them all, son.'

'I don't want to fight them all. Just Bowden and his friends. Leastways, they'll do for the time being.'

Arnie shook his head. 'I felt like you when I was young. Then I learned a lesson.'

'Oh aye.'

'I realised that I could advance maybe a couple of stepping stones across the river but I could never get to the other side, that would be the lot of someone long after me.'

Ben grinned. 'The trouble is the bastards keep moving the banks.'

Ben had hung his cricket boots round his neck by tying the laces together. He gestured to the nets that had been erected in preparation for the game. 'I'm working on a new ball.'

They walked to the nets and Arnie stuck some stumps in the ground while Ben pushed his feet into his boots.

'Where do you want me?'

'Bowler's end but ten yards behind the wicket.'

Arnie tapped out his pipe and took his position. Ben came gliding past him with his effortless run. He bowled his faster ball chest on with the minimum leap but his arm came over at twelve o'clock to give him bounce. His thighs passed inches from the bowling stumps and the ball smashed into the pitch half way down and reared head height as it passed the over the batsman's wicket.

Neither man said anything and Ben selected another ball from a small basket and repeated the process. This time the ball was even faster.

He turned to Arnie. 'What do you think?'

The old man levelled him with his watery eyes. 'Promise me something son, you're not going to bowl that at Bowden.'

'Why not?'

'Because you'll kill him.'

'He's got a bat.'

'He'd need a suit of armour, not a bat.'

'He says he's a top player. So do others. Experts who write in the newspapers.'

'I don't care if they're writing in the Bible. I know he's not, and so do you.'

'How come?' Ben sounded irritated by Arnie's objection.

'I know that you are the fastest bowler I've ever seen by at least a yard and I know there are a thousand better players of fast bowling than Peregrin Bowden. And I know what you are going to do.'

'Do you?'

'Aye. Tell if I'm wrong. You're going to pitch on middle and off, or middle. You're going to bowl short, with the ball cross seam, and you're going to bowl from stump to stump so that when the ball is screaming for his head there's nowhere for him to go.'

Ben nodded. 'Something like that,' he said with a small boy's defiance.

'And have you thought what will happen if you hit him on the head? If he's lying dead, what are you going to say? "He had a bat". Is that the plan?'

Ben said nothing for seconds, then. 'You said yourself the wicket's flat and slow.'

'They could put glue on it and you'd still be too fast for Bowden.'

Ben walked home that evening irritated and frustrated. He knew that he needed to humiliate Bowden and his friends in return for their sneers. He didn't just want their wickets, he wanted to destroy them. He wanted spectators to laugh at them, or at the very least to clearly see that these men, who thought that he had no place with them at social events, had no place with him on the cricket field.

His mother chattered to him with gossip of old friends and families he had left behind; people who in the main would live all their lives on the Boutilier estate where time had almost stood still.

He stared at his mother as she knitted away, talking all the time. Chickens clucked in the back garden and he could smell the purity of the air. He kissed her forehead and went out to stand in the porch that Jarvis had built her. The sun had set, but the land was still lit in its afterglow. He heard the bark of a single dog carry across the fields. The fox from the far woods, where he had harried the rooks, would be slinking along a hedgerow. Behind him, Busker, Jarvis's sheepdog, too old to guide the flocks, growled as it patrolled the chicken coops. Suddenly down in the valley, through the huge main gate there came a necklace of car lights looping slowly along the gravelled drive. The great and the good, including Lady Helen, were arriving ahead of the match. He felt the distance between them. He wanted to be in the limousine beside her, he wanted to be with her.

He remembered the Ben who had taken her blow from the whip with a quiet rebuke. That man had long gone, but the irony was that without him none of this would have happened. He flung his head from side to side in anguish at all the confusing thoughts helter-skeltering through his mind.

A mile away in the great hall, Helen dined with her father at opposite ends of the long table. Helen could see the glass pane, that covered the huge scroll, glinting in the flickering light of the fire and knew that her father had chosen this room for the meal as a tactic.

He'd announced that he would not be playing in this year's match. He looked fragile, and empty, incapable of the hedonism that had been a central part of his life, but in an odd way his frailty gave him a dignity that passed for strength.

She looked at him along the polished, oak table, over the heavy silver tableware and the embossed cutlery laid at all the empty places, and she was overwhelmed by a sudden feeling that he was dying, and that he knew it. All his life he had set great stock on courage. She remembered how he had spoken in admiration of Ben after Wolfie had been saved. Indeed he had also praised Ben's father for his courage in the war, a war he had missed, a war that could have defined him with his ancestors, who had fought or fall-en in other battles. Despite all his selfish indulgences, he believed himself to be a servant of his country.

He spoke little during the meal and dismissed the ser-vants when coffee was served. Helen regarded this as an extraordinary development, for her father had always spo-ken before the servants as though they did not exist. She knew it could only mean one thing. She was not kept wait-ing.

'Have you thought any more about Peregrin Bowden?'

'No.'

'Why not?' His voice had a slight croak to it.

'Because there's nothing more to think about. I don't love him, and I never will.'

'Love!' Boutilier gave a harsh laugh. 'It would seem that Bowden loves you. God help him.'

'Well, God might help him but I can't.'

Boutilier glared down the table. He could see the Boadicea coming out in his daughter and decided on a new line of attack. 'Perry believes that you are infatuated with this young man, Linden.'

Helen tried to keep the shock out of her face. So it had

come to this. No doubt it was Perry who had told the tale to Lowther as well. They made strange allies, with different goals, did Lowther and her father.

When she spoke her voice was calm. 'I once told Perry that one can choose one's friends, but never the man or men you fall in love with.'

'And are you in love with Linden?'

'Yes.'

'You stupid girl! And where do you think this love will take you, and for how long do you think it will last?'

'It will last as long as it lasts, and it will take me where it takes me."

Boutilier stared at her in horror. He recognised the strength in her that he wished was in his son. She had rebelled against him all her life, in revenge for his own dissolute behaviour. But this revolt had more substance. He began to cough and held a linen handkerchief to his mouth until the fit subsided. He replaced the handkerchief without looking at the specks of blood that he knew were there.

Only that morning he had written in his diary, 'Death comes to us all. It's just that I have more information than most.'

He wanted a Roman death in which his courage demanded a respect that counted against all his follies, indiscretions, and self indulgences. But most of all he wanted the peace of knowing his daughter was to follow the family path that had been lain down over the centuries. He did not need to look at the scroll to recite the great names on it, names that rolled down from the history of England. And now it seemed his daughter was intending to add Linden, the chicken trader, to that body of great men.

He looked steadily down the table at her. 'I know I have not been a good father. I know you have often gone out deliberately to hurt me because I have let you down, Helen. But I'm begging you not to marry this man.

'He may be better than Bowden in every respect, in every respect but one. He is not one of us, and never can be. If you marry him it will allow the enemies of our class to dance on our graves.'

Helen's eyes filled with tears. She had prepared herself for him to shout and rage, but not this. She summoned all the strength she had left. 'You should look to Charles for the heir you seek.'

Boutilier sighed. 'We both know that Charles finds women repugnant.'

'Well tell him to lie on his back and think of England. Or get the gamekeeper to stand in for him. The same names will still go on that thing.' She pointed to the scroll.

'You're talking like a naive schoolgirl.' Boutilier rose from his chair and then sagged back in exhaustion in his chair. She went to him holding him up by the shoulders. His jacket felt like a sack of bones.

They both knew they had gone too far. She held him to her talking softly. It was the first time they had touched each other in years. She tried to remember when she had stopped loving him and begun to hate him. She thought it must have been around the time her mother died. He was the easy target for blame and the easy outlet for her grief.

They'd planned to meet on the drovers' road by the old bowling pitch. On all previous occasions she had ridden Jasper up the old trail, but this time she set off walking up the hills at a fast pace, glad of the wind that wrestled with her hair, roughened her face, and watered her eyes.

She had to find the strength to leave him.

She wished it was in mid winter with rain to lash her as

she fought the battle in her mind. As it was, even the fierce wind could not keep the sun from warming her body, sending her into a drift of dreams. She saw him a mile away along the flat of the land, a stooped, forlorn figure, because she was half an hour late having forsaken the horse. His body stiffened at the sight of her and she knew in that instant she could not leave him. She would have to accept that, for the rest of her life, she would be haunted by the sight of her father, thin-faced, with spittle bubbling on his lips, making his last plea.

She found herself running toward Ben, until she had to stop to regain her breath. She stood panting, watching him move to her with that smooth, gliding run of his. She clung to him, hiding in the hugeness of his body. 'You must never leave me. Never. Never. Never.' And then she laughed at the words. How stupid they were. How pointless to try to exact such a promise, for who could say what would happen? Minutes ago she had been telling herself she must leave him and then, at the sight of him, she knew that could never be. Best just to live the day in good heart and conscience and to hell with everything else, especially family scrolls.

His fingers touched her lips. 'What's the matter Helen?'

'I love you. That's what's the matter. It feels like I'm on a wild leaping horse that I can't control.' Her thoughts were coming in a rush at her now. 'Arnie spoke to me this morning. He called at the house. He's never done that before. He says you are going to hurt Perry. You mustn't.'

His body had stiffened.

'Believe me if you do it will cause more trouble than you can imagine.' She looked at him. 'It's about Bunty's party, isn't it?'

'That and other things.'

'I know they behaved badly to you. I saw it, remember.

But if you bowl to hurt them, they'll just win support. Don't you see the only way you can win is to rise above them?'

He looked down at her and said in a low voice. 'The trouble is, I'm not sure I'll be satisfied with just that.'

She shook him in sudden anger. 'If I see you bowl killer balls at Perry Bowden . . . I don't think I'll feel the same about you. Think of the consequences, not just for you, but for me as well. It's all I'll ever ask you.'

They stood drained by the moment before turning back towards the cottage.

'You know I'm going to marry you, don't you, Mr Bowler?'

Her head was level with his chest and she didn't look up, but she knew that he was smiling.

'I think I knew it when I saw you watching me run to you.'

She punched him lightly in the chest. They'd come to the turn in the trail where she had left him with his blistered feet.

She turned into him and kissed him slowly and softly. From half a mile away ,although their bodies were no bigger than dots, Peregrin could see they were lovers in love. He brought his horse to a stamping halt and stared angrily up the hill, his breath whistling through his teeth in primeval rage. He turned his horse and galloped back to the stables, dismounting and sending the hunter at a trot into the arms of a hapless groom.

The youth steadied the horse and stilled its clopping hooves. He didn't look, but could hear Bowden leave, whacking his crop against his long, leather boots.

Chapter Twenty three

Helen left Ben in the lane leading to his gate. She walked along the leafy path, exhausted by the events of the last twenty-four hours. A blackbird swooped low across the road clucking its alarm call. A shotgun rung out across the fields and a flock of rooks rose like dust from the beech trees in the far distance.

She stopped dizzy with doubts. She felt she was in a boat being whirled around until she did not know which way she was pointing. What alarmed her most was that she had walked out of the great house, only two hours ago, resolved to leave Ben. How could she have contemplated such a move? The thought frightened her. She knew that this time he would never have allowed her back into his life in the way that he had twice in the past. He still had a childlike simplicity, but he was also a harder, more resolved man than the Ben of a year ago. He had grown and felt his worth; he had made new friends and new enemies. The man who had stood silent while Bowden had sniggered at the 'stone age bowler' was no more and in his place stood someone who had won his right to arms, and was ready for battle.

She still had doubts about the great match. She knew she had swung him with her arguments, but for how long? Or what would happen if Perry or his ghastly friends did something else to provoke him? Perry had only faced him briefly in the nets, in benign circumstances, and his friends had even less experience, and worse, were bolstered by the false confidence, gained from facing inferior bowling in university matches.

She turned a corner in the lane and shivered in a sudden breeze. Through the hedge she could hear Arnie tapping in the stumps at the nets. She found the gap that Ben had found all those months ago and walked slowly to the old man.

He waved which was unusual for him. She knew he too had seen the change in Ben and was anxious for news. Arnie put his pipe in his mouth and forgot to light it. 'Well?' he asked.

'I think he's seen sense. For the moment, anyway.'

They were standing in the middle of the ground and Arnie looked down at the wicket. 'I've put the heavy roller on it and been watering it just in case. It's as soft as a sponge and as flat . . . ' he searched for a simile that was not obscene or even merely rude, and failed. 'As flat,' he said, defeated.

She looked at him glumly. 'They're playing over five days. It'll wear.'

'Well,' Arnie sucked on his pipe and found it unlit. He reached into his pocket for his matches and found them gone. 'If he's such a fool, there's nowt more we can do.'

He was not speaking the words that Helen wanted to hear.

That morning was the first of two days of nets before the match. Ben made a brief appearance, bowling at three-quarter pace and staying well away from any of the Gentlemen. So much so that one of Perry's friends, having seen his relatively modest pace, called out to him waving his bat. Ben remembered the little man in glasses from Bunty's party and gave him a hard stare. 'No sir. I'm bowling to my like with all due respects. They need the practice, or so they say. Wednesday will be soon enough.'

The little man shrugged dismissively. He'd seen the great man bowl and heard the tales from Perry about how he'd struck him through the covers. He walked off with a cocky strut. Ben watched him go and continued practising his slower ball.

Sawyer had been made captain of the Players' team as a mark of respect after he'd announced that this was his last season.

He had no formal education, his vocabulary was bolstered by obscenities, but he had a shrewd mind and an instinctive judgement of character. He knew what greater brains did not know, that Ben was to be steered rather than directed. As such, he knew there were times when it was best just to allow him to do what he wanted. And if that included bowling slower balls in the nets all morning , that was fine. There were a couple of other nippy bowlers in the side who could give his batsmen the practice that they wanted.

He looked across at the little man who'd waved his bat at Ben. He'd played cricket with him and his like for a dozen seasons and had never ceased to wonder at how stupid an intelligent man could be. Anyone could see from Ben's body language, the slightly slower run, the lazy arm action and the loose follow-through that he was holding himself in reserve. But not these gentlemen, not even Bowden, who'd faced him in the nets and seen him play. It was as if they saw only what they wanted to see. Perhaps that was the way they lived their lives, cushioned from reality.

Ben bowled another couple of overs and then signalled to Sawyer that he'd had enough.

Sawyer nodded and walked across. 'Everything OK?'

'Yes.' The word came through a thick pullover that Ben was tugging over his head. He emerged with a grin. 'Everything's fine.'

Sawyer gestured to the small man who was busy cracking a spin bowler over the mid off position. 'What's with Little Lord Fauntleroy?'

Ben told him about his treatment at Bunty's party and Sawyer whistled quietly.

'What's he trying to do? Commit suicide?' Sawyer looked at the little man again. 'Cambridge isn't he?'

Ben shrugged. 'Dunno.'

Sawyer continued watching the little man bat in the nets. 'He likes to get on to his front foot. Quick feet too. But his right shoulder comes round as he moves across the wicket. Mainly an eye player.' He grinned. 'It's technique that matters against pace, so he won't last long eh!'

'No, he won't.'

Sawyer looked at him keenly. 'You know he isn't in your league.'

'People keep telling me this. So why does he get a bat and get to stand at the other end?'

'That's the way it is.' He rested his arm on Ben's shoulders. 'There's a chap just died. Huntingdon showed me his obituary in The Times. Arthur Begbie he was called. He didn't give a fuck for anybody and injured three amateurs in the nets. One of them was Lord Burnley. So he was banned by Lancs. Later he tried to bowl round the wicket to Fry and Ranji. The umpire stopped him after an over, so he bowled short and fast until he hit them both. He wasn't as fast as you though. Mind you, he might have been if he hadn't spent his time drinking and fighting.'

Ben looked puzzled. 'I'm not a drinker and brawler.'

'No. You're worse. You're political.'

'What are you trying to say?'

'Not sure really. If you're going to try to beat them you must play within their rules, or they won't accept that you've won. If they say bowling short is OK, it is. If they say it isn't, it isn't. And never forget, when Begbie went out and got drunk he was an appalling, ignorant hooligan. When the lads from Eton rioted at their school it was just high spirits. They make the rules. You can't beat them unless you make them accept that you've beaten them.' He took off his cap and scratched his head. 'Christ! My head hurts! How far to the nearest pub?'

During the early days, Arnie told him not to bother going on long runs over the hills to get fit. Bowlers, he said, got fit by bowling. Ben had accepted the advice even though he got great pleasure from running. However, he found that bowling led to stresses and strains because he was constantly exercising the same muscles. As the months went by he began to make his own decisions and one of those had been to take a run every day. Even in the streets of London, or in one of the city's crowded parks, he found he could lose himself in his thoughts. However, the drovers' trail offered him greater delights. He loved the great sweep of the high land, the lush turf, manured by tens of thousands of cattle over the years, the sweeping views tantalisingly obstructed by trees and hedgerows, and most of all, the clean pure air that fed his lungs.

His only occasional companion on these runs was Wolfie, who attached himself to him each time he returned to the estate. Some days he would follow Ben up on to the trail, bounding ahead and then tearing way down the road and galloping back. On others, he would lay in wait for Ben in the bracken and come bounding out in a mock ambush, snarling and snapping and then leap away down the trail.

Ben set off after a light breakfast heading towards the old cricket wicket he had built. He found this warmed him up admirably for the morning nets. There was no Wolfie waiting for him at the gates this morning and he made quick progress up the slope past the point at which Helen had abandoned him on her horse. He looked down at the great walls of the estate and beyond them the cricket ground, all but hidden by beech and elm trees. His feet flew over a long flat stretch of the road to the bend that led to the pitch. As he ran on he saw three men at the wicket bowling stones. He approached at half speed surprised at their presence, for although he'd been told that there were the occasional visitors to the wicket since the story about him had appeared in the press, it seemed strange that they were abroad so early. The three heard him coming and turned to face him. They were all burly young men, working men from their dress of dark, stained trousers, rough jackets, and flat caps.

'Mr Linden, isn't it?' The man at the front offered him a notebook and pencil. He smiled. 'Now here's good fortune.' His accent was from the North, Leeds perhaps, certainly Yorkshire. Ben was wary as he took the book to sign his name even though the men had appeared to be friendly.

One of the men who stood to Ben's right said. 'We didn't think you'd want anything to do with the likes of us.'

There was something odd about his tone, too tense for the pleasant words. Ben smiled. 'I am the likes of you.'

'Well, why are you fucking your betters then?' The big man in the middle swung a punch as he spoke. He was taller than Ben which was fortunate for he had time to duck so that the blow landed on the crown of his forehead. The knuckles spread and split and the man shouted out in pain, but by then the other two were at him. As soon as they gripped him he knew they were not average men. They were strong and well-balanced street fighters. Ben whirled his arms over their gripping hands using the leverage to break free. He kicked out and caught one man on the inside of his knee but his plimsolls were too flimsy to do much damage. The man flinched for a second, enough time for Ben to punch him in the mouth. He felt a sharp pain in his fist from the man's teeth and then took a thumping blow in the ribs from the last of his attackers who followed up with a left and a right. Both punches caught Ben static and off balance and he staggered away. For a moment there was a chance for him to run, but he didn't. He found himself standing by the disturbed pyramid of stones. The two men were steadying themselves for another attack and the third man, who he guessed to be the leader, was rising to his feet clutching his right arm to his side. His face was contorted with pain as he snarled, 'Get the bastard!'

Ben stooped quickly and grabbed two of the stones. As the men closed in on him he hurled one stone at the nearest man's groin. It hit him in the stomach and he fell winded, but by that time the other man was on him with a flying butt. Ben just had time to raise his elbow in protection but the man's momentum took him through his defences and he caught him a glancing, but heavy, blow on his right eyebrow.

As the two struggled, the big man closed in and began raining in punches to Ben's ribs with his left hand. Ben struggled to burst free and stamped his heel on a foot, but his light plimsoll had little effect on the heavy boot. The third man had recovered his wind by now and punches were raining on to his face and ribs. By instinct he clutched at a jacket, but he was weakening fast and he made an easy target for the men who had time to set themselves for heavy blows. He briefly passed out and came to lying on his back. One of the men had stretched out his right arm and the big man was holding a stone ready to smash it down on his fingers. His face was still contorted in rage and pain. Ben kicked up with his right leg bending from the hips and his foot caught the arm sending the stone looping away, but the big man merely laughed and picked up another stone. 'Hold him still, you fools!' Ben felt the tightening grip on his arm and the weight of the other man across his hips. He lay helpless and the panic must have shown in his face for the big man started to laugh. 'Not so brave now, eh!' He raised his hand clutching the stone. Ben gave one last frantic wriggle to escape, but the men held firm. He looked up straining every sinew and then suddenly the big man had gone. He heard the snarls from the huge dog. The claws from Wolfie's back paws lacerated his face as the wolf hound sought purchase to push towards his foe. The two men who held him captive loosened their grip as they became aware of this terrifying new threat and that was enough for Ben to break free once more. Ben found that in his panic he had kept hold of a stone in his left hand and he swung it at the head of the man holding his arm. He fell without a sound. The second man was already rising off him, trying to flee. By the time Ben rose to his feet he was fifteen yards down the track ignoring the screams for help from the big man. By now Ben was possessed by a cold fury and it was as if his mind had detached itself from his body so that, it seemed, he was watching himself pick up another stone. The man had run a further thirty yards when he threw the stone. He could have run a further fifty for all the good it would have done. The missile caught him at the base of his spine and he fell with a scream. His cap, which had remained on his head throughout the fight, fell to the ground a few yards on from its owner. The big man was still screaming for help. The great dog, consumed by a blood lust by now, was shaking his great head back and forward trying to tear off the arm at the shoulder.

The big man was past feeling pain and he caught Ben's eye. 'For the love of God, man he's going to kill me!'

'Who sent you?'

'What?' The big man started to scream again.

'Who sent you?'

Ben waited a second for an answer and then turned his back on the big man and began to walk away.

'I don't know. I swear I don't know. George hired me.' The big man was screaming. Ben turned round and saw him gesture with his head down the track. George was now three hundred yards away, obviously in severe pain, but limping with the speed of a man to whom fear had given wings.

Ben walked towards the big man with deliberate slowness and then shouted a sharp command to Wolfie, who was so enjoying his work that he didn't hear. He reached out and struck the dog lightly about the ears and motioned away with his hand. Wolfie backed off growling. Ben looked down at the man who was sobbing with shock. 'Not so brave now, eh.' Ben could see raw red flesh through the torn jacket. He pushed the man back with his foot until he was lying on his back and motioned for Wolfie to come closer. The giant dog advanced, snarling to a foot from the big man's throat.

'You were going to break my hand.'

The big man was broken. 'As God's my witness I'm sorry, Mr Linden. They gave me ten guineas. It's in my purse. You're welcome to it.'

Ben didn't answer. Instead he stepped on the big man's wrist and picked up a heavy stone. 'If you move the dog will have your throat. 'Oh Jesus! The big man thrust his free arm across his throat. Ben looked down and grinned but the dark eyes were full of hate. 'I can throw one of these over one hundred yards. I'm going to throw it at your hand. I might miss. I probably won't, but I might.' He spat on the turf. 'Remember, if you move the dog will have you.' And with that he hurled the stone downwards. Even if he had wanted to, the big man would not have had time to move which was just as well for him because the stone splatted a deep divot in the turf, an inch from his fingers before bouncing away.

'Looks like it's your lucky day!' Ben smiled, his eyes still full of hate, as the big man lay sobbing and defeated.

Ben raised his foot and released the arm. He walked away without looking back. He whistled for Wolfie and the great dog bounded to his side. Ben heard the sound of slapping feet as the big man fled. He looked down at the dog that seemed to be grinning at him with blood stained teeth.

As he moved down the slope and the adrenaline wore off he began to feel the battering he had taken. He wiped the cut above his eye with his torn running vest and found the movement of his arms caused pain to his ribs and stomach. The pain caused panic. Supposing it caused him to miss the match. He remembered the big man trying to smash his hand. That, of course, was the whole point of the attack. They wanted him to miss every match. They'd wanted to cripple him. The anger rippled through him, against those thugs and the man or men who'd hired them.

By now he could see the cottage and he stopped to lean against a tree. He didn't want to alarm his mother but his ribs hurt when he took a deep breath. The sweat from his running and the fight had turned cold and he shivered. He did not know how long he stood there. The shock of the events seemed to freeze him. He became aware of Wolfie barking deeply and his mother shouting 'Shut up you daft dog!' and then her call of alarm as she spotted him against the tree. She called to Jarvis and he ran to Ben, held him against his body and helped him into the cottage where he laid him on his bed. His mother stood in a panic. Her son needed a doctor yet the nearest was a ten-mile drive in her pony trap. Then she remembered Ben mentioning that one of the Gentleman players was a medical man. She called to Jarvis to put blankets over her son and ran down the path to the cricket field.

She found Arnie at the nets and told him of the attack. Five minutes later she was walking back to the cottage with a fresh faced young man who apologised for the fact that he was not a qualified doctor, merely a medical student. 'You'll do,' she said. 'It's cuts and bruises, I think. He's been banged about by three bits of scum. What's your name, young man?'

'Miller. John Miller.' The young man smiled. 'Your son's a bit of a hero of mine, actually.'

Beth didn't hear. She was wrapped in her own thoughts. 'They tried to bust his hand, he says. The dog saved him.'

'Dog?'

'Aye, more like a wolf. A great beast of a thing.'

They were at the door and she ushered him inside and led him to the bed.

Jarvis had got the running vest off Ben and Miller bent over him. The blow to his head had closed his right eye and his rib cage was covered in livid red marks from the punches and kicks he had taken. Miller pressed gently to Ben's body and noted the whoosh of pain. After ten minutes or so he turned to Beth. 'I don't think anything is broken. Fortunately he's as fit and strong as any man I've seen, which means he'll recover quickly. But he's taken an awful battering.' He noted Ben's cut knuckles and the blood-stained fur at the corners of the great dog's mouth. 'Between them, they've given as good as they got, by the look of it.'

Arnie and Sawyer were at the door before Miller left and they were closely followed by Helen, who burst in and ran to Ben's bedside, not caring about the looks she attracted.

Miller stared at her. He'd never been introduced but recognised her from pictures in society magazines.

Helen held Ben's bruised hands.

Her status allowed her to take charge of the situation without being questioned. 'How bad is he, doctor?'

Miller decided against going through the ritual of advising her of his qualifications and merely said, 'He's a very fit man, so I expect him to be up and about in a couple of days.'

'What about the match?' Sawyer got straight to the point.

'That's another matter. He'll certainly be in pain.'

Sawyer nodded. 'Can he play then?'

'I'm playing,' Ben spoke for the first time from his bed.

Miller looked down at the muscled young man. 'Have the police been called?'

Ben shook his head. 'They weren't from around here. They'll be long gone by now.'

Miller looked at Wolfie's bloodstained fur. 'It looks as though at least one of them will need hospital treatment.'

Ben struggled to sit up and groaned with the effort. 'Not round here though. They'll patch him up for the journey and deal with it when they get home.'

Miller was not impressed. 'I still think the police should be called.'

Ben looked up at Jarvis and his mother. 'Call the constable. I'm not going anywhere.'

Helen said quietly, 'I'll deal with the police.'

That afternoon a detective inspector, the most senior officer in the valley, arrived in a spluttering Morris. Lomax was a thorough man. He interviewed Linden as best he could, given the man's condition, and then walked up the drovers' road to the scene of the fight. He noted the scattered stones, the bloodstains on a couple of them, some scraps of blood-soaked cloth. Undoubtedly the dog had saved the young man from serious injury.

It seemed an extraordinarily vicious attack, and one with no clear motive. A runner out on the moor would not be carrying any money. Perhaps there had been an exchange of words and things had got out of hand. He looked down the long stretch of track. They'd run off down there and not stopped. He walked the road towards Wolviston and a mile on found some tyre tracks. So they'd been waiting for Linden, but why? The young cricketer had said he didn't know why they had attacked him. Was that the truth?

Lomax was a shrewd man. Linden was known throughout the country and as such might become a target for all sorts of reasons. This was premeditated and planned. That was just one of the unusual features of the case. Another was the original call to the station had come from Lady Helen Boutilier. My God, that had got their attention. He wondered what tale the young thugs could tell and how harmful it would be if their story ever got out.

Chapter Twenty four

After she called the police from the great house, Helen hurried back to the cottage armed with ice packs which she had taken from the fridge in the huge kitchen. The cook stood silent but open-mouthed as she piled the cubes into a cavas bag. Helen sat with Ben until late into the night holding the ice against his ribs.

Beth was alarmed by her presence almost as much as by the visit of Lord Boutilier long, long ago. She found comfort in repetition, and when that was disrupted by visits from the gentry, her instinct told her to keep on curtsying until they had gone, and hope that no bad would come from it. But as she watched Lady Helen's long, slim figure bend like a swan's neck over her son's bed, she knew that, for better or for worse, this was not merely a visit, this woman loved her son.

Beth herself had once fought off the women in the factory who'd chased after her man, but that was a different fight, between people of the same class. This went across boundaries that blurred the conflict, until no one knew what might happen. All she knew was that this love could not exist without a battle, the like of which she had never known. She heard Helen whisper, 'So what really happened?' and knew that no good would come of the answer.

The following morning Ben ignored his mother's entreaties to spend another day in bed and walked stiffly down to the cricket ground.

Arnie had more success with him. He had no ice, but he soaked towels in cold water and wrapped them round Ben's chest. Ben shivered, but didn't protest.

Arnie sat on a battered wooden chair in the corner of the room and asked the same question that Helen had asked a few hours earlier. 'So what really happened?'

'They were paid. They said I should stop seeing Helen.'

Arnie stared at him. 'Well, that narrows it down to a few thousand.'

Ben rose from his seat on one of the long benches in the changing room. Arnie saw the livid marks on his muscled body. Ben's voice was low, but full of anger. 'Fewer than that. There's not that many knew and cared about Helen and me enough to set a band of thugs on me. And there's even fewer knew about me running that road.'

Arnie looked for signs of pain as Ben rubbed the towel about his body shivering slightly. 'You think it was Bowden, don't you?'

'Yes. Or one of his friends.'

'So the plan is to maim the lot of them. You know you've no proof.'

'Yes. And I promised Helen that I wouldn't bowl at them.' He shrugged his shoulders. 'Hell, I may not be able to play anyway.' He reached for his clothes.

'If you go for revenge like this, you do know that you could lose her.'

'I know.' His eyes would not meet Arnie's stare. 'The trouble is I am what I am.'

'You've no proof.' Arnie said again.

'I'm hoping the police will give me a clue.'

'They'll only act on proof.'

Ben smiled. 'My guess is that they'll not get it. Not enough to satisfy them. But more than enough to satisfy me. If it's Bowden and his chums it'll never get to court. Some toff will make a phone call and that will be it. But I don't want them in court. I want them on the wicket.'

Arnie shook his head. 'You can't win like that Ben. Win Helen and you've beaten the lot of them. Helen is what this is all about. Not being better than someone at cricket.'

'No!' Arnie's words tapped into some deep sense of justice in Ben. 'It's about those bastards being able to do this and get away with it.' He gave a harsh laugh. 'We grew up in different times, Arnie. My father died shot to pieces trapped on some wire because their fathers fucked it up.'

'Their sons died too.'

Ben looked at his great friend, noted the anger in him, and retreated. 'I know I'm bitter,' he said.

Arnie shook his head. 'You're worse than bitter boy. You're obsessed.'

Ben dried his chest with a warm towel. 'Aye, maybe.'

'I've been thinking. You could have sent Wolfie after the man who ran away. My guess is that he was made of less stern stuff than the big man. If Wolfie had hunted him down he'd have talked. Why didn't you do that, Ben?'

The young man shrugged his shoulders. 'I'd just been in a fight. They'd just tried to smash my hand. I couldn't think of anything beyond that I'd escaped. And I really wanted to frighten the big man as much as he'd frightened me. That's what I wanted more than anything. There were three of them, but really it was between him and me.'

Arnie said nothing for seconds as he digested the words. 'Aye maybe,' he said at last. 'It's just I've never seen you freeze like that. So, maybe you didn't really want to know who'd done it because that way you could blame the whole bloody lot of them.' He stared at Ben. 'Don't drag Helen into this. She's given up more than you'll ever know, so that she can be with you. If you hurt her, you and me are finished.' He turned his back on Ben and strode off angrily to the wicket. There was time to give it one more watering.

Ben stared after him. This was a side of Arnie he'd never seen before. He whirled his bowling arm over and felt the pain from his bruising. Still it was less than yesterday. The ice was working.

Ben stayed away from the nets that morning. Sawyer called at the cottage in the afternoon and asked about his health. Ben told him he would struggle for a couple of days.

Sawyer nodded. 'They're insisting that you play. Apparently the whole valley is coming to see you. If I win the toss, I'll bat.'

'Thanks.'

Sawyer grinned. 'Nowt to do with you, young 'un. My rules are simple: Always bat first in a five day game. There's some who look at the clouds and the pitch and put the other side in. They're just trying to be clever buggers.' He looked at Ben who was clasping a towel full of ice to his ribs. ' Brrrr! Rather you than me.' He left the cottage whistling tunelessly.

Boutilier summoned Helen to breakfast that morning and then sat in silence until the second coffee was served. Yet again he motioned for the servants to leave with a wave of his arm.

Helen looked down the long table at her father. Her brother was absent and now the servants were dismissed.

'I hear Linden was attacked on the moors.' His voice was stronger than yesterday.

'Yes. They were trying to warn him off me.' She stared at her father.

Boutilier's head rose sharply at her tone and manner. 'Good God, surely you don't think it was me!'

'Tell me it wasn't.'

He stared at her. 'Of course it wasn't. Three bungling

thugs from Yorkshire. The sheer incompetence of it. Oh yes, I know all about it. I have instructed the police officer to report directly to me.'

She knew he was speaking the truth. She remembered the time a fading film star had grabbed her breasts in a seedy night club. A week later he sent in a resignation letter to Ealing and shortly after that he was seen sporting two bruised eyes working as a porter at Kings Cross. Boutilier wasn't just ruthless, he was efficient. The men employed to beat up Ben were just hustling thugs who hadn't even bothered to scout their target, or they would have known about Wolfie. No, if her father had been involved, Ben would not be playing for a month, or maybe forever.

Inspector Lomax had spent the drive along the river road to Wolviston working out just what he should do. He was man of keen intelligence. He'd left school at the age of fourteen despite the pleas from his teacher that he should be allowed to stay on for a scholarship at university.

'University! University!' His mother had echoed the word as though it was a dirty book found under his bed. He was needed to put food on the table and that was that. He was destined for life at the local mill, and then one day, shortly after his eighteenth birthday, he stepped in when a constable was attacked by two drunks. He was a big lad and a week later an inspector called at his home.

'Policeman! Policeman!,' His mother had bleated the word out twice, though this time it was as if she'd found a pound note in his room, a cause of suspicion, but not necessarily a bad thing. A week later he joined the force.

It didn't take a genius to work out that the motive for the attack was probably something to do with Lady Helen. The trouble was, if he was right, what sort of tale would they tell? Not one that would do his career any good if it ever got out.

When he got the phone call from Lord Boutilier in person he felt like a man trapped halfway through a minefield, who was suddenly given the route out.

He would find out what had happened and then the buggers could do with it what they wanted. If everything went well his lordship would have reason to be grateful to him. Chief Constables were made on weaker patronage.

It was with new enthusiasm that he made phone calls to police colleagues in all the major cities in Yorkshire. The following day an Inspector Hollins called him from Leeds. They had three men, he said. Well known faces and two of them didn't look very well.

'Lift them,' said Lomax.

'On what charge?' the man from Leeds didn't like being bossed around by an outsider.

'Any bloody thing. Attacking a dog's teeth with an arm. Just hold them till I get there.' He sensed a surly silence on the other end of the phone. 'Look I've told you as much as I can. It's either me telling you nicely or your Chief Constable being rather rude. It's a delicate matter, but I can tell you that both our careers are on the line.'

Hollins gave Lomax an address. 'It's a house we use away from the nick,' he said. 'I'll have them there.'

Lomax's next phone call was to the great house where he asked to be put through to Lord Boutilier. He told him briefly of the progress he had made and then chanced his arm. 'I think I can find out what happened your Lordship, but I'm not so confident of getting enough evidence to bring the matter to trial.' Who was he kidding? Linden could identify them, then there were the tyre tracks, then there were the injuries. A jury of worthy people would hang them twice before breakfast. Lord Boutilier would know that too. Lomax held his breath. Boutilier spoke in a smooth, calm voice. 'I feared as much, Inspector, though between you and me it's probably for the best. However I'd be very interested to hear your thoughts after you have spoken to the men.'

'Certainly, Sir!' Lomax kept his voice level.

He listened, heart thumping, as Boutilier added. 'I am grateful for your efforts in this depressing matter, Inspector.'

Lomax took the afternoon train to Leeds and was met at the station by Hollins.

'Two have done a runner,' he said shortly. 'We've got the boss man.'

He drove Lomax to a rambling terraced house near the Headingly cricket ground. Lomax took in the litter strewn streets, the shambling, overgrown gardens and the rotting window frames. 'This the posh end?'

Hollins didn't reply as he pushed hard on the ill-fitting front door and then walked down a narrow, dark passage, past a flight of bare stairs, and into gloomy room at the back. He turned on the light, a single naked bulb. The big man was sitting at a bare, wooden table flanked by two large constables.

His face was marked with minor cuts and bruises. His dark greasy jacket hung off the right shoulder and his arm was in a pristine white sling that contrasted vividly with his shabby clothing.

'Name's Eric Boyle. We lifted him at the Royal.' Hollins spilled out some sovereigns from a purse. 'He had these. Said he's won them on a horse. Wouldn't say which one. He's the top tough guy this end of the city. If you hit him he doesn't blink for a week.'

Lomax leaned across the table. 'Who hired you, Eric?'

The big man gave him a hard stare.

Lomax looked at the wounded arm. 'What's the matter, Eric? Once bitten twice shy?'

One of the constables eased himself on creaking boots and started to chuckle. Eric gave Lomax another hard stare. Lomax stared back into the slit eyes. He looked past the cuts and bruises and noted the scattering of small scars on the face, trophies of past conflicts no doubt. Leeds was a big city and, like many parts of the north of England, was suffering hard times. There'd be plenty of men trying to earn a crust on Eric's patch and there wasn't room for all of them. If what Hollins said was true, Eric had served one tough apprenticeship and the hard man's stare wasn't a bluff; it was what he was. He'd told Linden that someone else was the leader. But, of course, that was balls.

'Got a dog, Eric?' The question surprised the big man. 'No.' he said, a little too quickly.

'Don't like dogs, Eric?' Lomax could see that Eric did not like dogs. 'Especially big dogs, Eric? They've got memories, you know.'

The big man shifted in his seat, but said nothing.

Lomax continued in a pleasant voice. 'I could take you to see a famous cricketer. Or I could take you to see a dog. A fucking big dog. I prefer the dog. They never lie. I'm guessing his heckles will go up at the sight of you and he'll break free of the lead I'm holding.'

Eric's slit eyes widened. Lomax smiled. Then of course you'd run and the dog, well, the dog would chase you because that's what dogs do.' Lomax's voice hardened. 'And you know what big dogs do when they catch you, don't you, Eric?'

The big man's eyes shifted nervously round the room,

seeking comfort from somewhere. He failed.

Lomax looked up at the policemen. 'Time for me to talk with Eric alone, I think.'

Hollins hesitated. Lomax smiled. 'Don't be fooled by my soft country burr, Inspector. I could take on a two-armed Eric, never mind this cripple, who I'm told was getting a hiding from Linden.'

'No I wasn't.'

Lomax laughed. 'God, Eric. If you had a brain you'd be dangerous. Pride goeth before a fall.'

The policemen left the room leaving the two big men together.

Lomax sat staring at Eric for a few seconds that seemed longer.

'Judges sit on different circuits, did you know that, Eric?'

Again there was no reply. 'There's a couple of judges who sit on the circuit where I work, who love their cricket. They've never met Mr Linden but my guess is that they talk about him every day. When they hear that you tried to bust his hand they'll make sure you appear in front of one of them. And when Linden tells how your chums held him down while you tried to smash his hand with a rock. Well, it's not cricket is it? Their only regret will be that they can't hang you. You and your friends will go to jail for a very long time.' He stared at Eric again and saw the bruiser's face slacken for the first time. 'On the other hand you could walk away from this. Give me a name and this won't even go to trial. It's not you we want.'

Miller was right. Ben was so fit and strong that his body repaired itself at a remarkable rate. On the afternoon before the match he walked freely along the drovers' road with Helen and Wolfie. Helen insisted that the dog went with him everywhere. He laughed at her caution, but agreed because he realised it gave her comfort.

They passed the rise in the road where she had abandoned him and she clung to him with surprising strength.

'Can you bowl tomorrow?

He nodded. 'Not fast, but quick enough. I'll be OK by the second innings. I'll get them then.'

'You'll get their wickets,' she couldn't hide the alarm in her voice.

'Yes,' he said.

She looked up from his side. He was looking straight ahead. Sometimes he seemed from another world.

Wolfie came bounding into view barking in great woofs. A tatter of bloodstained cloth fluttered from his mouth. She stared at the dog and felt a deep sense of foreboding.

Chapter Twenty five

They came in cars, carts, buses, and taxis from throughout the valley and beyond to the Boutilier cricket festival. The great event had been held twice a year since the war and during that time Boutilier's influence and rank had attracted some of the country's finest cricketers. However, the newspaper correspondents who, being experts, seldom agreed on anything, were adamant to a man that this year Boutilier had excelled himself.

The Gentlemen versus Players match had no official status, but the array of outstanding players meant that it had a rank in its own right. In deference to the quality of the two sides, it was announced that Lord Boutilier would not be appearing for the Gentlemen this year, though his son, Charles, would be allowed to bat as a twelfth man. However, he would not field or bowl.

Some seven thousand people crushed into Boutilier's ground on the first day of the match. Those first in claimed the hard wooden benches that ringed the ground and after that spectators lounged on grass slope that made an amphitheatre of the cricket pitch. The players wore the brightly coloured blazers of their counties over their whites.

Ben was conscious that at the last festival match his role had been to help Arnie flatten the pitch. Now he was strolling round the ground in his whites and a splendid maroon blazer.

Spectators called to him and burst into applause as he passed them, and he had to pause frequently to sign autographs.

The sun was hot and high and with luck would dry out the pitch by the time he was called on to bowl, though he suspected that Arnie would water it each night and bring on the heavy roller.

The day started well. Sawyer won the toss and gave Ben the thumbs up sign as he strolled from the square.

Ten minutes later the Players' openers began to attack the Gentlemen's bowling on a placid pitch as Ben sat in the small changing room with a bag of ice packed against his ribs. He endured this for half an hour and then went for another stroll around the ground.

He looked more like a boxer than a cricketer with the deep bruising on his face, but it mattered not to the crowd who rose in applause as he passed.

Arnie was sitting at his usual position for match days, on a low wall that enclosed the rollers opposite the pavilion. He nodded to Ben. There was a distance between them since their quarrel. Arnie was alarmed by the change in the young man since he'd left the estate. Ben thought his old friend had judged him harshly on little evidence and he was outraged at the way the old man had taken it on himself to doctor the pitch in favour of the batsmen.

He perched on the wall signing some more autographs, saying nothing until the last of the boys had departed.

'You're popular today.'

Ben watched the bowling for an over. Scarcely a ball got above pad height.

'I see you've had the water on.'

'Aye. Best to make a match of it.'

'Aye you've definitely evened it up,' Ben said in a low voice. 'Both the batsmen and the bowlers are complaining. The bowlers say there's no bounce and the batsmen say they're put off by the frogs on the wicket.' He smiled deceptively at Arnie.

'Cheeky young bugger!'

Ben's look hardened. 'Why are you helping that lot against me?'

'You know why.'

Ben got up and continued his stroll round the ground.

Bowden's friend, Giles Smallwood, was fielding at third man. Ben watched him carefully and noted that he ran in small quick strides. He was fast on his feet, and Ben knew, from his performance in the nets, that he liked to get on his front foot and turn the ball in the mid wicket area. Normally that would have been suicide against someone of Ben's pace and bounce but on this pitch he might get away with it. As Ben approached round the boundary, Smallwood took off after a late cut with startling speed and returned the ball with surprising power for a little man. He turned back to his position with a jaunty stride and spotting Ben called out, 'Morning, Linden. Looking a little battered.'

'I'll have recovered by the time you bowl us out. In fact I might have retired.' The spectators who heard the exchange started to laugh and someone called. 'Good on you, Linden. Watch it though, the little 'un's too big for his boots.'

There was more laughter at this and the little man glared at Ben, not bothering to disguise his contempt. Ben gave him a hard stare and moved closer. As he passed within a yard of the fielder he spoke in a voice low with menace. 'Remember this Smallwood: on a cricket pitch, we're your betters.'

One hundred yards away from her seat among the good and the great Helen clutched at Bunty's arm waking her from a snooze in her deck chair.

'What's the matter?'

'My God! I thought Ben was going to strike Smallwood.'

Bunty looked out across the pitch at the two men. 'Giles

Ferdinand Smallwood! Surely not. He's the only man in the world whose name is longer than his body.'

In spite of her alarm, Helen gave a laugh that turned heads from the cricket.

Bunty smiled. 'You're missing your Big Ben aren't you? Why didn't you call on him this morning?'

Helen shook her head. 'It wouldn't do before such a big match.' She gestured to a row of spectators, all wearing loudly coloured blazers. 'They've all come to watch him.'

'And who are they?' asked Bunty in a tone that suggested her ignorance of them was very much to their detriment.

'The England selectors.'

'Hmm.' Bunty peered at the row of elderly men noting that many of them were clutching flasks. 'God help us then. They all look drunk to me.'

Helen gave a peel of laughter and reached out and grasped Bunty by the wrist. But her eyes were not on her friend, or the row of distinguished gentlemen in childishly vulgar blazers: they were on Ben Linden. She'd watched him as he moved away from Smallwood with his cat-like walk, and now, as he passed the crowd of distinguished guests, his eyes sought and found hers and her heart gave an involuntary leap. She heard Bunty give a low whistle. 'My God, he looks as though he's going to leap the seats and straddle you.' She turned to her friend smiling. 'What a lucky girl you are!'

Helen didn't hear her. She was looking down at Ben's bruised face.

Four rows back Lord Boutilier watched his daughter and though he could not see her face he saw her body go tense at the sight of Linden and he knew then that he had lost her, that if the thugs had killed the young man, he would still have lost her. His immediate concern now was to convince his daughter that he had had nothing to do with the attack. Lomax had been particularly useful in this respect. He seemed to be intelligent, diligent, and above all discreet, a very useful man to have. He had given orders that, no matter what the circumstances, Lomax's calls were to be put through to him immediately.

The policeman had telephoned that morning interrupting Boutilier's breakfast, usually a capital offence. His soft valley accent pleased Boutilier. There was no attempt here to disguise his origins, to put on false clothes. Even so, he believed Lomax to be an ambitious man, and that made him easier to manipulate. Boutilier's father, a noted soldier, had once told him that the British Army was built not on clever Generals, but on loyal NCOs.

Lomax had told him that they had the leader of the group in custody and had offered him immunity from prosecution in exchange for information.

He had a tale to tell. There was not much meat to it, but Lomax believed that at least it was the truth.

Boutilier listened to the inspector in silence and then asked a few questions. He thanked the policeman handed the phone to a footman, left the remains of his breakfast untouched, and went to seek his daughter. She was not in her room and Wolfie was not in his great basket in the hall.

A footman opened the great French windows at the back of the house as he approached. He walked past the man without seeing him. The great parkland of the estate was laid out before him. He sat on a cushioned swing. The canopy was swept back allowing the sun to warm him as he looked out over the vast estate that had been the family home for more than nine hundred years. Perhaps he was dying. Certainly his family, as he knew it, was dying. The times were changing too fast.

He had never approached the great cricket festival with such foreboding. He feared the Gentlemen were about to be overwhelmed and that the Players would not be gentle in their triumph. Even the loyal Arnie soaking and flattening the pitch could not save them. Linden, or no Linden, the new men would be too strong. Loud, bawdy men in the main, they were kicking at the door of the established way of things and who knew where it would end.

Boutilier knew he could not control them. He could not even control his own children. He accepted, of course, that he couldn't command Charles not to be a homosexual. But the boy could have done more to hide it. He could have married well, had a son and then buggered every male in the county for all Boutilier cared. Helen had always been hell-bent on revenge for the way in which he'd treated her mother. Ironically, her mother hadn't cared if he'd whored his way through London, but that didn't fit in with Helen's own agenda, so she'd conveniently ignored it as she'd embarked on her own campaign of bad behaviour. And now she'd fallen in love. One couldn't choose who one fell in love with, of course, which in Boutilier's opinion made it a potentially perilous business. However, if she had been able to choose and consorted with the devil for advice, she couldn't have chosen better if she was out to wound him.

Linden had admirable qualities, but the world Boutilier lived in wouldn't see it that way if Helen took him for her husband. They'd not even see a great fast bowler. No, the sniggering crew of them would not look past a man pushing a cartload of chickens and eggs.

He was filled with a sudden exhaustion. The world was losing its sense of order and who knew when and how it would regain it. Cricket was merely a symptom of the illness, but one close to his heart.

As the players came off for tea, which was served on long tables in two separate marquees, Boutilier and his distinguished guests were taken in a fleet of limousines for a meal in the great hall at the house. Boutilier waylaid his daughter on the steps leading to the entrance. 'We need to talk,' he said. She looked at him, alarmed by the thinness of his voice. 'It's about the men who beat up Linden.'

Helen sat through the evening session boiling with excitement. She had thought briefly of trying to get a message to Ben so that they could meet somewhere in secret, but knew that it was more practical to wait until close of play. The Players batted on and on. They'd lost only three wickets by the end of the day and had amassed four hundred runs. Arnie's placid pitch had been very much to their liking. Sawyer came up to Ben in the changing room. He'd been batting for two hours and his face was red and wet with sweat. 'I'm going to declare at lunch tomorrow,' he said. 'How do you feel?'

'Better by the hour.' Ben threw his right arm over in a bowling action. There was just a niggle of pain. He had another sixteen hours, that should be enough time for him to be near his best.

He handed Ben a note. 'This is from Bunty.'

'You know Bunty?'

'Not in the Biblical sense, unfortunately.' Sawyer advanced on one of the steaming tubs.

Ben read the note twice. It was in Helen's neat style and merely said. 'Meet you at Jasper's place at seven. PS Bring your own ice.'

He changed slowly and then sat waiting for the crowds to disperse.

The sun was settling behind some large clouds as he

walked across the pitch. Arnie was out with his hosepipe.

He called, 'If Wolfie falls in you can get him out yourself.'

'Fuck off!' Arnie didn't look up, but sounded cheerful enough.

Ben strode on through the gap in the hedge, past his cottage, and up the slope towards the drovers' trail. She was sitting on the edge of the bracken on a tartan rug. He glanced about anxiously for any stragglers from the crowd. She seemed unconcerned. He sat beside her and she tilted forward to lay her head on his lap.

'My father summoned me,' she said. 'He has some news about your attackers.'

She felt his body move slightly.

He says they were hired by a man who came from London. He would be an agent, hired by someone else. The agent had connections in Leeds. They were meant to merely beat you up a bit. Not damage your hand. They lost their tempers when you hurt them.'

So what are you saying?'

'This is way beyond Perry and his chums. And Inspector Lomax doesn't believe we'll ever get proof of anything.'

'You mean he's been told to call it off by your father.'

He felt her breath in sharply. 'It's possible.' There was silence between them and then when she spoke her voice was sharp with anger. 'Look, I know it's a disappointment to you that Perry was not involved, but the fact is he wasn't. He's guilty of being a stupid and rude snob who feels threatened, but he's not a hirer of thugs. Nor are his friends.'

She looked down at him. He was staring at the distance, trying not to heed her words.

Her voice faltered. 'You know, Ben, you are in danger of becoming as bad as they are, except that they have got their upbringing as an excuse.'

She got to her feet and walked away slowly weeping softly. He stared after her but didn't call out.

She paused briefly by the cottage and walked on down towards the cricket ground. She found Arnie splodging about the wicket and hung her head against his chest. 'He hates us all, Arnie. Me too. He just doesn't realise it yet.'

Arnie held her to him.

Ben stayed sitting on the bracken until the sun drifted down behind the long dark forest to the west of the vast estate. He shivered in the gloom. He couldn't remember any of his thoughts and supposed he must have been dreaming. He rose wearily to his feet and walked stiff and cold to his cottage.

The following day he stayed in the dressing room while the Players batted on and on. Sawyer reached his hundred just before lunch and declared.

Ben ate nothing and said nothing during the meal, not even a word to congratulate his friend on his hundred. They walked out on to the pitch through the Players' gate, their studs scratching on the stone steps and then digging into the soft turf. He glanced across to the new stand. She was not there, and nor was Bunty. Their places had been taken by two elderly men in garishly coloured blazers, who were already dozing after a heavy lunch.

Sawyer approached him. 'Do you feel OK to open?'

He nodded and took the shiny new ball. The crowd murmured in anticipation as he paced out his run. He saw Arnie watching him from the pavilion steps chugging on his pipe; he heard the crowd murmur as he started his run, a murmur that rose to a roar as he approached the wicket. The batsman danced on his toes as he approached, moved his right foot across the wicket, but kept a sideways on stance and was as still as stone just before Ben released the ball. He'd done everything right except he didn't have the reflexes of a top player and the ball was in the wicket keeper's gloves as his bat was still coming down. Ben glared down the wicket but the batsman didn't meet his eye. Instead he advanced out of his crease and patted the wicket where he thought the ball had landed. Ben turned and walked angrily back to his mark. The crowd were baying in anticipation now, but Ben knew that the batsman's incompetence had made him look fast and he was at least a yard off his pace. Furthermore his back felt stiff.

He ran in again, straining for strength and rhythm. Again the ball went past the bat, again the crowd gave out a sound like a beast coming in for the kill, and again Ben returned to his mark angry with himself. Four more balls followed and still the opener had not put bat to ball. The crowd applauded wildly and he walked off to third man.

Arnie had done his work well; there was neither pace nor bounce in the pitch.

Warren opened from the other end, all surly that he hadn't been given first go with the new ball. This bloke Linden was quick enough, but he, Warren, was an England player, not some new man.

Warren stormed in all muscles and power and slammed the ball into the pitch. It cut off the seam and rose hip height, striking the bat and rising high over slips and third man for six. Warren stormed back to his mark muttering obscenities. Even a wicket off his fifth ball did not appear to appease his wrath. Bowden came in and played the last ball comfortably. Ben noticed his back lift had shortened. Someone had been coaching him.

Ben bowled another maiden and then, at the start of his

third over, Sawyer went across and had a word. 'You're trying too hard,' he said. 'Your run isn't smooth.'

Ben nodded. 'My back's stiff. I'm hoping the sun will get on it.'

'Do you want a rest?'

Bowden had taken a single off Warren's last ball and was taking guard.

Ben shook his head. The bait was too strong.

His run in had lost its glide and in place of the grace and power there were only straining muscles and sinews. He pitched the ball on off stump, though a little short and Bowden played a block shot off an angled bat, forcing the ball through the covers for four. Bowden smiled at the applause and turned to face the bowler once more. He blocked the next four balls and then used the pace of the ball to take a single to mid off.

The two men stood a yard apart staring at each other in naked hostility, like two dogs about to go for the throat. The umpire, sensing something was amiss, broke between them and thrust Ben's cap into his hand.

By now there was a puzzled buzz from the crowd. Linden had not sent any stumps flying and he appeared to be no faster than Warren.

Sawyer signalled for him to take a rest and he walked back to his fielding position at third man, defeated. His flowing run had deserted him, his back felt stiff, and his mind was in such turmoil over Helen that he was unable to analyse the batsmen's movements. He looked beseechingly across to the new pavilion and saw for the umpteenth time that she was absent. He felt empty and weak, unable to defeat, or even fight, his misfortunes.

Arnie was standing by the boundary and Ben moved to within a few yards of him.

'This is the worst I've seen you,' he said shortly.

Ben glared at him. 'It's like bowling on porridge out there, thanks to you.'

'It's not the wicket. It's you.'

Their altercation was interrupted by a shout from Sawyer. Bowden had cut Warren through the slips and the ball raced to the boundary fifteen yards to Ben's right. He raised his hand in apology. From one hundred yards away he could see Bowden's white teeth as he grinned at him.

He threw the ball in hard and flat so that it smashed the stumps a yard from the batsman.

He turned back to the boundary.

'What's going wrong?'

He turned his back to Arnie to concentrate on the next ball.

'You're behaving like an animal. There's no strategy to what you are doing. There's no thought.'

'What do I do?'

'Keep your temper for a start. You're running too fast to the wicket so you're losing your balance. Run in like you always have done.' The over ended and Ben was moved to sweep the mid wicket boundary. His replacement, a young medium pacer, found the slow pitch suited him better than the quickies. In his first over he took two wickets, one an away swinger, and the other with a ball that cut off the seam. Bowden was joined at the wicket by Smallwood and both men found the slower bowling to their liking because they were able to get on to their front foot.

The day drifted on and still Ben was not called back to bowl. One of the spinners bowled Smallwood who had made a quick fifty and wickets began to fall regularly, but not before Bowden reached his century.

By close of play the Amateurs were eight wickets down

and still more than two hundred runs behind. Bowden walked off raising his bat and Ben trailed some thirty yards behind him, adrift even from his team mates, and unnoticed by the crowd.

Sawyer took him by the shoulders in the dressing room. Both men were aware that a silence had fallen round them. 'You can't win every day, Ben. But what you can do is do your best.'

Ben thrust him away angrily. 'I'm trying my best, dammit.' He walked to the door slamming it behind him. It was only when he'd crossed the ground and burst through the hedge into the narrow lane that he realised he was still in his cricket clothes.

Back in the dressing room Sawyer grinned. He'd watched Ben boil in a hot rage all day. Tomorrow he knew it would be cold.

Warren started muttering about 'prime donnas' and young lads who had a lot to learn.

Sawyer turned on him. 'Ten bob says he takes five wickets tomorrow.'

By the time Ben had got to the cottage the sweat of the day was running cold about his body. His mother handed him some large rough towels that had been warming in the sun and he disappeared into the little bathroom that Jarvis had built on to the back of the cottage. He soaked himself for ten minutes, and then pressed the last of the ice that Helen had stored in their cold larder. It was almost gone and melted quickly against his warm body.

He towelled himself roughly, almost angrily, dressed and announced that if anyone called, which he doubted, he was going for a walk.

He hadn't gone half a mile towards the hills before he heard her horse coming at the gallop behind him. He turned and she smiled weakly. 'I heard you had a bad day.'

'Who from? Peregrin?' He tried to make a nonsense of the name but failed.

'Arnie, actually.'

He looked up at her. She seemed all haughty on her horse. 'I'm surprised you're interested. You couldn't be bothered to come today.'

She looked at him as though he'd slapped her. 'You expect me to dance around you after the way you've been behaving. I'm not your bloody servant. How dare you!'

He blinked at her, surprised by her sudden anger. She was not finished. 'You're not my lord and master,' she waved her arm seeming to him to emphasise her family's lands and largesse, and through that his own humble background. 'You've changed, Ben. You're riddled with rage and it's going to hurt yourself more than anyone else in the end.' She turned her horse so sharply that it reared and swung on its hind legs. For weeks now she had been the weaker of the two, bending her own life to suit him, so that he now took her for granted. She was in a boiling rage and leaned down and hissed at him. ' Perry and Giles didn't hire those thugs. And if you hurt them tomorrow, I'll get father to blackball you from cricket.'

She kicked her heels into Jasper' ribs and disappeared down the slope into the gloom of the narrow lane to the sound of clumping hooves.

He stared after her, shocked by her sudden venom. His world was collapsing too quickly to make any sense of it. He clutched his head in anguish. He had control of nothing except himself and his ability to be a great bowler, and for a day he had even lost that. Tomorrow, he promised, would be a different day.

Chapter Twenty Six

For the first time in years he felt the need to talk about himself to his mother, but she had gone to bed by the time he returned to the cottage. He knew what she would say: that no good could ever come of a romance across such a social divide.

He slept fitfully knowing that he had lost Helen. In the morning, he kissed his mother softly on the lips and strode down to the cricket ground in his flannels. Today he acknowledged the crowds with the slightest of nods. He said nothing in the dressing room as his team mates changed and they, mindful of the spat of yesterday, said nothing to him. He stared at Warren as though he was a practice match for his aggression. Even Sawyer avoided his eye. On the way to the wicket though, Ben approached his captain. 'Give me the ball.'

'Your ribs OK?'

'My ribs were always fine. It was in the mind.'

Sawyer stared at him. He looked like a handsome hard man from a gangster film with his hair slicked back from his high forehead. 'There's some looking forward to you failing,' he said quietly.

'So what's new?'

Sawyer tossed him the ball, knowing that all eyes were on them. 'Don't let me down,' he said.

Ben walked to the wicket and began striding out his run. Sawyer passed him on the way to mid off and watched him closely. There was none of the anguish of yesterday; instead he saw the cold intent of a man focussed on destroying the batsmen. He ran in smoothly and Sawyer saw the fingers go across the seam to take the pace out of the ball. It pitched slightly over length and Bowden leapt on to his front foot and drove it into the covers for four. The next three balls were slightly quicker but still pitched up, on, or just outside the off stump and Bowden stretched forward striking the ball cleanly. The crowd shouted their appreciation of the batsman's elegant stroke play. Sawyer said nothing; he could sense that something was going to happen. There was no discernable difference to the run-up, but this time Ben bowled close to the stumps with his body more square. The ball pitched just past half way down the wicket. Had Bowden gone on his back foot he could have played the ball chest high, but he didn't. He pushed forward seeking to play his cover drive and found the ball way too short and lifting off the flat wicket at incredible speed. He tried to turn his body out of the way of the ball, but was too late and was struck high on his hip. His scream was heard all round the ground as he fell wriggling in pain.

It was minutes before he was able to regain his feet and reach for his bat. The crowd applauded his courage as he resumed his stance. They saw Ben approach and say a few words and again broke into applause. The Times man later wrote that this was an intrinsically English scene, a display of courage from one player, and of sportsmanship from his opponent.

Out in the middle Bowden's perception was a little different. Ben walked to him and said in a low, even voice, 'Just as well it wasn't a stone, eh!'

Bowden stood astonished at the bowler's effrontery, but most galling of all, was the knowledge that he had been tricked into a playing forward and that the last ball had been at least two yards quicker than anything else he had faced during his long innings.

He flexed his hip and put weight on the front foot. The

pain wasn't as bad as he'd feared. He had nothing if not physical courage, and he gave Ben a hard stare as the bowler ran in. The next ball was probably quicker than the one which preceded it but this was pitched up in his block. He jammed his bat down but the ball squeezed under its base, and on to the wicket.

Huntingdon, the next, and final, batsman for the Gentlemen, had been famously described by the Manchester Guardian correspondent as 'easily the worst batsmen in county cricket since the war.' Just in case he had not got his point across the writer had added, 'Mr Huntingdon would be hard pressed to bat number twelve in most teams'. Ben bowled him with another yorker which Huntingdon never saw.

Bunty, who was sitting on her own in the dark recesses of the new pavilion, shivered at the sight of Ben's display. Even with her limited knowledge of the game, she could see that Bowden had been out-manoeuvred. As the players came straggling off the pitch Bunty turned in search of Helen, only to be told that she had stormed back to the house.

Ben sat in the dressing room, shirt off, packing some ice against the dark bruises on his ribs. Warren stared across the room at him and nodded when their eyes met. He knew as well as anyone else in the room that they had just witnessed an extraordinary display of fast bowling.

Sawyer came across to Ben grinning. 'How are you if we make them follow on?'

Ben shrugged. 'I feel fine. It depends whether you want the match finished two days early. There's people booked until Saturday from all along the valley. There's people up from London and Manchester.'

'Right. We'll not make them follow on.' The decision was

not popular throughout the dressing room as some of the professionals had been anticipating a couple of days off. They'd already been disappointed to learn that Boutilier had decided not to provide them with women this year as the match had attracted so much attention, he couldn't risk word getting out.

Ben clamped the ice pack to his ribs as he watched the batsmen preparing to go out. As usual there was a false jollity about the room. These men played to put food on the table. To them it wasn't a game, it was a means of making a living. And when their performance declined through age, or any other reason, they would have to find some other means of surviving in a harsh world. They were playing for higher stakes than were their opponents who would return to the stock market or some family business.

There was a sudden silence in the room that lasted for no more than a second, as the opening batsmen advanced from the dressing room out on to the pitch like gladiators into an arena. One day they would make the last walk into the sunlight, but not yet, not yet.

Ben moved beside Sawyer who was padding up. 'I need to walk off the stiffness,' he said. It was a lie and they both knew it but Sawyer smiled and said, ' Don't stray too far.'

Leaving the ground during a match was highly irregular, but Ben needed time on his own. Helen had gone, Bunty was in the dim recesses of the new pavilion surrounded by the posh people, Lizzie was in London and his mother was away on market day. He walked without thinking past the cottage and up the slope towards the drovers' road, that strange place that drew him like a place of worship. There was a gentle breeze, pleasant in the warm air, and below him he could hear the noises from the crowd drifting up to him like a soothing wave. So many of the pivotal events of his life had taken place in this strange empty place that it seemed appropriate that he should walk here when about to make the biggest decision of his life.

This match would be his last. His talents had earned him enough money to keep him for years, but at a terrible price. Helen was right. He had grown to hate the posh people to the extent that his own values had become distorted. His mother had been right. He couldn't live in Helen's world, sneered at by her friends, and she couldn't live in his, working like one of the servants who had surrounded her for all of her life.

He walked lost in his thoughts until he found himself standing by his makeshift wicket of long ago. The stick stumps had gone, as had the stones, and the divots they had made in the turf. Nothing remained but his memories and the most potent among them was the sound of Jasper's clumping hooves as he had swayed semi-conscious on the great beast and then the feel of her hand as it slipped beneath his trouser leg and held his flesh. He turned with tears in his eyes back towards the cricket match and as he walked down the slope, past the cottage, the sounds from the ground seemed to rise in mockery of him and of his dreams. He steeled himself. He had lost Helen and so he had lost everything, but by God he would win a cricket match in such a way that he would leave a mighty epitaph. He strode along the lane, behind the hedge that looped around the ground. If he could have bowled in that moment, he would have bowled so fast that all that had gone before would have seemed just a prelude. But he wasn't bowling, he was walking along a lane, out of sight of players and crowd. The question was: could he sustain this surge of strength until his moment came?

He made his way through the gap in the hedge and

walked towards the pavilion. There was something about his stride that the crowd picked up. As he walked around the ground he wanted his last day to live on long after he had gone.

There were two sides to his fame, the one where he was pestered by strangers, where casual moments were distorted to fit some erroneous mythology in the newspapers, and there was the other, where through his deeds, he could create his own world, where people would say, 'Were you there when . . . ' That was the side that drew him. To be the best he could be, and for that to be better than anyone else could be. That was a statement worth making.

The fickle crowd rose at the sight of him. He waved back to them almost in mockery. Two quick wickets and he was a hero again. He wondered what they would be saying by tomorrow evening. He passed Huntingdon who was squinting short-sightedly from the third man boundary. Ben smiled as he passed. 'Mr Huntingdon.' He had a natural respect for the quiet, clever man who played the game purely because he liked it. Huntingdon was a gentle man who could shrug off defeat like a change of clothes providing the match itself had been enjoyable. He was playing here among the best because he happened to be among the best amateurs in the country, but that was not his ambition. He could just as happily spend his days playing with friends on a village green. That was something Ben could envy in others, though he knew it was not for him. Ben enjoyed the game, but he needed something beyond that. He needed to win; he needed to be the best because his whole history and the history of his family was a story of struggle and conflict.

For the first time since he entered the ground he looked at the scoreboard. The Players were one hundred and three for one. He looked out on to the pitch. Both Bowden and

Smallwood were watching his stroll round the ground. He felt the elation of the huntsman. He would have his day.

Sawyer declared The Players' innings thirty minutes before the close, but Ben passed over the offer to open the bowling arguing that it would be better to give his body another few hours to recuperate.

His team mates noticed that his demeanour had changed; he seemed to be living in a world of his own, rarely speaking, and then never on casual matters.

He refused to drift off to the pub with the rest of the players, or even approach the great house for food and drink. There were some who said that the great Bradman was a similar sort of loner and that Ben was preparing himself for their great battle when the Australians came on tour the following summer.

As he served out the last minutes of the day's play in the deep, Ben glanced once at the new pavilion hoping to see Helen. Then, with cold resolve, he concentrated on his business, watching the batsmen closely as Arnie had taught him. Was he still when the ball was bowled? Where was his right foot when the bowler reached his delivery stride? Did he play down the line of the ball or move his bat out to in? Did his left shoulder keep him in line to play straight? In which areas did he try to score his runs? What were his favourite shots?

As he watched he felt the cold thrill of a card player with a good hand.

The two openers survived the six overs before close of play and walked off to polite applause. One of them glanced across at Ben as he skipped up the steps and the young bowler knew he was on his mind.

Ben changed in silence. Sawyer came across and patted him on the shoulder. 'Ready for tomorrow?'

Ben nodded and squeezed the older man's arm. 'See you tomorrow.' And with that he left the dressing room and walked out into the square. The pitch was rolled and flat waiting for another soaking. He didn't want it any other way. He hoped the wicket would remain as placid as it had for the previous three days, so that no one could have any excuse.

As he stood a lone straight figure in the centre of the pitch in the fading sun, Arnie watched him from the little pavilion and knew, as he always had known, that this was where Ben Linden belonged. The gladiator had found his arena, and it was as though the one existed for the other.

He found himself drawn to the centre of the ground. He nodded to Ben. Ben smiled and held out his hand which Arnie took warmly.

'You once told me that you put a ball through Grace's whiskers.'

'Aye. The Gentlemen match. He was way past his best and I was in my prime,' he said modestly.

'What did he say? The Doctor.'

'He said, "What's this then?"'

'And what did you say?'

'Me? I said nothing.'

'But you didn't bowl short again?'

'No.'

'So he made you bowl where he wanted. He could go on his front foot whenever he wanted and know there was no risk because you wouldn't bowl short.'

'Yes.'

'He tricked you then. He used his reputation to make you bowl where he wanted.'

' The Doctor was the Doctor.'

Ben looked at his friend and mentor and smiled, 'Times

have changed Arnie. They're not going to tell me what to do.'

'I saw what you did to that prick Bowden today. Helen's probably bathing the bruise on his bottom as we speak.' He turned to walk away but Ben caught hold of him. 'She's going to get me blackballed from the county game.'

'She said she wouldn't piss behind my pavilion when she was five. Then she changed her mind. She used to tour the gardens in a chauffeur driven Rolls when she was eight. But a few years on she was organizing a soup kitchen for workers' children in the Great Strike. She's as stable as a feather in the wind, but her heart's in the right place.'

Ben gave a deep sigh. 'Maybe. But you can't say that about her friends and family. They hate me, Arnie.' He looked at the wicket. 'How many gallons has Boutilier told you to put on tonight?'

Arnie smiled, but didn't take the bait.

Ben bent and felt the wicket. 'It's dried out again. I could have gone after them this evening, but I didn't.' He shrugged and turned to Arnie. 'Tomorrow's my last day.'

'Probably.'

'No Arnie. My last day. I'm packing it in. Tell his lordship not to bother getting me blackballed. I'm finished with cricket and with that lot.' He gestured to the great house.

Arnie stared speechless as Ben turned and walked away. He watched him push through the gap in the hedge and disappear from view. He stood there in the velvet light of the setting sun and couldn't think of a word to tell Ben, to tell Boutilier, even to tell himself. The boy would go. Of that he had no doubt, and with him the finest bowler he had ever seen.

Ben walked slowly to the cottage, half expecting to hear Jasper's thumping hooves. His mother sat waiting inside with a chicken stew filling the rooms with its aroma, and spuds bubbling in a boiling pan. He hadn't the heart to tell her he wasn't hungry and dabbled with the food when she laid it on his plate.

'I'm giving up cricket after tomorrow, Ma,' he said at last.

'About time,' she said. 'Daft bloody game.'

He laughed for the first time in days, but this only encouraged her.

'Where's it got you, eh? All the important people hate you. Strangers pester the life out of you. Gangsters want to beat you up, and your picture is plastered all over the papers. That's no way to live.'

'We got some money out of it,' he reminded her.

' I'll grant you that, though money's not all it's pumped up to be.'

'It is when you haven't got it.' He smiled. During the past year he had changed beyond recognition, but, it seemed, his mother had not changed by a comma. He admired her for it. At her age perhaps it was easier not to change.

He rose with the light the next morning. He left a brief note for his mother inviting her to watch him play. He knew she would give a little snort as she rejected the request. She had better things to do, though breaking the necks of chickens wasn't one of them.

He remembered how she had reacted to his imminent departure to become a cricketer. Playing games wasn't proper work, she'd said. Humping dead chickens on a barrow was work, and would remain so in her mind.

Games had never loomed large in her life. She'd taken him to church a week after she'd got the telegram and she'd knelt in the tall empty church, a bent, dark figure that frightened him with its frailty. He'd heard her pray, just the sounds, not the words or the meaning. She'd never spoken of that day, but much later, he'd known with sudden clarity, that she was praying to survive.

Outside the cottage, the air was clear and sharp, though he could see the mist lying like bad breath on the distant fields.

The rooster had been going for an hour and it stared at him cocksure from a fence post near the gate.

He was first in by an hour and he sat in the dressing room, staring out at the pitch, pressing some ice cubes to his ribs. They were half melted and a cold trickle ran down inside his trousers. He'd changed into his flannels by the time the first of his team mates came in, farting and yawning, with tales of drink and ribaldry from the night before. They were better than the Gentlemen and they knew it, to the point that they didn't believe they had to work at it.

He gave them a hard stare. God help any of them who dropped a catch off his bowling on this day. He was the youngest in the team by two years, but his prowess gave him an authority that only Sawyer could rival. Yes, they were on another planet to the other lot, but there was only one of them who could win the match in a day, and he was sitting in a corner giving them hard stares.

He wanted to be clear of them and rose suddenly from his seat and walked out on to the balcony.

'What's with him?' Warren motioned after the retreating figure.

Someone else said,' Don't care, so long as I don't catch it.' There was a brief laugh and then they forgot about the man outside.

The crowd were coming in dribs and drabs now and some called out when they saw Ben on the balcony. He nodded because it was the easiest thing to do and then walked round the back of the pavilion where he found a bench to sit on. He sat like a fighter, focussing his rage and then Sawyer came down the back stairs his studs scratching on the steps.

He sat heavily beside Ben and nudged him with his elbow. 'I've been speaking to Arnie.'

So he knew. Ben turned to his friend. 'Say nowt. Just give me the ball and we'll be finished by tea.'

Sawyer thought he had never seen such certainty in a man. 'Lunch,' he said. 'Lunch would be better.' He rose and walked halfway up the stairs. 'There's no arguing with you then? The season is over. Why not wait the winter and see how you feel?'

Ben shook his head. 'Time for me to move on. Don't tell the others.'

'The Aussies'll be pleased.' Sawyer stamped up the stairs and into the dressing room.

Ben got rid of the openers in his first three overs when the ball was still hard and had bounce in it. The first with a ball that reared short of a length, forcing the batsman to parry from chest height. The second, a Yorker that spat into the wicket, sending the bails flying like bullets.

That brought out Smallwood to join his friend, Bowden.

The little man raised his cap and said 'Good morning,' to the fielding side. Ben snatched the ball when it was lobbed back to him and strode fuming from the wicket. Sawyer chased after him. 'What's the matter?'

'Good morning, is it? I said "Good evening" to him once and he ignored me because I didn't belong with my betters. Well here, he's with his fucking betters, and he doesn't belong here.'

Sawyer stared, astonished by the outburst. 'Calm down, man. Concentrate.'

Ben was gripping the ball so hard his knuckles were white. Sawyer pointed at the ball in his hand. 'I hope you're going to remember to let go.'

Ben stopped at the end of his run. 'For the record this one's going to bounce head high outside his off stump. So if he wants to come down the wicket like a fucking matador he knows he'll get pinned.'

Ben moved in quickly and, though his leap to the wicket was long and low, his arm action was slightly higher than normal. Smallwood danced forward with nimble feet as Ben's arm reached the peak of its arc. The ball pitched halfway down the wicket and reared up outside the off stump. Smallwood should have left it alone, but his momentum took him towards the ball which flicked the peak of his cap and whacked into the wicket keeper's gloves. Smallwood stood frozen a yard outside his crease and, twenty yards back, the wicket keeper bowled the ball slowly at the stumps. Smallwood was still standing in shock when the ball removed the bails.

As Smallwood turned back to the pavilion Ben looked across to the main stand and was gratified to see Helen and Bunty in their seats. Well, he'd give her something to remember him by.

So involved was he in his own battle that it was not until he turned at the end of his run that he saw the incoming batsman was Jepson, resplendent in his Harlequins cap. The England Captain took his stance, his feet balanced about a foot apart. His long, lean head rested on his left shoulder as Ben began to run in.

The first ball was short, fast and on the off stump. Jepson moved his back foot to middle and off as Ben approached the wicket, but at the point of delivery his head and body were perfectly still. He shuffled a few inches into line of the ball and with no back lift played a dead bat and dropped the ball at his feet. He played the remaining four balls with similar lack of ambition and did the same the over after that. Ben had now bowled seven overs and Sawyer came across to him. 'Time for a rest.'

Ben looked across at the England captain, who'd seen him off and protected Bowden from his bowling. He smiled. 'I'll be back.'

Jepson nodded, 'I'll be here.'

'I hope so.'

They were both correct. Ben was brought back from the same end half an hour before lunch, and Jepson was still playing as coolly as he had at the start of his innings. The contest was more in his favour now. He had had time to play himself in and the ball was softer and the seam frayed so as to restrict bounce and movement.

Ben's favourite tactic in such circumstance was to trust in the pace of the ball through the air and pitch at the batsmen's feet. Jepson was on to him though and again blocked the first three balls. The fourth ball was slower and moved slightly away off the seam, enough to find a thick edge and run down to third man for a single.

Like Jepson, Bowden was well set, having just got his half century with a sweeping late cut off Warren's bowling. The correspondents had noted an improvement in his play from the previous summer. His back lift was shorter now and he played straighter than in his more flamboyant days at university.

Ben too had been watching him, noting that he still had weaknesses, one of which was a compulsion to hook short balls, almost as an act of bravado. One shot off the bowling of Warren had reared off the top of his bat over slips for six. Ben opened with a bouncer at three-quarters speed.

Bowden was on it with a swivel of his hips sending the ball high over the square leg boundary. The next ball was the same pitch and line but two yards faster, Bowden, possessed by the desire to kill the bowler, swung his bat but knew as soon as he played the shot that he was trapped. The ball hurtled down wicket to wicket rearing chest high. He ducked in alarm and wafted his bat to protect himself. He felt a blinding pain in his left hand and fell to the ground as the ball looped slowly into the wicket keeper's gloves. He had to be helped from the wicket, his face contorted with pain.

Boutilier's son Charles was next up and he lasted just two balls before Ben found his edge with a fast short ball that made him freeze. He walked from the wicket, some said, with an indecent haste.

Jepson farmed the bowling for the next two overs and then walked off for lunch with his bat tucked into his ribs like a baton, looking neither right nor left.

Ben had no desire to eat and he sat out the back of the small pavilion on his wooden bench feeling his ribs gently. There was no pain.

He heard her feet approach, the thin heels of her shoes tapping on the stone slabs. He saw the shiny dark blue shoes and her slim ankles coloured in peach stockings, but he didn't look up, not even when she said, 'You swine. You've broken his hand.'

'Aye well, he's got another one to hold you with.'

He felt the stinging slap to the side of his head and reeled at the sudden venom of her attack. He looked up angrily. 'You'll do that once too often.' He rose to his feet and she took a step back. 'You know nowt about cricket, Lady Helen.'

'What I do know is that I matter for nothing in your

mind when set against your insane desire for revenge. You've turned into a monster. I want nothing more to do with you.'

He watched her walk away. His mother had been right all along. No good could come of it. He turned slowly and stepped up the rickety stairs into the pavilion.

He took a further three wickets that afternoon, the last of which was Jepson's, shortly after the captain had reached his century.

The Gentlemen had come away from the match with two players scoring centuries, yet they had been routed by as ruthless a display of fast bowling as anyone could remember.

The Players, with no women to amuse them at the great house, had departed en masse to the pub and were halfway to getting drunk by the time Ben had iced his ribs and changed. Only Sawyer remained behind. They walked slowly across the wicket.

Ben knew why his friend had stayed with him. 'There's no changing my mind,' he said.

Arnie came out of the old pavilion where some thought he now lived. Before he could speak Ben said. 'I never bowled at them.'

Arnie smiled. 'I know.' He gave Ben a hug. 'Well, you showed them. Even Mr Jepson at the finish.'

'He's a great batsman,' Ben said. The three of them talked quietly about the match and then Ben, who throughout had been strangely subdued, left them saying he had things to take care of. They watched him stride away to his mother's cottage. Sawyer was overtaken by another thought, which was that his team mates were at least six pints ahead of him.

Chapter Twenty seven

Ben rose early in the morning, roused by the sound of his mother clattering about the kitchen, scolding the big tom cat she had taken in after finding a mouse in her cold store room. The cat had shown little inclination to chase after mice but it did enjoy attacking the paper spills she rolled to light the fire.

'Get off, you stupid bloody thing,' she wagged a spill at the cat which promptly pounced on the paper tearing it with its claws. His mother laughed like a little girl until she saw him at the door and then she rose from her knees, slightly embarrassed. 'I've boiled you some eggs.' She nodded to the table.

He told her he planned to set up a little business. He didn't know where or what. He needed to return to London. He wanted time to think.

He left his cricket kit and his clothes in his room and walked into town to the railway station along the river road. From time to time the lane swung right up to the river bank and he could see the round white stones on the dried-up bed; his practice balls, he'd called them. The station was almost empty. The visitors who had travelled to see the cricket match had left the previous evening..

He arrived in Kings Cross by lunch time, bought the *Evening News,* and was startled to see his picture on the back page, next to a report of the great cricket match. The correspondent described his performance as one of the most ruthless displays he had seen in the last ten years. He wrote: 'One assumes that Linden does not target the head and body of his opponents, but he comes perilously close to being accused of doing so.' Ben threw the paper angrily into a bin and walked away. He had begun to despise the majority of the cricket writers. He remembered the same correspondent giving Arnie the benefit of his views in front of the pavilion. The veteran cricketer had listened solemnly, and then destroyed him with a wink.

Ben stormed out in front of a taxi. The driver was about to yell abuse, and then he recognised the man who was hailing him.

His flat had a hollow feel to it, even with the sun shining through the front window. Dust danced in the sunbeams. He tried to shrug off his sense of gloom. He told himself that a new life beckoned him; he had money and he was young. But these thoughts were blown away by the sight of a stocking she had left hanging over her kitchen chair. She never had got used to the idea that someone was not five minutes behind her picking up everything she dropped. He went through to the bedroom and began putting her clothes and soaps and scents into the dainty case she had brought to his home. His resolve reeled with regrets and the rooms seemed emptier than before. He pulled himself away from the moment. He told himself that, as he stood here with her ghost, she and her father were probably starting their campaign against him.

He slumped at the kitchen table his head heavy in his hands. The wooden chair wobbled. How many times had she asked him to level off the lengths of the legs? He needed to get out of his flat, and to never return

That afternoon he took her belongings to Bunty's apartment. Bunty was wearing her silk kimono which she called a dressing gown. She yawned heavily, but then stared at him as though he was a specimen in a zoo. She said she knew about his row with Helen.

He held out the case as confirmation. Bunty recognised

the soft leather. 'Oh,' she said. 'I rather hoped it was just Helen in a temper.'

'She's trying to get me thrown out of cricket. She and her father.'

'She said you were trying to hit Perry and his friend.'

He shook his head. 'No. I wasn't. I just stopped them from going on their front foot.' He could see that Bunty didn't understand. 'It doesn't matter. I've got a story for you. I'm quitting cricket.'

Even Bunty understood the significance of this. 'But why? Helen doesn't mean what she says. She always falls well short of her fury. She'd never try to end your career.'

Ben shrugged. 'That she even considered it is enough. Anyway she needn't bother now.'

'But why?'

He gave a harsh laugh. 'Come on, Bunty. You've seen the way they treat us. You've had some of the same.'

They looked at each other and both began to laugh. He gave her a hug. 'You've been a good friend, Bunty. Don't make the quotes too outrageous. That's all I ask.'

The Wagnerian maid came down the spiral staircase with Bunty's breakfast tray. She smiled at Ben. Apparently, she had read about his attempts to kill the gentry and approved.

'What are you going to do?' Bunty stroked his arm.

He shrugged. 'I don't know. Maybe go away on my own for a while. I'm selling the flat and moving out of London.' He was aware that his thoughts were so wild that he was giving one plan to his mother and another to his friend.

'And what about Helen?'

He looked down at the floor. 'You know that can never happen. She hates me now. And anyway her father, her friends, her whole world, apart from you, would turn their noble backs.'

'Well, what about me? You can't just disappear from my life and banish yourself to some dreadful place in the dreadful provinces.'

'I know that in the dreadful provinces there's little chance of me coming across some sleazy film star, or some night club drug dealer, and all the other wonderful people who inhabit your world. But there are other consolations.'

The arrow hit home and Bunty wrapped the kimono tighter round her body. 'I'm not bored here, Ben. Boredom is my one great fear. So, not being bored is good enough until I can find something that engages me more.' She looked at him. 'But you. You were born to play cricket. You have already found your place.'

'There are too many true enemies and too many false friends.'

Bunty tied her belt into an elaborate bow. 'Absolute nonsense,' she said with a sniff.

'Huntingdon says there's a cottage I can have on his estate. It's in Northumberland.'

'Good God! That's at the other end of the country, isn't it?'

He smiled, 'They don't play much cricket up there. They won't know me with a bit of luck.'

He held out his hand and she took it and pulled him onto her. She clung to him. 'Send me an address,' she whispered.

He left her with a heavy heart for he knew that, despite their different circumstances, they were fellow travellers.

He wanted to say one more goodbye: to Lizzie. He took a cab to the ground, only to be told she was not yet at work. He scribbled a note, and left by the back of the pavilion. Suddenly, Lizzie appeared across the road on the arm of a young man in a flat cap. She waved hello to him and he waved goodbye to her. She disappeared round the corner. Their paths would cross again someday. That was the basis of their friendship. They were passing ships. They didn't throw hooks to haul each other in.

Back at the flat, some coherent plan began to form. He needed to disappear quickly because once Bunty's story got out, the world and his mother would be after him.

He caught the train to Wolviston and spent a last night at his mother's cottage. In the morning he picked up the drovers' trail. He carried a mighty pack of sandwiches, a large flask of water, a change of clothes and a toothbrush in a rucksack. His mother had stitched a little pocket inside to hold the medal safe. Her eyes were large suddenly. 'He'd have wanted you to have it.'

He headed north. The trail was pockmarked with the hooves of the Sniper's beasts and littered with crusts of dung.

It was on the second day that he saw him, standing still, next to his pony, as his dog, bored with the lack of beasts, chased sky larks. The three figures were silhouetted against the bright sky line, the last position in which you expected to find John Bart.

The Sniper hadn't seen him in years, but knew him in a second. 'You move the same,' he said with a sniff. His eyes were hidden under the broad-brimmed hat, but Ben could see the face had thinned and the lines were deeper. The long gun case was still at his back. The Sniper reached into a pack that was strapped across the pony and pulled out a small wooden carving. Ben started at the sight of the sniper peg from all those years ago.

'You nicked it, John Bart.'

The Sniper smiled showing strong white teeth. 'Sorry,' he said. 'I was going back, and suddenly, I felt sure, that if

I took the peg, I would survive. I needed that peg like some need a Bible.' He looked at Ben expecting him to laugh. 'Maybe it worked eh?' He held out the peg. Ben took it and then he reached into his rucksack and held out the medal.

'He'd have wanted you to have it.'

The Sniper shook his head at the offering. 'Don't like their medals. Nor did your dad. Throw it away Ben.'

Ben shook his head. 'I can't. I need it to remember his worth. My worth.'

'You already have his worth, and your own worth.'

There was a silence and then Ben told him of his decision to quit cricket.

The Sniper sniffed again. ' Going north?' He moved back towards the pony and they sauntered over the soft turf.

Ben remembered telling Helen that the drovers' road was no man's land, a place where they could meet as equals. Fanciful stuff! He smiled and then glanced at the figure of the man in front of him, moving with slow certainty, and he remembered that, not so long ago, John Bart had plied his trade in his own no man's land, where everyone had lived or died by their own skills.

They moved north for two weeks. Progress was slow. The Sniper made a detour at each town to deliver perfumes, stockings and trinkets he'd bought to order, using the cash from the sale of his beasts.

Often he didn't speak for hours which suited Ben's mood. Once he turned to Ben and said suddenly, 'This is not the life for you.'

'It seems a strange life for anyone.'

The Sniper shrugged. 'It was either that, or back to the gangs. I'm best on me own.'

Two days later they parted. The Sniper headed north to Dumfries and Ben turned east to Bamburgh and Huntingdon's vast land.

Chapter Twenty eight

Now that Ben was gone from the estate, Helen felt free to ride the trail every day with Wolfie woofing his way into the wild hills. Sometimes the wind brought tears to her eyes, sometimes it was her memories. She had spoken to no one about his departure, no one except old Arnie. She was startled to find that his interpretation of what they had seen was very different from her own.

She had watched a sleek, ruthless bowler of incredible speed almost kill two of her friends. No. No. They were not her friends. Perry was the boring, posturing golden boy who had buggered about with her brother, and Smallwood was the breast –biting, potential rapist whose father had bought him out of trouble all his life, and who had shown a psychotic lack of remorse for any of his excesses.

Arnie had not known the personal details about the men, but he did know cricket. He'd told her that basically what had happened during the match was that 'Ben had shown them that they were two posh sods who didn't belong on the same field as him.' He'd sucked on his pipe. 'Pardon my French.'

She'd smiled. 'You don't know a word of French.'

He'd nodded. 'But I do know cricket and I'll explain to you if you want to hear it.'

'Go on.'

'They both like to get on to the front foot, which they can do against most bowlers. Bowden likes to hook as well. All Ben did was deny them those shots. He said basically: "You'll play off your back foot and you won't hook me either." Your friends almost got badly hurt because they're two arrogant fools who think they are better than they are.'

It was the longest speech that Helen had ever heard from Arnie. 'He knocked Smallwood's cap off. He could have killed him.'

'Because the stupid little man charged down the wicket at the fastest bowler who's ever lived. Ben never bowled to hit him, that ball pitched outside the off stump.'

'He planned to hurt them.'

'Maybe at one stage he did. But he saw sense. When he bowled at the match he intended to intimidate them. It's the modern way. The problem is that Ben is much faster than anyone else. He bowled the same to Jepson. The difference is that he belongs on the same pitch.'

Arnie had sucked on his pipe seemingly unaware that it was not lit. 'Have you ever considered, Helen, that all he is demanding is the right to be treated with the respect he deserves? He's one of the greatest bowlers who's ever lived. He's used on the cricket pitch where he's useful, but off it they turn their upper class backs on him. They make him change in a different dressing room, walk on to the pitch by a different gate. They make him stay in the humblest rooms at the hotels, or lodging houses, take buses instead of taxis. As he sees it his father won a Victoria Cross, gave his life for his country, and this is how his country treats him.'

He looked up and saw that Helen was crying softly.

'You can't accuse me of that. Not once I got to know him.' She wiped her eyes. In the schism that existed between herself and Ben since the cricket match, she had come to realise that the real core of contention between them wasn't the hostile bowling; it was something much more profound. She blurted out the thoughts that had lain in ambush at the back of her mind. 'Whatever the rights and wrongs of all of this, he was turning into a monster. He was obsessed with the injustice of it. And that became a stronger emotion than anything he felt for me. There were times when I wasn't a person to him. I was one of the posh people. Snobbery works two ways, you know.'

Arnie said nothing.

'He just took me for granted, Arnie. I can't forgive him for that,'

She rose to her feet. He watched her sad figure stride away across the cricket field, and up the long slope towards the great house.

The long velvet notes of the clarinet rolled out like a call from the lost through the haze of smoke. Bunty inhaled deeply on her cigarette as her eyes worked the room. She'd never liked Freddie's; it was too sordid. On almost every night she had been there she felt she could have taken a photograph and entitled it, 'And Two Minutes Later the Orgy Started.' Bodies leaned into each other on the dance floor, hands slipped under clothing, legs rubbed under tables, and all to the background of talk charged with love and lust as the notes from Freddie's clarinet glided out like a siren embracing them all, intoxicating them, and enticing them with yearning for something less empty.

Bunty watched Helen staring into the gloom. She'd hardly spoken since arriving on the evening train, and Bunty knew from past experience that this was a bad sign. Helen had not asked a question, not even when she saw her little case that Ben had left. 'Let's go out,' she'd said at last.

'Where?'

'A club.'

'Which one?'

Helen had shrugged. 'Something seedy.'

'Seedy?'

'Yes. The seedier the better.'

Bunty had stared at her friend. She looked exhausted but fuelled with a desperate energy. Bunty had guessed she had had little sleep but she knew it was pointless to argue when Helen was in this mood. She rose from the couch. 'Come on, then.'

And that was how they came to be in Freddie's. Bunty sought sight of a friendly face in the subdued lighting of the club. She failed. She knew from past experience it was only a matter of time before Helen walked slowly to the dance floor to become the object of the collective lust from all the men in the room as she danced, hands clasped above her head in a slinky coil. Usually she walked away unscathed, but Bunty knew that tonight was different; Helen was past flirting with danger, she was ready to embrace it.

'This is not a good idea,' Bunty said coolly.

'And what is that? Helen sent a gray spume of cigarette smoke into the grey cloud that hovered from the ceiling. Her honey-blonde hair hung in natural coils to her shoulders which, together with her large, wide eyes, gave her a wistful, fragile appearance. Bunty knew this to be an illusion; she recalled the first time she had watched the slight figure, dressed in men's hunting clothes, riding Jasper. It seemed impossible that someone so small could control something so large, but she had, without fear or doubt, in the manner of a person who had been born to it, which of course she had.

Even so, Bunty knew how to deal with the little girl in Helen. She moved her arms suddenly to catch Helen's attention. 'Well, speaking purely from my own point of view.' She paused and saw that Helen was listening, 'The only reason that I didn't try to screw Ben Linden was that I knew you were in love with him.'

'Yes, I WAS,' Helen attempted a yawn.

Bunty overcame the urge to reach across and slap her friend and, with great effort, kept her voice steady.

'WAS? WAS? Well, that had better be WAS. Because once you get up on to that floor and play your role of the lost innocent girl, you'd better be damned sure you're right.'

'I am right.'

'I don't think so. If you were, there would be no need to go through this nonsense.'

Dammit Bunty! I know myself better than you. We're finished, Ben and I.'

'So you won't mind if I pursue him myself then?'

'Not at all.' The hesitation in Helen's voice made the words sound false.

Bunty took heart. 'Fine then, get on with luring these dregs. But know this: When you wake up in the morning with someone whose name you can't remember, there's no going back.'

'What do you mean?'

'I saw Ben shrug off the attentions of dozens of women when he first came to London because he loved you. But the trouble with faithful men is that they're less likely to shrug off the indiscretions of their partners. He'll never trust you again, you see. And he needs to trust. So come the day when you go sobbing back to him begging forgiveness, well, it'll be too late then. The sight of you will merely remind him of his misery, and he'll probably be physically sick, hopefully over you, because you'll certainly deserve it, you bloody little fool.'

Bunty feared she must appear ridiculously pompous. There was a positive however. Helen wasn't speaking. In fact she avoided looking at Bunty and stared out on to the dance floor. Bunty decided to play her last card. 'I'm not sitting here and watching you wreck your life. I'm leaving.'

And then she was out on the street. A sudden shower had cooled the air and the street lights danced on the damp paving stones. She walked slowly away from Freddie's, aware that she was also walking away from her greatest friend. Then she heard the clop of high heels and suddenly Helen was clinging on her arm, her head buried into Bunty's fox stole.

'You're wrong about me loving him,' she said. 'I think I hate him.'

'Hate will do for the moment.' Bunty waved at a cab.

'But you're right. It's belittling to randomly seek sex for revenge.'

Bunty clasped Helen's little, cold hand. 'Revenge? Revenge for what?'

'He's hurt me, Bunty. To the heart.'

'Yes, he has. And he has been very foolish. But you can't believe that he planned to.' She put a finger to Helen's lips. 'Let's leave it there for the moment.'

As they settled in the back seat of the cab, Bunty looked at her friend and smiled. She recalled a columnist's description of the flapper girls from almost ten years ago. 'They dance until they're dizzy and then they dance some more, ever closer to a half-seen edge, not caring of consequences, a state which they see as a sort of freedom.'

Despite Helen's protest, Bunty believed she had saved her from herself. But for how long? She knew her friend was hell-bent on something.

Chapter Twenty nine

Far from sinking into his illness, Boutilier seemed to be regaining his strength. He was up walking every day now, his eyes bright and alert, fuelled by the fight ahead. Ironically, the stronger he got the weaker his arguments became to Helen. She walked slowly to her room leaving a trail of clothes to her bathroom. She ran the water and crossed to the window where she stood naked, looking out from her vantage point over the great estate.

Her grandfather had had the elms chopped down at the end of the paddock to afford an uninterrupted view over the rolling fields and across the valley. It was the canvas for much of her life: the road where she had been driven as an eight year old pretending to be queen, the pavilion where as a five year old her uninhibited toiletry habits had been interrupted by Arnie, and the paddock where she had first mounted a pony. She could have stood there all day and not repeated one memory. She could hear the taps rushing and guessed the bath was near to full. She stayed at the window as her mind fixed on something out of sight. Down in the long sweep of the land, hidden by the alder bushes, lay the remains of the old river where Ben had startled her horse and she had struck him with her whip, and in the valley beyond that, still out of sight from the window, the flat strip of turf by the river bank where she had watched him run with such grace and beauty.

She ran white and nimble to turn off the bath, dressed quickly and marched down on the great hall. .

The huge fire was crackling already. As a child she had stood in the fireplace and tried in vain to see up the chimney. Martha, her nanny, had told her stories of children who long ago had to climb the chimneys to clear them. 'But not you, my darling,' she whispered as the child's eyes had widened with terror for surely there were monsters up there in the dark.

She'd been wrong. The monster was there out in the open, spread over the huge mantelpiece, a stretching legacy of shields and names that filled the framed glass for forty feet or more. And at the end of the frame, her brother's name and then her own.

She hated it with ascending anger. Why not attach the names of the thousand prostitutes or serving girls her father and his ancestors had enjoyed over the centuries? Her father had endured her ranting. He'd told his friends that his daughter had spirit. She'd vote socialist for a couple of years and then she'd see sense. 'We all do. We all do.' He'd laughed gently and so had his friends.

As she locked the great door that guarded the hall she felt a clarity of purpose. She could hear the muffled clatter of crockery as the servants prepared breakfast down the passageway. The gardeners too were up, mowing the long lawns to the percussive sound of Big Bella, the burliest of the downstairs maids, beating dust from Wolfie's muddied rug.

Helen put a chair against the wall at one end of the fireplace and unhooked the frame, working her way to the centre until the weight of the glass and wood brought it smashing down, splintering across the oak floor. She plunged her hands into the broken glass, tore out her name, and threw it into the flames.

She heard herself laughing wild as a witch, heard the servants knocking on the door; and most pleasingly of all, heard her father calling, pleading. She noticed her blood on the key as she unlocked the door.

She confronted her father as he stood stiff with shock surveying the damage.

'Damn you and your stupid bits of paper!' She rushed past him. The bath water was still warm.

Boutilier left the great house for his flat in London the following day. He said only one thing to Helen, but it gave him savage pleasure. 'Your peasant lover will never play again.' As he stormed from the room he had time to note the shock on her face.

From his apartment in St John's Wood, he telephoned Lowther's secretary to arrange a meeting at Lords ground the following day.'

'Can I ask what it is about, your Lordship?'

'No.' Boutilier replaced the phone. 'Impertinent lackey.' He was sure that Lowther would come as summoned. The filthy little Jew would find the importance of the host and the venue too much to resist.

So it proved and prompt at three o'clock Boutilier ushered the business magnate through the historic Long Room with contrived indifference and into a small office past the dressing rooms and up one flight of stairs.

Lowther was becoming increasingly irritated. First the arrogant call and then Boutilier had taken his proffered hand as though he was grasping a wet fish. He was under no illusions about Boutilier's motives, and that his own role was merely to form some cog in a plan. Even so, Boutilier's opening statement took him by surprise.

'Linden is to be blackballed from cricket after his disgraceful performance at the recent match on my estate.'

'I don't know much about it. I wasn't invited,' Lowther said cuttingly.

'Selectors only, I'm afraid,' said Boutilier, knowing that was Lowther's exact ambition. 'However, I am sure you will have read about the controversy.'

'And why should this concern me?'

'Because you have a certain influence with a number of newspaper proprietors.'

Lowther's dark eyes glinted with menace. 'I think you exaggerate, Lord Boutilier.'

'No I don't.' He reeled off a list of four names, all new-money men. 'I can go into great detail if necessary.'

Lowther's large face tightened. Why was Boutilier going to all this trouble?

The answer wasn't long in coming.

'When the news becomes public I don't want these sensationalist rags starting some Bolshie campaign in support of a man who could have killed two fine young men.'

Boutilier and Lowther were sitting across a small dark table. From outside came the pleasing sound of bat on ball at the Nursery end. Lowther was in the inner sanctum of the great game. He had dreamed of sitting here at the centre of power, and the reality was he'd been invited here to be a lackey. All his loathing for the men who had mocked and thwarted him distilled into pure hatred.

He gave a harsh laugh. 'And why should I help you, Boutilier, in your futile escapade? Why should I help you and your chums who told spurious lies about my family; you and your foolish friends who want to lock everyone out of your little club? Why should I help you in your futile efforts to stand against time?'

'Because if you don't you will certainly go to jail.' Boutilier reached into the desk drawer and pulled out a green folder. 'I have here a report from a police officer who investigated the attack on Linden. I have also a subsequent report from a private detective who followed up certain leads and obtained a statement from a Mr. Jacobs, who lives in London, but who, as you know, has connections in Leeds.'

Lowther tried to keep his face impassive but his mouth felt dry. 'Why on earth should I have the boy harmed? I have been his greatest supporter.'

'Oh yes, you gave him money to let him loose among his betters hoping he would create a scandal. But when you discovered he was having an affair with my daughter, it was an opportunity too good to miss. Working class bowler warned off by hired thugs. The stuff of dreams for your seedy newspaper friends.' He paused, aware that Lowther had been too shocked to attempt an interruption. The two men looked at each with mutual loathing. 'The trouble was that the thugs lost their tempers, and it went too far. It became a police matter.'

Lowther glared at Boutilier, but he knew the aristocrat wasn't bluffing and that, in this fight at least, there was nothing else he could do. At least now their hatred was out in the open. In future there would be a frank exchange of views and Lowther had little doubt that his arguments would prevail. He contented himself with an opening salvo. 'This isn't really about Linden himself, or your daughter. You and your kind are frightened of him, or rather of what you imagine he represents. There's a new world coming, one based on merit, not class and privilege. Cricket is merely a microcosm of that.' He rose stiffly from his chair and walked away.

Ironically, after all his efforts, Boutilier's plans to wreck Ben Linden's career were overtaken by events. Bunty's article announcing Ben's retirement meant there was no longer any need to mount a campaign to vilify him.

Instead, under Boutilier's direction, the Establishment gave a muted, but dignified, defence against complaints of unfair treatment.

The fastest bowler in the history of the game had walked away. Some of the more conservative papers likened Ben's disappearance to desertion, with the Australian team set to visit the following summer.

Ben himself was alarmed by the furore, eloquently described in Bunty's letters to him. His replies to her, which she quoted in her articles, dwelt on a single theme. He had only ever asked for one thing: to be treated with the same respect off the field as he was on it.

Boutilier joined in the debate both in public and private. In public he used coded language. He accused Linden of reckless bowling, of taking intimidation too far; of displaying a desire to win at all costs that was not the spirit of the game.

In private he used more direct language. Linden, he said, had deliberately set out to hurt his betters, driven by a hatred of the upper classes. Yet, it was those very same classes who had given him the opportunity to excel.

For a while the power of his position rather than the power of his arguments held sway.

And there the debate would probably have faded to be replaced by other topics, had it not been for the tour of the Australians the following summer.

Sawyer was the first to lift his head above the trenches. Safely ensconced as a professional with Pilkington in the Lancashire League Club, he told the Manchester Evening News correspondent that he had seen his new teammates play in the nets and they had limitations. 'Would you set a man like Ben Linden to bowl to them in a match?' he asked. 'The simple answer is No. He's just too fast. But the same is true for the Gentlemen. However, they own the game so they want him to bowl to order so they can still play. The simple truth is that he is far too fast for them. Most of them just aren't good enough to face him. There was no intent to hurt them; the aim was to intimidate them, but that is the nature of fast bowling. It's dangerous.'

Ben remembered Huntingdon's face when he showed him the article. 'A reporter's concoction, if ever I saw one,' he said. 'Intimidate! Sawyer has a vocabulary of fifty words, and a least half of those are unprintable.'

Ben laughed. 'Maybe, but between them they've summed it up quite well.'

Huntingdon had given Ben an empty cottage on his father's land near the Northumberland coast. The previous occupiers, a shepherd and his wife, had lived into their eighties and then died within weeks of each other, a common occurrence, Huntingdon told him.

The remote cottage suited him while he took stock of his life. He lost himself in the vast estate. He took to running over the round Cheviot Hills, pausing on a peak to look along the soft valleys where ancient peoples had once lived in their thousands, seeking the sanctuary of the hills from the beasts below. When the farmers and shepherds saw his distant figure moving as smooth as a bead over the rich grassland they he told him that he should run in the great fell races in the west. But Ben only smiled at such an idea. The last thing he wanted at that time was to be in the public eye once more.

In addition to his running, he joined the estate workers chopping trees or digging thin drainage trenches across the sprawling fields. At first the men had looked at him in suspicion. This was not cricketing country and they knew him only as a friend of the great family. They could not comprehend why he should want to join them. But as the days went by and he worked with the best of them they came to respect him. Some days he drove himself to exhaustion so that when he returned to his cottage he could flee into sleep and from the haunting memories of Helen. He thought of her every day. At first the cottage had been a sanctuary, but, as time passed, he realized he had to move on.

The turning point came when Bunty ambushed him in her fourth letter. Without warning she broke off from giving him news of her life in London to warn him, 'She'll not come to you, Ben. You must realise you took her for granted. That was unforgivable after her own sacrifices. Sorry, but I've got to say this, even if it means the end of us.' That was the only letter he kept. He carried it with him in his battered wallet and every day it called to him, numbing him with a strange power as he read it. It took him a week to reply in his careful neat hand. 'Bunty,' he wrote, 'Please help me to get her back. I don't know what to do.'

He retreated from the letter box like an accused man waiting for the jury. When he arrived back at his cottage he could remember nothing about the walk. His gate was ajar, which was unusual and in the porch lay a pristine copy of The Times. Huntingdon had left a brief message above the masthead in his sprawling hand. 'Thought page 32 might be of interest.'

He turned the pages in chunks. Huntingdon had drawn an arrow in heavy pencil directing him to the headline 'England Captain declares himself a modern man.'

The article consisted mainly of an interview with John Jepson who said that in future his county would no longer follow the custom of having separate dressing rooms for Gentlemen and Players, nor would they have separate gates. Furthermore selection to the county side would be on merit only. Indeed they had already gone some way down this road by refusing to allow members to play for the county as a matter of right during their university vacation.

He hoped that this modern approach would find support elsewhere. No doubt there would be many complications and arguments ahead, but his overriding belief was that the game had to change. He had no doubt that many people would be adversely affected, but the public should take comfort from his belief that most of them would be Australians.

'About bloody time!' Ben chucked the paper into a corner and made himself a sandwich from the ham he had bought during his trip to the village.

He slept fitfully and was awoken by the sound of a tooting horn. Huntingdon was waiting in his car. As he climbed in the passenger seat of the little Morris he noticed the gleaming, mahogany gun case on the back seat. 'Off for a day's slaughter are we, Hon?'

Ben occasionally referred to Huntingdon as 'Hon' in mocking reference to his status.

Huntingdon took his revenge by driving towards the coast at an alarming speed along the winding lanes.

Ben gripped the dashboard trying to control his concern. 'I thought you said this was just a runabout car.'

'It is. It runs about sixty on country lanes.'

Ben smiled in spite of his nervousness. 'Where are we going?'

'Alnwick. One of the guns needs the sights realigning.' He nodded towards the back seat.

Huntingdon stared ahead. 'Do you know what Napoleon said about his generals?'

'I don't know what Napoleon said about anything.'

'He said, "Don't tell me they're good. Tell me they're lucky.' Huntingdon turned to him and smiled. 'You're both.'

Ben gestured to him to look ahead. 'I don't feel to be either at the moment.'

Huntingdon glanced across at him before negotiating a double bend. 'Jepson's article means that Boutilier is a busted flush.'

'Really. I can't see that.'

'Jepson's as stiff as one of his collars but he's obsessed by one thing; to captain a side that beats the Australians. He knows he needs you to do that. That's the first thing. The second is that the mere fact that The Times printed his views after Boutilier's outpourings shows that you have support among the establishment.'

'I find that hard to believe.'

'Jepson and others have let it be known that you didn't go out to maim anyone. Jepson batted for hours against you, so who can argue with him.' Huntingdon grinned. 'They don't know, of course, that you had thought long and hard about it, but that's another matter.'

They careered in through the Bondgate and Huntingdon sent the Morris rearing up the slope to a parking spot.

'Back in a minute." He left Ben in the car and disappeared though an old coaching gate, with the gun case tucked under his arm.

Ben sat deep in thought until Huntingdon returned. 'Ready Thursday.'

He whistled tunelessly as he started the car and reversed into the open road. The driver of a passing milk wagon had the temerity to honk at him.

Ben waited until they had left the town and were heading west before he spoke. 'Boutilier will get me blackballed.'

'Too late for that. He should have done it when the pot was hot. He's missed his chance. Now it would look like pure malice. He could have killed you off three months ago.

Now it's too late. The mood of the great herd has changed.'

Ben stared out at the winding road. Huntingdon glanced across at him. 'Welcome back.'

Ben continued to look ahead. 'I can't stop thinking about Helen,' he said. 'I can't make myself care about anything else

That evening he sat at the table by the front window of his little cottage and wrote her a letter in his careful hand. He told her he was to visit his mother the following week end. 'I know I've been an arrogant fool with you,' he wrote. 'Bunty helped me see sense. I am going to walk the trail on Saturday morning at ten. Please meet me there, where my pyramid used to be. Even if it is just to say goodbye. I Love You, Ben.

P.S. I wrote to Bunty asking her to plead my case, but that was wrong.'

His hand was shaking when he put the letter in the post box near the castle. He felt as though he had summoned a dreadful jury to give their verdict. For months he had sustained himself on the hope that Helen might find her love again. Now the letter would set off a chain of events and the risk was that at the end of it, he might have no hope left.

A week later Huntingdon drove him forty miles to the Central Station in Newcastle. Neither of them spoke for much of the journey. Huntingdon parked under the portico and shook Ben's hand at the entrance to the station. 'Good Luck.' He noticed that Ben's face was white and strained. 'Hon, you have been a true friend to me.' He had not gone two yards before he drew out a handkerchief with the speed of a gunslinger and retched into it. He stared at the aristocrat like a little boy asking for help, before turning to walk to the platform. As Huntingdon watched him go, he was overwhelmed with envy.

Ben arrived in Wolviston late that afternoon and took a taxi to the estate. His mother held him quietly. She knew the real reason for his visit but she did not speak of it. He refused to eat and slept fitfully, waking early. He had three hours to wait and that was too much. He told his mother that he needed to go for a walk and headed for the door before she could ambush him with a breakfast. Ben thought of visiting Old Arnie, but he was afraid the old man would know more about Helen than he did and betray his fate with a look or a gesture. He found himself heading along the drovers road, past the old bowling wicket towards Wolviston.

The thugs' car had gone of course and so had the gouges left by the tyres as they'd fled. The hoofmarks from the Sniper's beasts still pockmarked the trail though. He walked on and on, he didn't know for how long. In his hurry he had left his watch by his bed. He turned in panic and walked back towards the estate. As he drew closer to his bowling pitch he began to run, but there was no one there. Was he early? Had she been and gone? Had she never even come? He blinked numbly into the empty space and stood as still as stone for minutes. Then he walked into the bracken and began to pick up the round, smooth stones that he had bowled so long ago.

He built them into a small pyramid by the place where he had started his run-up. Still she didn't come. He tried to take comfort from the stones. Some day she would ride past here, and at least she would know he had tried. He sat at the side of the trail looking along the valley. A thin mist hung around the trees. Sirens called to him hurting him with memories: the little girl in the tiara; the arrogant young lady with her horsewhip; Wolfie fighting for air in the swamp; the young woman who had left him injured to avoid gossip, and later her tearful regret; the day he had set out for London leaving her sobbing in the lane. Well, the world had turned the full circle now. He closed his eyes. Above him some sparrows chattered ever fearful of the dreaded hawk. But that was all. No stamp of Jasper's hooves, no snort from the flaring nostrils. His body slumped in misery until his head rested on his raised knees.

He knew that eventually he must get to his feet and begin the walk into the rest of his life. But not yet. He felt too tired, too afraid.

He buried his face hard into his knees. Cricket beckoned once more. Perhaps one day he would see her in the crowd, on the arm of Peregrin, or someone like him. He shuddered at the thought.

He did not know how long he had remained hunched like that, nor did he know how long she had been standing behind him before he became aware of her presence. He turned. She was just out of reach. He tried to put on his male mask but failed completely. There were tears in his eyes and his voice was weak.

'Where's Jasper?' He tried to keep his voice steady.

'I walked.'

'Aah. I was listening for him.'

She stood stiff. There was no welcome in her face; she was angry and tired, emptied by what he had done to her.

'You took me for granted, Ben Linden.'

'I've been a fool.'

'You distorted everything to the point that you forgot what you had.'

'I know. I can't turn back the clock'

'No, you can't.'

He closed his eyes and waited for her to leave. He decided that he would wait until she had disappeared down the slope and then he would have to follow the same path. He would walk slowly so that by the time he reached the dip she would be hidden by the leafy lane and by the time he approached the threshold of his mother's cottage she would be past the drained-out pond from which he had rescued Wolfie. She would leave only her ghost behind. The thought of losing her made him shake with grief, but her feelings for him had faded. How could they have done anything else after his appalling behaviour? She was right; he had taken her for granted.

He sat there, hunched, hands over his ears so that he could not hear her departure, his eyes closed, not wanting to see the empty space that would confirm that she had walked out of his life.

Helen stood silent and still, watching the abject figure. The proud lady in her wanted to walk away. That would hurt him and he deserved the pain. But she knew that without him she could not eat. She did not want revenge, but she needed his remorse, so that she could believe that he would never treat her as badly again.

She started to cry softly and reached out to touch his hair. His face turned up to her.

She leaned into him and whispered, 'I've missed you, Mr. Bowler.'

THE END

By The Same Author

The Brothers

Two brothers from Northumberland stand at the threshold of their lives at time of the Great War. One chooses to fight at the front, the other goes to live in the wilds. Both are united by one thing... the fight for survival.

> I loved this book which really captured the era. Wonderful depiction of life in rural Northumberland and the impact of war on a tiny community. The scenes at the Front were well done. I thought the ending of the book was superb. Thoughtful and well researched.
>
> Anne Jones
> World Speed Reading Champion

By The Same Author

The Sixties Man

Kel Adams was tough and good looking. He was made for the hedonistic Sixties. But he was bored.
Then he met the tough guy of Newcastle and a film star, and suddenly he was surrounded by murder and mayhem.

Critics said:
'A wonderful read.'
'A remarkable insight into violent times.'

By The Same Author

The Net

Football Chairman Maurice Oaksley was king of the cons when it came to sleazy transfer dealings. But his best signing was a soldier called Joey.
Maurice did the deals. Joey killed people, though on good days he just hurt them.
Together they made a great team. They had to if they were to survive, because they'd become unwitting pawns in a game of spies.
To win was to survive.
To lose was to die in The Net.

> A fascinating thriller that reveals a deep knowledge of how football works at the highest level and how it can be open to corruption.
>
> John Gibson
> Executive sports Editor, Evening Chronicle, Newcastle